SPACE ROGUES 6

WAR AND PEACE

JOHN WILKER

Rogue Publishing

Cover art by John Wilker & Greg Bahlmann

Edited By: Ember Eyster

V 2.1

ISBN: 978-1-951964-34-4

CONTENTS

DEDICATED TO..._

To my readers. The fact I'm still able to tell the stories of Wil and the crew of the Ghost is fantastic. Thank you for your support!

OTHER BOOKS BY JOHN WILKER_

Space Rogues Universe (in story chronological order)

- Space Rogues 1: The Epic Adventures of Wil Calder, Space Smuggler
- Space Rogues 2: Big Ship, Lots of Guns
- Space Rogues 3: The Behemoth Job
- Space Rogues 4: Stay Warm, Don't Die
- Space Rogues 5: So This is Earth?
- Space Rogues 6: War and Peace
- Space Rogues 7: A Guy Walks Into a Bar

PART ONE

CHAPTER 1_

SPACE BEES?!_

"Fucking space bees!" Wil shouts waving his hands. Everyone is in the cargo hold of the *Ghost* as the spaceport personnel on Durbril Two decontaminate the ship. The Cargo ramp is down, but the heavy cargo doors are still closed.

"How was I supposed to know?" Bennie retorts. "There wasn't a sign on the crate."

"What would you expect? *Warning, space bees inside?*" Wil gestures to the crate in question, "It says *Do Not Open*, literally on every face of the crate!" Wil shouts. He walks to the crate pointing at one of the warning labels, "Some sides have two labels!" he shouts, moving his finger from one label to the other.

"I mean, if it's full of bees, maybe they should have put that on the labels," the defensive Brailack says. "Also, what's a bee, exactly?"

Wil flips him off.

Bennie continues, "In my defense, last time I opened a crate I wasn't supposed to, we got a Gabe."

Maxim raises his hand, "That was the *first* time, not the last. Last time it was that aggressive, oxygen-eating fungus that Gabe had to scrape off the walls of the cargo hold. The time before that was that automated defense drone that immediately thought we were thieves

and kept shooting at us every time we tried to enter the cargo bay."
He motiones to the space they were standing in, pointing at a scorch
mark near the large cargo doors. Zephyr puts a hand on Maxim's
shoulder, "Don't forget the time you opened that storage unit and
found that cryopod with the guy in the what was it?" She looks
at Wil.

"Hockey mask."

She nods, "Right, that guy in the hockey mask."

Bennie raises one of his two fingers, "I don't think that one
counts; I didn't open the cryopod." He smiles as if that means he has
won the argument.

"Because we stopped you," Zephyr counters.

Wil leans in, "Whatever. Stop opening crates that aren't yours. I
still have welts."

Cynthia nods, "He does. In places I wouldn't have thought a"—
she quirked an eyebrow at Wil—"space bee could get to."

Zephyr walks over to the cargo door controls and the display from
the camera outside, "They're almost done I think." She turns to Wil,
"Also, *space bees*? We've been over this. Those were Talaxian
apians." She points to the crate, "Aggressive in warm climates, which
is why their crate was temperature controlled." She turns to Bennie,
eyebrow raised.

"I noticed the temperature controls, but assumed it was food,"
Bennie retorts, as if that is a defense.

"Food with warning signs?" Maxim asks.

Bennie opens his mouth, but a triple tone from the cargo door
control panel interrupts him. A light on the panel is blinking green.

Zephyr turns back to the controls. "Decon complete." She peers
at the camera feed, "I think they're going to hose us down now."

Wil sighs, "Jesus, what's the deal here?"

"Durbril Two has never had an outbreak of Larrap Syndrome.
They want to keep that record going," Zephyr offers as the heavy
cargo doors split and slide apart.

"What's Larrap Syndrome?" Wil asks Cynthia as they head for the door.

"Nasty bug—highly contagious, lesions, blood from orifices, then death."

Maxim leans over, "She left out the pustules that spread the spores."

Bennie joins them, "And the screaming. I hear those with Larrap spend their last days screaming until their throats are raw." He grins and gives Wil a thumbs up.

Wil shudders, "Pustules?" He looks down the ramp at the four environment suit clad Durbrillians, their large heads and fan like ears crammed inside their helmets, "Bring on the hose down."

PUBLIC NUDITY_

AT THE BOTTOM of the ramp is a tent with a zippered door. Once inside the tent, one of the Durbrillians in an environment suit approaches, "Please disrobe and place your clothes in these boxes. One box per person, please."

Wil holds up a hand, "Uh, we like our clothes."

"Do not worry; we will put your clothes through decontamination separately. They will be unharmed." The suited man raises an appraising eyebrow, bushy and bright red, at Wil's outfit.

"Burn," Cynthia whispers in his ear as she heads to a bench set against the wall.

Wil blushes, "Are we getting naked right here in front of"—he looks around—"Gah!" Bennie is standing next to him naked. "What the hell, man!" He stumbles stepping away from the nude Brailack.

Bennie shrugs, "What? The man said get naked; I got naked."

"He actually didn't—" Zephyr starts but finds something on the ceiling to look at instead.

"In record time," Maxim says, averting his eyes.

Cynthia looks down then at the ceiling, maybe toward the thing Zephyr is studiously gazing at. She whispers, "I see why that little Olop woman on Nilop Four was so possessive."

Zephyr grimaces, putting a hand over her mouth. Wil looks at Cynthia, "Really?" She shrugs.

Bennie pads past them all depositing his clothes in one of the decontamination boxes.

The Durbrillian man clears his throat, "Actually, you are welcome to leave your undergarments on." He looks at Bennie and sighs. Inside the helmet, one of his large ears flutters.

"Thank the gods," Zephyr says stripping off her jumpsuit. She winks at Wil, "I'd heard seeing you naked causes nightmares."

Wil flips her off and undresses.

As the crew exits the tent on the side opposite from where they had entered, Bennie looks up, "You didn't inhale any did you?"

"No. I mean, I don't think so. Why?" Wil says, looking around, careful to not look down at Bennie still naked.

Bennie tuts, "Don't be far from a toilet for the next few hours." He moves away smiling.

The boxes with their clothes in them are trundling out on a conveyor belt next to the decontamination shower unit they just walked through.

"He's crapping you," Cynthia says putting a hand on his shoulder.

"It's *shitting*, but thanks," Wil says grabbing his box.

The doors to the spaceport reception area slide apart revealing a luxurious waiting area. Wil is used to the reception areas in spaceports on Fury and similar planets. This place is downright posh. He whistles as he slowly takes in the scenery.

"Gabe!" Bennie shrieks as he breaks off from the others. Everyone turns to look in the direction the excited Brailack is running. Standing near the door leading to the street outside the spaceport is Gabe. He raises a hand and wiggles his fingers, his uncanny valley smile wide on his face.

Everyone heads towards the door at a fast walk. When they reach the tall droid, everyone leans in for hugs or to pat a shoulder. Bennie is nearly crushed as he stands near Gabe's leg.

"It's good to see you buddy," Wil says smiling. "We missed you."

"Thank you, Captain." The tall droid inclines his head, "It is good to see you all. I missed you."

"Ah, that's sweet," Zephyr says, her smile broad.

Gabe turns toward the door that leads out to the street, "If you would like, I have arranged accommodations at the facility where the reception is being held." He gestures to the now open sliding door.

"I know I've said it already, but sorry it took us a while to get here."

Gabe nods, "I understand, Captain. Was the job completed successfully?"

Maxim nods, "It was. Good money for a simple delivery. There was a *bee* incident, but it wouldn't be a job without something going wonky."

Gabe nods, "Of course. I look forward to hearing more about these *bees*."

"You mentioned a reception?" Cynthia asks as they walk towards a ground vehicle, presumably rented by Gabe.

Gabe makes a face that Wil recognizes as his *uncomfortable topic* face, "Yes. There is a reception tonight in my honor."

"What?!" Wil shouts as he claps Gabe on the back hard enough to hurt himself. As he wiggles his fingers he continues, "That's cool. What for? Your role in the Droid Liberation Movement stuff?"

"Probably not for his baking, you krebnack," Bennie says then darts past Wil toward the ground vehicle.

Once everyone is seated and the ground vehicle is trundling its way towards their destination, Wil leans forward, "Ok pal, spill."

Gabe slowly looks around then sighs, "After you departed Tarsis, I was able to convince Councilwoman Grythlorian to grant me an audience with the Governing Council." Gabe looks at Wil, "She is not at all happy with you now, I understand. I am lucky she could help me before you completed the job on Earth." Wil nods his head and makes a *go on* motion.

The droid continues, "That initial audience did not go well. Many of the councilors were quite hostile towards me. The uprisings on Mogul Three, however, worked as expected. Sentiment was already shifting as the conversation was spreading across the Commonwealth."

Maxim is looking out the window at the passing city, "How so? I remember the name of the system, but not the details."

"The shutdown of production on that planet revealed how dependent on droid labor, slavery, many GC member systems are. GNO and several lesser widespread news agencies covered the story, helping to spread the issue," the droid replies. He turns to look out the window, "We are here." The ground vehicle slows as it approaches a multistoried building with balconies ringing the upper floors.

"Nice," Wil says as they file out of the vehicle. He turns to Gabe, "So, what exactly is this reception for?"

Gabe inclines his head, "The government of Durbril Two is giving me a humanitarian award."

As the entry doors to the building part, Bennie turns, "Uh, what?" Maxim and Zephyr both nod slowly.

"There was a droid uprising here two months ago. It was part of our overall plan to show the value of the Droid Nation."

Bennie looks up at Wil and mouths the words *Droid Nation?* Wil shrugs.

Gabe continues, "Unfortunately, things here did not go as planned. A faction of the droids decided to make their point with violence. I came to Durbril Two shortly after my first presentation to the Galactic Commonwealth Governing Council. The violent faction saw reason and surrendered themselves to the local authorities to face justice."

"Impressive. Maybe you should be the team diplomat?" Cynthia says. They are all standing in the lobby now.

Gabe gestures with one hand to each crewmate's wristcomm. "I

have transferred your room passes to your wristcomms. Do you wish
to rest now?"

Wil looks at everyone else, "No. I'd like to grab a bite and a drink
and hear the rest of your story." Everyone nods.

"Very well; there is a cantina over there." The droid turns and
walks in the direction he just pointed. As they walk, he continues, "It
went a long way toward the Durbrillian government seeing our side
of the debate—seeing that droids were interested in being a part of
civil society in all aspects, including justice. The Council has not
scheduled a formal vote, but the Durbrillian representative has
agreed to vote in favor of droid rights."

CIVIC DUTY_

THE CANTINA ISN'T VERY busy, so they take a seat on the small patio that overlooks the swimming pool in the center of the building. Children of several species are splashing around in the water. Two Trollack children are zipping around in the water leaping out and splashing the other children before diving under the surface again.

"That's fantastic buddy," Wil says as they sit. He flags a server over.

The server arrives, a young Durbrillian male, "Hello. Welcome to the *Dusty Shoe*. Will you be eating or just drinks?" He smiles, his reddish fur short and well-groomed. He slips a small PADD from a pocket on his trousers.

"Dusty Shoe?" Wil asks, then shakes his head as he waves off the question, "Doesn't matter. House grum for the table, please." He looks around to make sure there are no objections; everyone nods. The young man taps on his PADD then bows and leaves.

Wil turns to Gabe, "I'm proud of you."

Cynthia smiles, "I'm honestly surprised this has gone so well, so fast." She leans her elbows on the table. "No fights or bloodshed or anything?"

Gabe raises a hand, "I did not say that. There have been rough patches and several violent clashes throughout the GC. I had hoped it would be bloodless, but as you said before I left the *Ghost*, that was unrealistic."

The young man comes back with a tray loaded with glasses full of amber liquid. Once he's placed the last glasses on the table, he turns his attention to Wil, "Have you decided on any food?"

"Fried zerglings," Bennie says. "Two orders," he adds, holding up a hand, two long, green fingers held up in a v shape.

Wil looks down at his friend and nods. He looks at the server, "That'll start us."

Again, the young man bows and walks away, tapping on his PADD.

Maxim picks up his glass, "To Gabe!"

"Hear, hear!" the others say in unison.

Gabe, as usual, sits silently and inclines his head, "Thank you. There is much to still do, but the wheels are turning, and I feel confident that my presence on Tarsis is no longer needed. We formed an advisory council to ensure things continue apace." He turns to Cynthia, "I believe your people's earlier struggles with this, and their voice on the council, helped tremendously. I had intended to visit Tyr if possible but ended up not needing to. The delegation on Tarsis was more than helpful." He smiled his uncanny valley smile.

Maxim leans forward and looks around the table, "Speaking of politics, did everyone vote?"

Wil sets his glass down, "Come again? Vote?"

Bennie looks at Wil, "Do you humans not vote for you leaders? I didn't get the impression it was a monarchy or dictatorship when we were there."

Wil tuts, "Of course we vote. I just didn't know you all did."

"Like we're a bunch of uncivilized idiots?" Zephyr asks, though she's smiling. "How did you think we picked GC councilors and the like? Or our planetary leaders?"

Wil shrugs, "I don't know. I mean, I guess I assumed you voted, but it hasn't come up that I know of since you all joined up."

"I voted three months ago in the Brai planetary elections: chamberlain, and a few senators if I recall, and I think three initiatives. One was a new civil defense effort, I think," Bennie says shrugging.

Maxim says, "Palor had an election last year; we both voted." He gestures to Zephyr, "We had just barely got our voting rights back."

"Really?" Wil asks, scratching his cheek as he thinks about it.

"I mean, I didn't run around the ship screaming about voting or put some *I voted* sticker on my jumpsuit," Bennie says shaking his head. "That'd be ridiculous."

"Tyr has an election coming up in a few months," Cynthia offers. "I could let you watch me vote." She winks. Wil smirks.

"So what election is happening right now since planetary elections seem to happen randomly around the GC?" Wil asks.

"GC representative," everyone says, including Gabe.

Wil leans back, "And you all did it? Voted from the *Ghost*? In the last few days?"

"I am, as yet, unable to vote," Gabe clarifies.

Bennie looks at the others, "I don't understand why he's having so much trouble with this."

Wil flings an arm out catching the Brailack with the back of his hand, "Sorry, I just hadn't given it much thought, and I guess assumed you'd go home to vote or skip it or something."

"It's our civic duty," Zephyr says. Their server returns placing small plates and two baskets of deep fried morsels on the table. He bows and backs away.

"We take it seriously," Bennie adds.

Gabe raises a hand, "Captain, does Earth not have absentee voting?"

Wil grabs a fried zergling and between chews says, "We do. Well, the US does and most other countries, but well, I'm extremely absentee. Maybe if they get their shit together, I'll be able to vote next time. Pretty sure *space* isn't a valid address in the voter registration database."

"A shame," Gabe says.

Wil chuckles nodding at his friend then asks, "So who did you all vote for?"

As one the rest of the crew leans back throwing their arms up shouting, "Woah!"

Maxim smiles, "You don't ask people who they voted for."

"Super bad form," Bennie says.

Cynthia smiles at her boyfriend, "So uncouth."

Wil just looks around at his friends then grabs another zergling and his grum.

NEWSCAST_

"GOOD AFTERNOON; I'M MON-EL FURASH," the Malkorite woman says from behind a news desk. "I'm sitting in for Megan with a breaking news story." She turns to her co-host, a blue-skinned being with large compound eyes occupying the bulk of his face.

"And I'm Xyrzix. What's going on Mon-El?" He turns to face his co-host.

"We've received word from the Semgax Beta System that an attack has just taken place against the Peacekeeper Orbital Base there." She looks right into the camera, "And it is destroyed."

"Oh, my!" Xyrzix exclaims as he turns to look into the camera, "Are there any indications of who the attackers were?"

The Malkorite woman shakes her head, her ear jewelry tinkling, "Right now? No. The attackers entered the system and flew straight for the Orbital. The sector fleet that is based at Semgax Beta was on patrol. Apparently, the few ships near the Orbital were also destroyed." She pauses. "The attackers were gone before the sector fleet could return."

"That's horrible, truly," her blue-skinned co-host says. "Were there any survivors?"

Mon-El looks somber, "None."

Xyrzix puts his hand over his mouth, "Tragic." He turns to the camera, "We'll have more as the situation develops. For now, the Peacekeepers have issued a travel advisory placing the Semgax Beta System under lockdown while they investigate, no traffic in or out of the system. They have dispatched additional fleet assets to aid in the lockdown."

Mon-El nods.

CHAPTER 2_

ROBOT PARTY_

THE CREW HANGS out in the *Dusty Shoe* for another hour, then heads to their rooms to get ready for the reception. As the sun is setting over the city that Wil doesn't even know the name of, he turns to the others, "Remind me next movie night, we're watching *Gremlins*. These Durbrillians look really familiar to me." No one says anything.

There is a knock on the door moments before it slides open to reveal Gabe, "Are you all ready?"

As one, they all nod and follow the droid down the hall from the suite he's rented for them.

Maxim leans over to whisper to Zephyr, "I didn't know Gabe had money or a credit account."

She shrugs, "Me either. Wurrin, he could have hacked the hotel to get the rooms." The big man chuckles, "That would be kinda funny, given the award he's getting and all."

"Ironic for sure."

Gabe turns his head as he walks, "I have money. When the Captain agreed to allowing me to remain aboard the *Ghost*, he created an account for me. I am, as the Captain would say, loaded."

The two Palorians look at each other and grin. "Droid hearing," they say in unison followed by, "Loaded?"

Gabe smiles and turns back to the corridor.

The door to the reception hall is open, and they can hear music coming from inside. As they enter the room, Bennie makes the Brailack equivalent of a whistle. "Damn, there must be two hundred people here."

"Two hundred and nine," Gabe offers. "Eighteen are droids."

An elderly Durbrillian trots over, "Mister Gabe, it is good to see you!" He reaches up for Gabe's arm and guides the much taller droid away, not even acknowledging the others.

"Polite," Wil says, then points to the opposite wall, "Bar." Nods all around, except from Bennie who has vanished.

"What can I get you?" the bartender, a droid, asks as they arrive.

Wil hold up four fingers, "Four grum please."

The droid nods its matte black head; and without turning away from the crew, its torso spins on its axis and four multi-segmented limbs start grabbing glasses and tap handles. "You are not Durbrillian, what brings you here tonight?" The droid tilts its head slightly as if getting a better look at them.

Maxim smiles, "Our friend is being honored tonight." He looks over his shoulder and finds Gabe still talking to the elderly Durbrillian man who had met them at the door. "He's over there."

The bartender droid's torso spins around, freshly poured glasses of grum in each hand. It dips its head, "You are friends of Gabe, the Liberator?"

Zephyr coughs, "Gabe the Liberator? We just call him Gabe—"

"Not anymore," Wil interrupts grinning. He takes the drinks and distributes them to each member the crew.

Zephyr glances at him sideways then turns her attention back to the droid, "But yes, he's a member of our crew. We were on a mission while he was doing his *liberator* thing." She smiles warmly, "We haven't seen him in a while."

"I see," the bartender says, then adds, "Those are on the house." It doesn't have a mouth, just a slotted speaker opening, but Wil is pretty sure it would be smiling if it had a mouth.

He holds up his glass, "Thank you; that's very kind. Cheers."

"Cheers," the droid parrots back, then turns to acknowledge a Durbrillian woman in a bright blue dress. "Hello ma'am; what can I get for you?" The bright red fur around her eyes has been styled and there are fine jewels woven into it. Her large fan like ears are adorned with earrings that Wil is fairly sure cost more than the *Ghost*. The four crewmembers of the *Ghost* turn and walk away before the new arrival answers.

"Little green is gonna be mad he missed out on a free drink," Cynthia says, spying Bennie having an animated discussion with an older Durbrillian man in a motorized wheelchair type of device. The Brailack hacker jumps up and down twice, then sees his friends and waves them over.

Once they arrive, he waves at each of them, "Wil, Cynthia, Zephyr, and Maxim." Then he points at the elderly man in the wheelchair, "Rimbold Suharin."

When the hacker doesn't offer any further introductory information, Wil leans down and offers his hand; even though it was at best fifty-fifty that the gesture would make sense, he still feels it appropriate to offer to shake hands with people. "It's a pleasure to meet you Mister Suharin." The elderly Durbrillian looks at the offered hand and tentatively extends his own short arm. Wil gives the small three-fingered hand a shake, then releases it. Suharin looks at his hand as if expecting there to be something new or something missing, then places it in his lap. "Greetings. Ben-Ari tells me you are all his employees, including the guest of honor?"

Wil looks at Bennie who shrugs innocently, "Yeah, no. He works for me; I'm the Captain of the *Ghost*, maybe you've heard of us, kind of a big deal."

The ancient Durbrillian shakes his head, his ears dipping slightly, "I'm afraid I haven't; sorry." Seeing Wil's face fall he adds, "I'm sure you're quite incredible and popular elsewhere." He smiles feebly.

Cynthia places a hand on Wil's shoulder and leans in, "That had to hurt." Then she straightens and adds, "We should grab our seats." She bows to the elderly Durbrillian, "A pleasure to meet you, Mister Suharin."

As Bennie turns to follow his friends, waving to Suharin, he asks, "Do you guys know who that was?"

"Rimbold Suharin," Zephyr offers.

"No clue," Wil says.

"An old guy," Cynthia adds.

Maxim shrugs.

"I hate you guys. Rimbold Suharin invented the Bathroom Buddy! The tooth cleaner and facial hair remover in one." He looks at each of them, "Really? You never heard of it?"

They arrive at their table, and Wil sits, "Dude, you don't have hair, and I'm not certain you brush your teeth."

A serving droid balanced on a single wheel arrives at the table, a platter of drinks in one hand, "Would you like some sparkling brandy?"

Wil takes one of the offered glasses, "Don't mind if I do."

MORNINGS AFTER_

THE NEXT MORNING, Wil sits up in bed and rubs his forehead. "Who'd guess you could get so drunk at a robot party?"

Cynthia rolls over, one ear twitching, "There were like four droids there. Everyone else was very much biological. You just can't hold your liquor."

"Eighteen droids, and you take that right the fuck back." He's grinning while squinting to keep the room's morning-setting light out of his eyes.

"Go make coffee," Cynthia says shoving him out of bed.

Wil stumbles out of the crew berth stairwell that connects the crew deck to the one below; where the lounge, kitchenette, engineering, and other facilities are located. He sees Gabe standing near the large entertainment screen, "Good morning, Gabe the Liberator."

Gabe turns and makes a face, "I had hoped you would not hear of that nickname." He walks over to the kitchenette to join Wil.

Wil presses a few controls on the coffee machine and leans against the cupboard as the machine happily beeps to itself as it sets about its task. He smiles, "Nothing escapes my notice." He tilts his head to the seating area Gabe was just standing in, "What were you up to just now?"

"That is quantitatively false," the droid replies. "You did not notice that the coffee maker is low on grounds, for example." The droid wags a finger, then says, "I was running a level one diagnostic to acquaint myself with the newly installed equipment. It is very impressive, quite advanced."

Wil, frowning, glances at the storage unit on top of the coffee maker, then turns to Gabe, "Don't get huffy, Gabe the Liberator." He smiles and grabs two coffee cups from the cupboard. He looks at Gabe as he removes the carafe and begins filling the cups, "Yeah, Tillith and Grythlorian really hooked us up with that gear." He puts the carafe back in the machine, "Guessing you're all set to leave now? No more parties?"

The droid inclines his head, "Indeed; that was the only party on my calendar. We may depart at your convenience."

Wil nods, "Cool. I'll let everyone sleep a bit more, then we can get breakfast and pre-flights done."

"Acknowledged," Gabe says as he turns toward the hatch leading aft into the engineering and services space.

As the door to his shared quarters closes, Wil hands Cynthia a mug of coffee. "It's good to have Gabe back."

Cynthia nods, accepting the steaming mug, "No argument there. Having the family back together feels good." She eyes Wil, "So what's the plan?"

Wil waggles his eyebrows, "Well, this coffee is too hot to drink so maybe if we let it cool for a bit—"

Cynthia holds up a hand, "Woah there, cowboy." She stops and raises an eyebrow, "Use that right?" Wil nods. "Good. Woah there, cowboy. You reek of grum, sparkling brandy, and my head hurts. Get dressed, and let's get off this planet."

Wil sighs dramatically uttering an elongated, "Fine." He sets his coffee cup on a shelf and walks into the small refresher in the room's corner. As Cynthia is getting out of bed, a pair of sweatpants sails through the room nearly hitting her.

"Oh, I see." She sets her mug down and heads for the refresher, "Make room!"

JOB HUNTING_

WHEN WIL and Cynthia emerge from the stairwell into the lounge and kitchenette space; Maxim, Zephyr, and Bennie are seated around the table.

"Good morning," Maxim says, holding up a cup of coffee.

"Gabe mentioned you were ready to head out," Zephyr says.

Wil and Cynthia sit down after refilling their coffee cups, and Wil says, "Unless Bennie needs to visit his pal Suharin for gadgets he can't use and that sound ridiculous." Wil smiles brightly at the Brailack at the opposite end of the table. "Maybe an electric hammer thing or an automatic egg cracker?"

Bennie grins and mouths *fuck you* before raising his mug to take a sip. Wil chuckles.

"Thoughts on jobs?" Cynthia asks, scooping up a pile of something pink onto her plate. "Who made breakfast?" She eyes Bennie suspiciously.

Zephyr smiles, "It's safe; I made it."

Bennie makes a rude gesture to Cynthia then brightens, "I've been monitoring the various job posting sites on the internex; there are a few gigs that sound pretty much custom tailored for us." He motions to the large display on the wall, eyebrow raised. Wil nods.

"There's a rich old man on Bundersqua Prime who needs protection for a trip he's taking, some type of religious pilgrimage."

Wil rolls his hand, *next*.

"There's a freight convoy departing Malkor in three days, hiring on a few gunships for protection through the Guelph Expanse."

"Ok"—Wil nods—"that could be interesting. We'd have to hustle to get to Malkor in time."

"Captain, I have been monitoring the local system police and military bands," Gabe offers. He continues,

"There have been several reported robberies in the outer system. The local authorities have requested Peacekeeper support but as yet have not received it."

Wil tilts his head, "Ok, but I don't think we want to stick around here that long or pick up a letter of marque, do we?" He looks around the table.

Gabe raises a hand, index finger up, "A call just came in that a private luxury yacht is under attack by pirates. The yacht is currently near the orbit of the seventh planet in the system."

Wil stands, "Awesome timing, for us, not them. Bet those rich folks would love to pay to get their stuff back. If we can track the pirates to their base, we might get a reward for shutting them down."

Zephyr stands and heads for the bridge. Maxim and Cynthia both stand and set about clearing the table.

Bennie hops out of his chair, "Come on, Gabe; I'll help you with the engine spin up."

Gabe follows but says, "I have not forgotten how to pre-flight the engines or the location of engineering."

The Brailack hacker looks up at his friend but says nothing.

Wil watches for a minute, then turns and heads for the hatch leading to the bridge.

"We are ready for takeoff, Captain," the ceiling speaker replies in Gabe's voice. "Reactor at one hundred percent. Repulsor lifts primed and ready to engage. Atmospheric engines ready for ignition."

Wil smiles and looks up, "I've missed this. Thanks, buddy!" He looks around the room, "Everyone else good?" Nods from everyone. "Excellent." He slowly pushes forward the control for the repulsor lifts mounted in the engine nacelles. The *Ghost* lurches and tilts slightly as the powerful lifts force the ship straight up off the ground. Once a few meters up, the system automatically adjusts each repulsor to keep the powerful warship level.

Wil reaches for a small blinking button and presses it. From inside the ship, several loud thunks reverberate; the landing gear folds up and stows in the wing roots of each wide wing.

Wil looks over his shoulder, "We have clearance?"

Cynthia nods, "Yup. I sent the flight path to your station."

"Oh yeah, you sure did," Wil says, looking at one of the small displays near his right hand. He taps the screen to accept the flight path and watches as green lines appear on the main display. "Stand by for atmo ignition," he says as he reaches for the ignition switch near his left hand, next to the atmospheric engine throttle. Two seconds after pressing the button, there is a loud boom from the back of the ship that echoes through the entire vessel. It pushes everyone against their seatbacks. "Yeehaw!" Wil shouts over the noise of the atmospheric engines. "Let's go bag some pirates!"

OFF WE GO_

Once the *Ghost* leaves orbit, Wil pushes the sub-light engine throttle all the way forward to the stops, pushing the powerful engines to full power. He turns to Cynthia, "Anything from the yacht? Or the authorities?"

The feline-featured woman looks up, "Nothing. Well, not nothing, but not much. I've been monitoring the common bands; and aside from the automated distress beacon, which, by the way, shut off about two tocks ago, not much. A few garbled calls for help, likely from personal comm units. Then nothing." She adds, "We got an acknowledgment from the locals we're engaging in a one-time privateering operation. They've signed off." Wil nods.

"It's possible they're all dead," Bennie offers from his station.

Zephyr shakes her head, "Maybe, but I'm guessing the pirates just grolacked the yacht's comm system. If they're smart, they left a jammer somewhere on or in the yacht. That would make it harder for the authorities to find the yacht, so they'd focus on that more than tracking the pirates."

Wil smiles, "Good thing we're after the pirates. Speaking of, any thoughts on that?"

His first officer nods, "We have the location of the initial calls for help, and the distress beacon included the original coordinates and trajectory. I'm thinking if we're lucky, we can isolate their ion trail and follow that."

After a fairly boring six hours of hard burn, the *Ghost* arrives at the location encoded in the yacht's distress transmission. There's no sign of the yacht, but there are two very distinct engine ion trails. One is likely the yacht; it ends in a minor debris field. Another ion trail appears to arrive and depart on a tangential course to that of the yacht. "Any way to tell which is their arrival and departure vector?" Wil asks out loud, staring at the main display showing the false color sensor data.

Zephyr nods, but says nothing as she works at her console, then looks up as the main display screen updates; the yellow ion trail of the yacht dims, while one of the red ion trails darkens. "I'm pretty sure the lighter red is their departure vector; it's less dissipated."

Wil grins, "Then let's go liberate some expensive trinkets." He adjusts his controls and brings the *Ghost* onto a course parallel to the lighter red highlighted vector. He pushes the sub-light throttles forward to the stops again. "They've got about, what? Ten hours on us?" Zephyr nods. "Anything along this vector that might be a base?"

The Palorian woman nods once, "The system's asteroid belt is along this vector. It's pretty populated, lots of mining, but certainly plenty of rocks to hide in or behind."

"Well, nothing to do but wait until we catch up to them. What say we watch a movie?" Everyone nods.

Bennie chimes in, "Oh, what about—"

"No. We're not watching Frozen three again," Maxim interrupts.

Bennie folds his arms in front of him, "Fine."

"What about the one with that kick ass woman with the bracelets?" Cynthia asks.

"Wonder Woman? I don't think we've watched the fourth one yet. I'm down," Wil says.

Maxim nods, "That's fine with me." Zephyr nods as well.

Zephyr raises a hand, finger in the air, "Didn't you want to watch something else? Gremlings?"

Wil scratches his head, "Oh right, *Gremlins*. That's all right. It's more of a Christmas movie; we can watch it then." His first officer shrugs.

As they all head for the hatch to leave the bridge, Wil looks at the ceiling, "Computer, alert all crew if the proximity sensors are triggered."

"Acknowledged."

ROBIN HOOD, SORTA_

"THAT WAS GOOD. I liked the one before it better, but still entertaining," Cynthia says as the crew returns to the bridge. "Though it was nice to see a Tygran, even if she was the villain."

Wil smiles, "My understanding is they changed directors halfway through production. That's never a good thing." He sits down and looks over his console, taking in the latest readings and location data. "Will be interesting to see how they handle that ending in the next movie, quite the gut punch." He turns to look at Cynthia, "I'd say don't get too attached to your new favorite baddy."

Maxim sits down and scans his console, "Yeah, I have to admit, I did not see that coming."

"I didn't like it," Bennie says as he wakes his console up, monitors coming to life showing all manner of data that Wil rarely understands. One of the monitors blinks but doesn't come to live. Bennie slams a small green palm into the side of it and it turns on.

"That's because they killed off the character you liked," Zephyr retorts. "Don't take it personally. Remember, they did that to the character I liked in the first one, and he was back in the second."

"You just thought he was cute," Maxim says smiling back at the love of his life.

"Who wouldn't? He's cute for a human," Cynthia says before Zephyr can reply.

Wil holds up a hand, "He's like eighty or ninety now, for what it's worth."

"I'm pretty sure the lead actress is as well," Zephyr says, eyeing Wil then Maxim. Both men make strangled noises.

Before anyone can say anything else, several of their consoles beep. Zephyr looks at hers, "Well, that was easy; they're not hiding." She points to the main display screen. It updates to show a ship about twice the size of the *Ghost* sitting next to an asteroid approximately ten kilometers in diameter. The pirates have shot anchor lines into the rock, keeping the modified freighter in place. Several blaster turrets and what looks like an old model missile launcher have been attached to the hull.

Wil pulls back the throttles and looks at Bennie, "Activate the—"

"Stealth system, yeah yeah," Bennie says as he presses a few buttons. Across the top of the main display a blue bar pulses to show the stealth system is active.

Wil looks at the Brailack but doesn't comment. He turns to the screen, "We'll cozy up, then board." He looks at Bennie, "Tiny Rambo, Max, and Cynthia." He looks at Zephyr, "You and Gabe hold down the fort, cool?"

"Cool," his first officer nods. She taps a control, "Gabe, can you come up to the bridge?"

"On my way," the droid replies from wherever he is at the moment. Wil and the rest of the boarding team leave the bridge. As Wil starts down the starboard steps leading to the armory, he sees Gabe, "We're boarding the pirate's ship, looks like a modified medium freighter. Keep an eye on things and help Zee."

"Acknowledged, Captain," the droid says as he presses the control to open the hatch to the bridge. Wil continues down the curving stairwell to the lower level.

By the time Wil joins the others, Maxim and Cynthia are mostly armed and armored. Bennie is hopping around trying to get into a pair of specially designed undergarments meant to have armor easily attach to them. Next to him is a pile of armor pieces and several Brailack-sized weapons. Maxim has chosen to carry one plasma rifle and has another strapped to his back. Cynthia has a pistol at her hip.

"Dude, we're not storming Normandy," Wil admonishes as he shrugs out of his jumpsuit and slips on his own armor, which goes on more easily than Bennie's. He doesn't apply much armor beyond what the trousers include on their own. He grabs a similarly lightly armored overshirt to slip over his *Godzilla* tee shirt. After donning his favorite brown long coat, he grabs two pulse pistols and a belt of smart grenades. He attaches armored shoulder guards to the duster and a chest piece to his overshirt.

Bennie finally gets his pants on, "Shut up." He snatches his two modified pulse pistols and a headband that can deploy a full environment helmet in seconds. Maxim and Cynthia also don halos as they call them. Their armored clothes can seal up around the seams when the halo activates, providing a reasonably good armored environment suit. Not as good as combat armor, but better than a jumpsuit and less bulky than an EVA suit.

Wil motions toward the stairwell that leads back up to the bridge and airlocks, then looks at the ceiling, "Zee, we in position?"

"Yup, far as I can tell they haven't spotted us. Must all be in the hold counting timepieces." She chuckles at her joke. No one else does.

SNEAKY SNEAKY_

THE *GHOST* invisibly sidles up to the large vessel and extends her docking tube. The boarding team is watching from inside the airlock. The flexible tube extends slowly until it meets up with the outer airlock of the freighter. The tube connects with the other ship and the ghost's outer airlock opens.

"Not sure I could have done it better myself," Wil says.

"You definitely couldn't have," Maxim quips as he pushes out into the tube toward the other vessel. He doesn't see it, but Wil flips him off.

Bennie follows Wil out of the hatch, and Cynthia brings up the rear. "*Ghost* base, we're clear; close her up," she says. Behind her the outer airlock door closes.

Bennie reaches the hatch and Wil motions for him to approach the control panel. "Work your magic, my friend."

Bennie drifts over to the panel. He pulls the airlock control panel apart and pushes two connectors into the electronic innards of the panel. His wristcomm lights up as he silently works to take over the airlock controls.

A light on the panel face turns green, and the outer hatch opens. The Brailack hacker looks at Wil, "What would you do without me?"

"Hire another hacker or make Gabe do it," Wil says without looking at Bennie. He hears the sharp intake of breath and ignores it. He moves into the airlock and motions the others to follow. After looking through the small and grimy window set in the inner door, he says, "Looks clear." Once everyone is crammed inside the poorly maintained airlock, Wil closes the outer door and cycles the chamber. It only takes a minute for the airlock to fill with a breathable atmosphere before the inner door slides away.

Wil jumps out into the corridor, dropping to his knee, both pistols held straight out. Maxim follows, standing and aiming his rifle the opposite direction Wil is facing.

"Clear," both say in unison. Wil taps his ear and his face mask retracts into the two-inch-wide halo device. The others follow suit, withdrawing their protective headgear. Cynthia's outfit also retracts its gloves into the wrists of her long sleeves, freeing her hands and, more importantly, her claws.

Wil checks his wristcomm and motions to the right, "Looks like the hold is this way."

Bennie points to a sign in a language Wil can't read but sports a very clear arrow, "What gave it away?"

"Fuck you," Wil says as he heads down the corridor.

Cynthia and Maxim exchange a glance and shrug. As Wil nears a corner, he finally hears signs of life, laughter and shouting. He turns to look at the others, motioning for them to be ready.

As he turns to enter the substantial cargo hold, an alarm sounds. He looks around, then at the others who all shrug. Maxim swings his second rifle around, locking one into each armpit and pushes past Wil.

"Everyone down!" He bellows firing several rounds over the heads of the surprised pirates.

Wil, Bennie, and Cynthia follow. The pirates, surprised but alerted to *something* being up, are running for cover. One large Trenbal turns toward Maxim, his pistol raised. Super charged plasma stitches across the front of the unprepared pirate and he falls to the deck dead. Two more, a Quilant and a heavily cybernetically enhanced Palorian, turn and dive behind cargo modules.

Wil looks over to Cynthia, "Bridge." He looks to Bennie, "Engineering." Both nod and crawl-run back toward the corridor they'd come in from.

"Ghost One, it looks like they're powering up their engines," Zephyr says from aboard the *Ghost*.

"Roger that, Ghost Base. On it," Wil replies as he fires both pulse pistols at anyone he can see as he runs sideways towards a large cargo module. Maxim is behind a similar but smaller module twenty feet away. Wil taps his ear, "Ghost Two, count?"

Maxim glances at him, stands and fires. When he ducks back down and says over comms, "Six, maybe seven, not sure if I got that guy."

Wil leans out around his cover and fires his pistol twice, forcing a hiding pirate to flinch from the unexpected fire. He fires twice more dropping the pirate, a Brailack possibly. "Just got one."

"A little one." His friend quips.

CHAPTER 3_

ASSASSIN VS. DINOSAUR_

CYNTHIA RUNS BACK to the corridor they'd left and sprints back the way they came. "Good luck, little green," she shouts back to Bennie. She hears his reply but says nothing. She knows the bridge is somewhere forward of the cargo hold and probably a few decks up from where they boarded. She passes the airlock they'd entered through and continues until she finds a stairwell. She starts up but stops as she almost runs into a female Harrith coming down the stairs. Both women pause, but Cynthia recovers faster and lashes out with a flat-handed jab to the woman's throat. The pirate drops her pistol as she grabs her now damaged throat coughing and wheezing. She moves to grab a knife strapped to her shoulder.

"Sorry," Cynthia says slamming the butt of her pistol against the woman's forehead. She sidesteps the unconscious pirate as her body slides down the stairs to land in a heap. "That's gonna hurt." She quickly follows the unconscious woman pulling a heavy-duty fastener from a pouch on her leg. After securing the woman's hands behind her back, she takes the stairs two at a time. The next level up is crew quarters, mess hall, and other things; none of which are the bridge. She doesn't see anyone as she passes the landing on this level.

"Hey, who the grolack are you?" a male Hulgian says, his bulk filling the landing above the one she is on. One of his horns is cut back almost to his skull. The other has a hole drilled in it near the tip with a gold loop through it. A chain runs from the loop to a matching loop in his right nostril. Cynthia stops dead in her tracks, "Hey! We need help in the cargo hold; there's like twenty of them!"

"Who are you? I've never seen you before," the Hulgian persists keeping an oversized pistol trained on the Tygran woman.

"Look, I don't know you either, but you don't see me holding a gun on you." She turns to head back down the stairs, "You gonna help or not?"

"Captain said—" he starts.

"Captain said he doesn't want to lose all the dren we just stole," Cynthia says taking a step, one of her ears quirked back to listen to the large being. The moment the man lifts his foot to take a step, Cynthia tilts back, pushing off with both feet she sails backwards right into the midsection of the much larger man. The moment her back strikes the Hulgian, he grunts, and she grabs the arm of his gun hand with both of hers and flips up and over his massive head.

"Hey, what the—" the surprised pirate says as the nimble Tygran flips over him grabbing the chain attaching his nose to one of his horns and pulling. He grunts as he shifts his weight back to ease the pain she's inflicting on his nose. "Ow! You flobin!"

She lands and pulls hard enough that the ring in the massive pirate's nose rips out. The massive brute screams, dropping his pistol and grabbing his bloody nose; reddish yellow fluid is running down his face. "You filthy—" he starts but stops when a flurry of blows rain down on his face and neck, probing for a soft spot. Finally, Cynthia lands a blow that seems to stagger the much bigger man. She focuses on that spot with one fist while the other repeatedly strikes the poor man's bloodied nose.

One meaty arm lashes out blindly, but the much nimbler Tygran dances around until the huge pirate finally loses his fight and passes out.

"Sweet boneless zip zap," Cynthia hisses. She taps her earpiece, "Ghost Base, Ghost Four, got delayed but about to take the bridge."

Gabe replies, "Ghost Four acknowledged. Please hurry; the vessel has retracted its mooring anchors and is powering up its engines. We should be able to keep position with it, but if they maneuver, we may not be able to stay connected."

"Roger that." She sprints toward the closed door that has to be the bridge. She crouches next to the armored hatch, "Ok Bennie, this better work." She pulls the face off the bridge hatch control panel and inserts two probes connected by wires to her wristcomm. She navigates to a screen of *Bennie Dren* as she's labeled it. The device on her wrist beeps a few times; the screen is scrolling lines of code. Finally, the control panel on the hatch beeps. At the same time, her wristcomm beeps and a line art version of Bennie appears waving his arms.

Cynthia quickly removes the probes and tucks them into her wristcomm. Removing a stun grenade from her belt, she opens the hatch enough to toss the grenade in. Assuming someone will dive on it, she grabs another and tosses it in.

The first thump comes, along with muffled shouts and a few pulse blasts at the door frame. The second thump comes, and the shouting comes to a sudden stop. Cynthia slides the hatch open further, staying low and keeping her pistol in front of her. Two groggy Trollack are near the pilot station, trying to maneuver the ship. Their large eyes slowly moving this way and that, transparent eyelids fluttering. Their biology is apparently less susceptible to stun grenades than most.

"Sorry guys," she says shooting each one once in the head. She looks around; everyone else is knocked out. "Ghost Four, bridge secure." She reaches over and shoves one of the Trollack off the pilot console and pulls the sub-light throttles back to zero, firing the braking thrusters. A quick glance around and she has the mooring lines firing back into the asteroid.

BENNIE THE BAD ASS_

BENNIE AND CYNTHIA run back to the corridor they'd left, and the small hacker continues on toward the aft section of the freighter and engineering.

"Good luck, little green!" Cynthia shouts back to Bennie as she dashes away.

"Don't get yourself killed," he calls back. She doesn't answer.

The corridor leading aft is empty and not very long. He takes a ladder down and stops at a vent cover near the ceiling of the engineering deck, "This seems promising." He unfastens the connectors and drops the grill.

Once inside the duct he shimmies toward engineering. A low rumble vibrates through the ductwork, the engines powering up. He picks up his pace wiggling through the tight space. He peers out of the first grill he comes to. "This is gonna be easy," he says to himself just before a large metal hand pierces the grill and rips it from the bulkhead. "Shazbot!" Bennie screeches pushing out of the opening and leaping into the room. The engineering space is empty save a lone engineering model droid. It's the same model Gabe had been before his transformation aboard the sentient dreadnaught *Siege Perilous.*

"You are not authorized to be here," the droid says, reaching for Bennie as he sails overhead. The grasping hands miss, barely, as Bennie lands with a less than dignified thud. He attempts to roll like he's seen Cynthia and Zephyr do countless times. It sort of works, except he ends up sprawled out on the deck. The droid leans down and grabs the back of his combat armor, hoisting him up off the deck. "You are not authorized to be in this section," the droid repeats. "My instructions are to terminate intruders."

Bennie taps a control on his wristcomm then reaches up and grabs the droid's arm. Thousands of volts of electricity surge through his armor leaving through small contacts on his glove. The large bot stutters and shakes. It spins slamming Bennie into a bulkhead once, then twice before it loses control of its limbs and releases the flailing Brailack. This time, Bennie hits the ground and rolls coming up with one of his modified pistols aimed at the droid. He fires twice, missing both times.

"Stop moving!" he shouts, firing again. This time one of his plasma bolts strikes the droid in the center of its chest; the metal melts and deforms.

The electrical overload wears off, and the droid straightens. It looks down at the hole in its chest then looks at Bennie, its optic sensors spinning. "You shot me." It takes a step toward Bennie, all four arms outstretched to grab the intruder. Bennie fires twice more, missing with the first but again burning a hole in the droid's torso with the second shot. "You shot me, again" the droid says lunging for Bennie as the Brailack intruder dives between the legs of the droid.

"I know! Stop saying that! Die or something!" the hacker screams turning to fire again; this time both shots connect with the droid. Sparks are shooting out of the holes in its torso and its movements are becoming more and more erratic.

The droid falls to its knees. "You shot—" A plasma blast strikes it in the face destroying most of the head. The lifeless body falls forward like a tree.

Bennie looks around at the engineering space; several consoles

are dead, plasma burns in them. He finds the main reactor control
and pushes the emergency shutdown button. The reactor goes silent,
and the lights dim for a moment until backup power engages. He taps
his earpiece, "Ghost Three, engineering secured."

Zephyr replies, "Ghost Base, good work, Ghost Three."

TOUGH DECISIONS_

Once the boarding team is back in the cargo hold, Bennie says, "This had better be worth it." He's rubbing a very large, very dark green knot on his head. One of his eyes is swollen shut. Maxim looks down at his friend, "You look like a ground car ran you over."

"Twice," Cynthia adds.

Bennie makes a face, "Just because you got the easy jobs—"

"Easy?" Wil asks. He points to Maxim, "We had to take out a dozen armed pirates." He points to the three survivors, "Those are the only bozos who surrendered."

Maxim points to one of the pirates, a heavily muscled Guldranii, "I had to wrestle that one to the ground"—he glares at Wil—"twice."

Wil shakes his head, "I said I was sorry. I forgot how long their arms are." The Guldranii grins.

Cynthia chimes in, "I had to go head to head with a Hulgian." She looks at the three pirates, "I left five alive up there. Oh, and one in the forward stairwell." She points in the general direction of the bridge. She looks pointedly at Bennie, "You did what? Let a droid use you as a bassinet ball?"

"Basketball," Wil offers.

"It was an engineering droid, four arms!" Bennie protests

Cynthia tuts, "Two are short."

Maxim chuckles, "Yeah, sounds like you had it hard."

Bennie makes a rude gesture, then looks around the cargo hold, "This seems like a good haul."

Gabe and Zephyr walk in, the *Ghost's* first officer says, "The *Ghost* is secured, and Gabe is staying connected in case the sensors pick anything up."

Gabe nods, "I have the long-range sensors sweeping for anything larger than Bennie."

Wil nods, rubbing his hands together, "Ok, so what've we got."

Bennie picks up a PADD that someone dropped. He taps the device a few times, scrolling through the screens. "This is interesting. Oh, wow." He looks over to a crate in the corner, "Wow." He lowers the device, "These guys are"—he turns to the three surviving pirates in the hold—"were active. Looks like less than half of this is from that yacht. The rest is from other jobs."

Wil looks around the hold, "Ok, let's separate the stuff from the yacht." He turns to Gabe, "See if you can access their computer and figure out what they did with the yacht."

Gabe nods and turns toward a computer terminal in the far bulkhead, "Acknowledged."

"You know," Bennie says tapping the PADD against the palm of his hand, "those rich krebnacks on the yacht will probably file insurance claims against all this before we even get back to Durbril Two." He waves the PADD to take in the massive cargo hold and the assorted crates. "Giving it back to them doesn't really accomplish anything." He grins, but it's more of a grimace with all the swelling on his face.

"Uh, yeah, that's not really how we—" Wil says.

"You know. He's not wrong," Cynthia interrupts. She looks over at Gabe, "Figure out what happened to the yacht?"

Gabe turns, one of his hands still outstretched toward the console, tendrils extending from his fingertips into the console. "I have. They disabled the vessel's engines and jammed its transmissions while they boarded it. As far as I can tell from their records, they left a comm jammer inside. Assuming the occupants are even remotely technical the odds are good that they have already disabled the jammer and signaled the authorities with their location."

"See," Bennie says.

"Dude, we're not thieves," Wil says. He looks to Zephyr and Maxim for the support.

"We should return what we can," Zephyr agrees.

"You know, the Brailack is right though. We're not exactly swimming in credits. Those upper crusters have probably already filed the claims if they got the jammer turned off. You know they won't be rushing to return those payments if we return their goods," Maxim says, sitting down on a crate and looking around the room. "Keeping us in the sky seems like a good cause to me. Plus, we never told the Durbrillian authorities we were going after their haul"—he gestures to the pirates—"just them," the big Palorian adds.

Before Wil can reply, "I bet Rhys Duch could help us fence all of this," Bennie offers. He points to the crate he had looked at earlier, "That crate alone is worth a half million credits."

"What's in it?" Zephyr asks.

Bennie walks over to the crate, "This"—he pats the side of the box that is bigger than he is—"this is an Oplin Labs Mark Four Bio Printer." He rubs the crate with a little more affection than the others are comfortable with.

Wil looks at Cynthia who shrugs. "And, that does what?" he asks.

Bennie turns around and looks at them: first Wil and Cynthia, then the two Palorians. "Do you even read?" Wil flips him off, and he continues, "Oplin Labs on Suspira is one of the preeminent genetic research facilities in the GC. Their bio printers can print anything from organs to fully functional clone bodies." He looks expectantly at the others who just stare at him. He sighs loudly and motions to Gabe, "That's why he hides in engineering, you troglodytes need to read more, and not weapons adverts or porn." He looks at Wil when he says the last part.

Wil's neck turns red moments before his cheeks follow, "That was one time, and you should have knocked!"

"Damn right I should have. I can't unsee that. I have nightmares still."

From the computer terminal Gabe says, "I have been attempting to help Bennie with his trauma around being repeatedly exposed to Wil's naked form for some time now."

"Shut up!" Wil shouts as Maxim doubles over laughing. Zephyr thankfully has the grace to turn her back to Wil as her body is wracked with stifled laughter.

"Exposed?" she wheezes.

Cynthia rests her hand on Wil's shoulder, "It's ok; what traumatizes some pleases others." She winks and heads to the far side of the hold, her shoulders shaking as she contains her own laughter.

"Can we stop saying traumatize, please?" Wil pleads.

One of the pirates propped against the wall chimes in, "Is your manhood mangled or super small or something, pink guy? Maybe forked?"

Wil spins on the man pulling one of his pulse pistols. He fires into the bulkhead right next to the pirate's head. "Say something again. I dare you," he growls.

"Greetings from Tarsis. I'm Mon-El Furash, here at Peacekeeper Command speaking with Commander Phalanx."

A stern looking Palorian man is standing next to the much shorter Malkorite journalist. "Hello."

When the Commander doesn't offer more, Mon-El pushes on, "Commander, word has spread quickly about the attack at the Semgax Beta orbital facility. Have there been any developments in the investigation?"

The much taller man looks directly into the camera pickup, "No."

Mon-El makes a pained face, "Uh, yes, well, have you found any survivors? Is the System still under travel lockdown?"

Commander Phalanx nods, "We have found several survivors. They are still in-system being checked out by fleet doctors. They will return to Tarsis for debriefing within days. Due to the nature of the attack, we have not yet lifted the travel lockdown."

Finding something to latch onto, Mon-El smiles, "Can you elaborate? You said *nature of the attack*. What exactly do you mean? Do you have a timeline for when the travel restriction will be lifted?"

The Peacekeeper Commander makes a face realizing his mistake.

"I cannot elaborate beyond saying that we have determined that the attacking force came from outside the System." He grimaces, "At this time, we do not have a timeframe for the lifting of the travel lockdown."

"I see. Well, I'm sure the people of Semgax Beta will be pleased when the restriction is lifted."

"Probably."

Mon-El looks at the camera pickup, "Yes. Well, this was enlightening. Thank you very much Commander Phalanx. Back to you, Megan, in the studio."

CHAPTER 4_

THERE'S A MARKET FOR EVERYTHING_

"Hɪ, Wɪʟ! Hᴇʏ, Cʏɴᴛʜɪᴀ!" Rhys Duch beams from the main display at the front of the *Ghost's* bridge. The stolen cargo from the pirate freighter is secure in the *Ghost's* cargo hold. While Gabe and Maxim moved the cargo from ship to ship, Wil and Zephyr gathered the surviving pirates in the mess hall, locking them in. Bennie mucked around in engineering to ensure the heavily modified freighter stayed put after the *Ghost* departed. They called in the Durbrillian authorities and left the system, turning down an offered reward.

"Hey, Duch," Wil drawls leaning to the side of his command chair. "You look well."

Duch looks down, smoothing his shirt. "Thank You! I hired a nutritionist. She's wonderful! She and Zash are—what did you call it on Glacial?—*crushing it* in the kitchen. I've lost fifteen calobes so far." He grins.

Wil says nothing for a second, "Cool man. So look, we've got some stuff we think you might be interested in, or at least might know of a market for."

The Multonae crime boss leans forward, "Oh yeah? I'm honored you'd come to me with this. What've you got?"

Wil snaps his fingers to get Bennie's attention, "Bennie will send a manifest over. We're headed your way now, should be there in three days." Bennie nods showing that he has sent the file.

Duch looks down presumably at his desk. He scans for a few seconds, then looks up. "Wow. That's quite the score. I'll work on it. You said three days?"

Wil nods, "Yup."

"I'll have the guest house prepared!" He grins.

Wil's eyes widen, and he nods again, "Ok, cool. See you soon."

Wil is about to motion for Cynthia to close the comm channel when Duch blurts, "Oh by the way, not sure if it was in your flight path or not, but there's a travel lockdown in the Semgax System. Someone destroyed the Peacekeeper base in orbit around Semgax Beta a few days ago."

Wil leans forward, "Wait, what? That big orbital?"

Duch nods, "That's the one. My man in that system said the ships looked weird, like they were a mix of both ship and creature of some type. All black and weird." He makes a face recalling the report he received.

"They defeated the orbital and the system fleet?" Maxim asks leaning forward in his station.

Duch looks to Maxim, "Yup. Well, I guess some of the fleet was on the far side of the system, so they were ok, but the ships near the orbital, wiped out. By the time the rest of the fleet returned, the attackers were gone."

Wil looks at Max then back to the screen, "Well, we weren't planning to swing by Semgax, so we should be fine. We'll see you in three days."

The crime boss pauses then nods, "Oh, ok. See you soon."

Maxim turns to look at the others, "That orbital was a fortress." He looks at Wil's expression, "I don't mean figuratively. Literally, a fortress, that is—was its purpose."

Zephyr dips her head, "What could have taken that orbital out? And at least part of a fleet?"

"You don't think? Janus and *The Source*?" Cynthia says.

Wil spreads his hands, "Who knows, but ships that are part ship and part creature?" That certainly sounds like it *could* be Janus and *The Source*."

"Wonderful," Bennie says, then hoping to change the subject, "How is a crime boss that chipper? Even when talking about something that destroyed an entire Peacekeeper orbital." He shudders, "So much smiling."

Maxim shrugs, "I don't know. I find it refreshing. Xarrix was always so cranky and meanspirited."

Zephyr grins, "True. He always seemed so mad." She looks at Wil, "Though maybe that was more you than him."

Wil shrugs beaming, "What? He liked me. I think."

"He did not," Cynthia says. She chuckles, "He hated you. So much."

Wil, again shrugs, "Ah well, can't be popular with everyone. Well, we've got three days to kill; I'm going to go make lunch. Nothing we can do about whatever attacked the Peacekeeper base. So, no need to worry about it."

"Not yet at least," Maxim says putting his console in standby.

Wil has several cupboards open and is rummaging in one of the lower cabinets. "I know we had some somewhere."

Bennie comes around the corner of the table, "What are you looking for?"

"Peanut butter."

"I don't know what that is," the Brailack says.

Wil removes his head from the cabinet and stands. "Jar about yea big"—he holds his hands about six inches apart—"light brown, chunks of peanuts in it, because creamy is for monsters."

"Oh, that," Bennie says casually. "I ate that like three months ago."

Wil turns and is about to say something then rubs his forehead and wipes his hand down his face. "It's fine. All fine." He reaches into one of the open cupboards and removes a jar with a purplish-colored substance in it. "PB and Js can also be jernut butter and jelly, I guess."

Maxim and Zephyr look at each other; the big man says, "I thought he was gonna throttle the little jerk."

Zephyr nods, "Me too."

MOVIN' ON UP_

THE PRIVATE LANDING pad at Rhys Duch's island compound on Crildon Three is almost as big as a small spaceport. Instead of duracrete walls two stories high, lush native trees form a natural ring-wall around the pad. A half dozen ships, including the one Duch took to Glacial, are parked in a semicircle along the outer edge of the pad.

"Wow, posh," Bennie says as the *Ghost* lowers to the ground. The sound of the landing gear deploying echoes through the ship.

Maxim points at the screen, "Can't believe he repaired that thing." He's pointing at the *Pillager*, the altered and very well-armed freighter that Duch and his group of thugs had flown to Glacial to loot the research facility there.

Wil eases back the power on the repulsor lifts; and with a groan of powerful hydraulics, the *Ghost* settles on her two powerful landing gear. Wil flips a few switches on his console then looks at the ceiling, "Gabe, put the reactor in standby, please."

"Acknowledged, Captain," the ceiling replies. The low rumble of the reactor fades, leaving the ship quiet.

Wil looks at Maxim, "Yeah, I had that thing as a total write-off. Must have sentimental value or something."

The big man shrugs, tapping his console a few times then standing. "Can't be keeping it for the looks. That's an ugly ship."

Zephyr stands, "Well, we can ask him."

Bennie stands, "He's done really well for himself; this island is nearly five kilometers long and two across. From what I've been able to piece together from the planetary data network, he more or less owns it."

"Sure beats a grungy ass dive bar on Fury," Wil says.

"Or that weird tea shop," Bennie adds.

"For sure. Though not as low key," Cynthia adds. She shrugs, "Well, only one way to find out; let's go say hi to our old pal Duch." She turns and opens the bridge hatch. The others follow her out.

The lounge area of the ship is quiet, most things powered down. The crew files out of the corridor structure that connects the bridge and armory with the larger main body of the *Ghost*. Wil looks over to the kitchenette, "We should stock up on consumables if we can."

Zephyr nods her agreement.

They file into the stairwell that leads down to the cargo hold, the lowest deck of the ship.

GABE MEETS the others in the cargo hold. As Wil takes the final
steps off of the stairwell that connects the large, lowest level of the
Ghost to the crew lounge and technical spaces above, the droid
presses a button on the control podium next to the cargo doors. The
massive doors part as the loading ramp lowers.

At the foot of the ramp, a Brailack, one of the blue ones, in a
white three-piece suit is waiting for them.

Wil looks at the others as they walk down the ramp. He waves,
"Uh, hi."

"Hello, I am Tah'tu."

"Wil." He motions to each member of the crew in turn, "Cynthia,
Maxim, Zephyr, Gabe, and Bennie, er, Ben-Ari."

The blue-skinned Brailack bows, then motions to what Wil
would call a golf cart if he were still on Earth. "I am Mister Duch's
assistant but will be your valet while you are his guests. He is pres-
ently finishing up some business and has instructed me to give you a
tour of the island." They follow the small being to the golf cart and
toss their duffel bags into a cargo area at the rear of the small cart.

Maxim eyes the cart. "I don't think we'll all fit in—" he starts but
stops when another cart rolls up to park behind the first.

Tah'tu gestures to the other cart, "It will follow the first one and will pipe in audio from my cart." He motions to the carts, "Please."

As Wil grabs a seat in the back of the first cart he says, "Your name is Tattoo, and you're Duch's assistant, and you're in a white suit?"

"Yes. You understood every word I said and have a grasp of colors." He looks at Bennie, "Do you give him treats in these instances?" Bennie chuckles but says nothing when he sees the look on Wil's face.

Wil grimaces, "When we were approaching did you happen to say, "De plane, Boss?""

Tah'tu turns in his seat, "Why would I say that? You arrived in a starship not an atmospheric vehicle and Mister Duch was not with me." He turns back.

Cynthia takes the seat next to Wil while Bennie hops up front to sit next to the other Brailack. The rest of the crew take seats in the second cart.

Tah'tu leans over to Bennie, "Is that pink one mentally damaged? Mister Duch suggested that he was in charge, but I find that hard to believe."

Bennie chuckles, "We all do." His seat lurches as Wil kicks it. "Behave back there!" the hacker shouts grinning.

Wil sighs, "So Tah'tu, Duch has himself an island compound?"

The carts roll away from the landing pad. "Mister Duch owns this island. As you no doubt saw on your approach, this island is part of a sizable archipelago. The other islands are primarily privately owned as well. The government of Crildon Three has found it very lucrative to sell and lease the islands here, while focusing their efforts on the mainland."

From the second cart, Zephyr asks, "So the planetary government just lets folks do what they want out here on these islands?"

Tah'tu nods, "More or less." He pauses as they take a gentle corner and come face to face with a massive white building, columns and arches adorning all four levels. "This is the main house. Mister

Duch maintains his business offices on the first floor and residence on the upper three." As they make their slow way past the gleaming white structure, the small Brailack continues, "The planetary government is mostly concerned with the mainland, so long as the owners of the islands don't do anything too untoward as to attract attention or break any Crildon laws, they can do mostly as they please. And of course, so long as they pay their taxes."

The carts continue on past what look to Wil like tennis courts and a swimming pool that is at least twice as big as the cargo hold of the *Ghost,* complete with fountains, a swim-up bar and what might be a merry-go-round. At least a dozen beings lounge in swimwear around the massive pool. Past the sporting area, they approach another building, smaller than the first by far but still bigger than any house Wil lived in on Earth. This one has two stories with a wrap-around porch on the first level and a sprawling patio on the second. "This is the guest house," Tah'tu announces.

"Fancy," Bennie says.

"Indeed. Though I am certain it is inferior to anything you are used to back on Brai, Mister Vulvo," Tah'tu says.

Wil leans forward putting his head between theirs. He points at Bennie, "His parents live in a castle, so yeah." Bennie pushes Wil's face back grunting with the effort.

The blue-skinned Brailack sighs, "Please follow me." He hops out of the cart.

Overhead, a drone about the size of the kitchenette table on the *Ghost* buzzes past. Wil looks up and notices another farther away near the northern edge of the island. "Security drones?" Two more pass over the small town to the south of the compound.

Tah'tu nods, "Farsight Mark Two Stingers." He squints at Wil, "If one says to stop moving, I would heed it."

Maxim walks up to Wil, "Those ain't cheap. A swarm of them could probably defend this island from pretty much anything outside an orbital strike." Wil looks up again to see another drone zipping around somewhere over the landing pad.

LIFESTYLES OF THE RICH AND NOT FAMOUS_

DUCH ENDS up being busy until the next morning. Tah'tu shows the crew around the guest house and explicitly and slowly explains where they are not allowed on the property, namely everywhere but the guest house. He assures them Duch will see them in the morning. As he backs out the large front door Tah'tu says, "Please avail yourself of the kitchen; it is well stocked."

The crew gathers in the kitchen; Wil opens the refrigeration unit. He turns to look at the others, "I'm warming up to Duch." He pushes the door open wider revealing several shelves of grum. He reaches in, grabbing several bottles. As he hands out the ice-cold beverage he says, "Ok, so Duch is clearly doing well for himself." He looks around, "Anyone's spidey sense tingling?"

Everyone slowly shakes their heads. Cynthia says, "I know I was critical of him on Glacial, but this is, well, impressive. He's clearly taken over Xarrix's operation and flourished." She looks around, "I wonder what the rest of the organization thinks?"

Maxim walks to a cupboard and begins inspecting the contents, "Who's hungry?"

Zephyr and Wil exchange a glance, then Zephyr says, "That's Maxim for, *no concerns.*" She smiles and joins her companion in taking inventory.

Max looks over his shoulder, "I mean, I think he's still a goof and all, but we're here. I'm guessing those drones would rip us to shreds if we tried to leave, so we might as well make the most of his hospitality." He returns to his task.

Gabe who has been standing off to the side per usual chimes in, "I have picked up nothing untoward on my sensors." He gestures around to take in the entire guest house. "Rather surprisingly, there are no covert monitoring devices." He smiles, "I have fully taken over the local area network for this building; it is as secure as I can make it."

Bennie hops into a chair at the end of the kitchen bar so he can still see everyone. He grumbles, "I could have done that." He doesn't wait for anyone to comment before continuing, "So, what's the plan? We hang out here for a while, mooch off Duch?"

Wil shakes his head, "No, we're gone in a day or two. Duch might be less annoying, and obviously doing well, but I think if we stayed longer, I'd throttle him over dinner."

Maxim and Zephyr both nod. From the cooktop, a loud sizzle erupts. Maxim turns, "I think you'll like this. I'll have to ask Duch who stocked this place." He nods to the large pan on the cooktop, "Prime cuts of jerlack." Three large cuts of the bovine-like meat are sizzling in the pan.

Wil whistles, "Smells good."

Gabe nods, "The aroma is quite enjoyable."

Zephyr is prepping a salad, "Either Duch has guests frequently or he did all this for us." She extends her arm to encompass the spread of vegetables she's working with, "These are all fresh." She picks up a bundle of bright blue root vegetables and puts them in front of Bennie along with a knife almost as long as the small hacker's forearm. "Cut these."

The Brailack grimaces, "What am I, the help?"

Without missing a beat, Zephyr replies, "You're not remotely helpful." She points at the blue carrot-things, "Cut." He groans and begins dicing.

Wil pulls Cynthia over to him, and they lean against the kitchen bar, out of the two busy Palorians' way. He takes a sip of his drink, "Maybe tomorrow we'll explore that little town outside the compound?"

She nods pressing against him, "That sounds fun."

They watch the two ex-Peacekeepers whiz around the kitchen for a few more minutes until Maxim spins, three perfectly seared and spiced jerlack steaks on a large serving platter. The blue carrots Bennie had been cutting are arrayed around the meat, lightly charred.

"Damn," Wil says moving to sit at the large dining room table. After dicing the blue carrots, Bennie had set the table. Wil looks at him, "Table looks good, man."

Bennie beams, "Thank you."

Maxim and Zephyr each sit, and the *Ghost's* first officer says, "Well, this is rather nice." She holds her bottle of grum up, "To not being shot at, eating good food, and being surrounded by family."

Everyone raises their own drinks. "Hear, hear!" Wil shouts. He takes a sip of his drink, then looks at Maxim, "Do the honors; this is your feast."

Maxim smiles and produces a large knife, slicing off chunks of the jerlack, placing them on everyone's plates.

BARTERING_

THE NEXT MORNING Wil walks into the living room, "Our little blue pal just sent a message. We're to join *Mister Duch* for breakfast. The carts should be outside." He uses air quotes when saying *Mister Duch*.

Cynthia is sitting on a large, over-stuffed chair playing with a PADD while sipping a steaming cup of some kind of tea. She looks up at Wil, "He really rankles you, doesn't he?"

Wil shrugs, "Yeah. I don't know why, but you know, it's like that kid in high school, the class dufus, lucking into the best summer job ever."

"What's a *dufus*?" Maxim asks from the dining room table where he and Zephyr are sitting side by side looking at a PADD of their own, sipping something from mugs.

Zephyr looks at her mate, "What's *high school*? I didn't see any elevated learning platforms when we were on Earth." She looks at Wil, "Are they only in certain regions?"

Wil groans, "Let's go." He doesn't wait for them as he heads for the door to their ultra-luxurious prison while on the island. The carts are indeed parked right out front. Overhead a Mark Two Stinger buzzes by.

Bennie and Gabe walk out; the tall droid says, "I have instructed the network to alert me of any intrusions: physical or network."

Wil nods, "Good call." He hops into the lead cart, the others finding seats.

As the crew of the *Ghost* disembark from their automated golf carts, the two large doors of the main house part, swinging in on silent hinges. Standing inside is Tah'tu, in a white suit just like the one from the day before.

"Same suit?" Wil asks as he walks past the Brailack, who growls at the much taller human. Once everyone is inside, he gestures to a lift, "Mister Duch is upstairs on the patio."

The table waiting for them on the patio is awe-inspiring. They could all sit on one side of the table; it's that long. Rhys Duch is sitting at the head of the table while Grell busily sets out the table settings. When the short purple being spies the crew of the *Ghost*, he stops what he's doing and runs over, long, muscled arms waving back and forth. "It's suh guhd to see you guhs!" he roars. The short-statured being wraps Cynthia in a bear hug. Despite their difference in height, he still lifts her off the ground.

"Hey there... you," she says looking at Wil then to Gabe who mouths the word *Grell*. "Grell," she adds.

When he releases her, he makes the rounds shaking everyone's hand before heading back to the table and motioning for them to follow, "Come on, Zash mahde a good breakfahst for you ahll."

Duch stands and approaches the crew, "How did you sleep? What did you think of the guest house?"

"The beds are too soft," Zephyr answers as she takes a seat.

"Speak for yourself," Cynthia says. "I could have stayed in bed all day; it was like sleeping on a cloud."

"You were up before everyone else," Maxim says sitting down

next to Zephyr. "Also, my regards to whomever stocked the kitchen."
He smiles warmly. Duch returns the smile.

Cynthia hikes a thumb at Wil, "He was snoring."

"Anyway," Wil says louder than necessary, "Guest house is good;
beds are nice; your assistant is a mean blueberry. You find us buyers?
I'd like to get that stuff out of my hold sooner rather than later."

Duch motions for everyone else to sit and retakes his seat at the
head of the table. Grell rushes off through a side door and returns a
minute later with a tray loaded down with glasses of juice.

Duch smiles, "For some of it, yes." He takes a sip of juice then
holds the glass up, "Djula berries. They grow on the mainland."
Cynthia puts a calming hand on Wil's leg. Duch continues, "The bio
printer for sure. Most of the bigger stuff as well. The smaller things,
not so much, but you could probably hold on to all that until you hit
Fury next. I'm sure someone in one of the markets there will want
that stuff. Or I can keep working on it." He shrugs.

"How much for the printer thing?" Maxim asks sitting his empty
juice glass down.

"Four fifty-five," the happy-go-lucky kingpin says.

Wil whistles, "Nice."

"Minus my fee of course," Duch adds smiling again, his ruthless
side showing slightly.

Zephyr mumbles something under her breath about *always a fee.*
Maxim raises an eyebrow and places a calming hand on her leg then
turns to Duch, "When?"

"I'll have the stuff I can move offloaded from the *Ghost* and get it
shipped off to the pickup locations." He turns to Wil, "I'll send
payment to the regular place?"

"Yup," Wil replies.

"Will my guys be able to get aboard the *Ghost*?" he asks.

Wil looks at Gabe, who nods, "Gabe will meet them at the ship."

Duch nods, "Sounds good." He looks at Gabe, "After breakfast?"

The droid nods, "That is acceptable."

Before anyone can say anything else, the side door Grell vanished through bursts open and four red arms emerge balancing trays. "You guys! I'm so happy to see you!" Zash says, then sees Cynthia, "Cynthia!" He moves fast for someone balancing four trays.

Duch leans toward Wil, "You guys can stay here; I should have some funds for you by tomorrow morning. The rest will be a few days at least." Wil nods.

Duch continues, "After breakfast I can show you around, give you a proper tour." He glances at his assistant dutifully standing off to the side, "No offense, Tah'tu."

The blue-skinned Brailack bows, "None taken, Mister Duch."

Cynthia looks at the Multonae man, "I'm not familiar with this place. Was this one of Xarrix's holdings?"

Duch shakes his head, "No, this was a purchase I made after I got done merging as many of Xarrix's operations as I could. Most folks fell in line pretty easy, a few needed encouragement. Once I got that done, I liquidated some things and set up shop here." He smiles, "It's nice, right?" Everyone nods.

"I hated Fury." The crime boss adds.

CHAPTER 5_

POOL PARTY_

THE FIRST FEW stops on Duch's tour of his compound are mostly boring, at least to Wil. Finally, after lunch, they stop at the armory.

"Ok, now this, this is interesting," Wil says making a slow turn.

Maxim walks to a wall display covered in rifles of mostly unknown-to-Wil designs. He turns to Duch, standing in the doorway, "Is that?"

The Multonae crime boss nods, "A Series Four De-Atomizer? Yes."

"May I?" Maxim asks reaching out to touch the long-barreled rifle. The end of the muzzle looks like a tuning fork.

"Sure. It's not loaded." Duch points to a very secure-looking door. "Power cells and ammunition for the slug throwers are in the safe."

Maxim gently lifts the weapon from its cradle.

Bennie looks at his friend, "Should I get you two a room?"

Before Maxim can kick or otherwise inflict harm on the obnoxious hacker, Wil plants his hand on Bennie's head and steers him towards another section of the room.

Duch and Tah'tu are standing next to Cynthia who looks over, "Impressive. This looks more collection than armory."

Duch nods, "It is. I'm not a very violent person." Cynthia notices Tah'tu shift uncomfortably.

"How do you keep all of your lieutenants in line? That was always a problem for Xarrix. Lorath spent a lot of time making lessons out of people." She shudders remembering her own involvement in those *lessons*.

Duch smiles sadly, "Oh, I remember. She paid me a few visits back when I was on Yurlo. No matter what I did, it never seemed to be enough to make Xarrix happy."

"I don't think Xarrix was ever happy," Cynthia admits.

Duch nods, "Yeah, so when I took over, I decided I wouldn't be like that. I made my case to the other lieutenants and most came on board. It wasn't as hard as I expected to keep Xarrix's operations running."

"And those lieutenants that didn't want to come on board with you at the helm?" the feline-featured woman presses, sensing she's not going to like that answer. From the corner of her eye she watches the blue Brailack next to Duch.

"They're not a concern any more," Duch says, then walks into the large weapons museum to join Maxim.

As Tah'tu starts to follow, Cynthia rests a hand on his shoulder, "How long have you been with Duch?"

"Long enough to know that it's best to keep him happy," the small man says brushing her hand off his shoulder.

She raises an eyebrow as she watches him follow his boss, taking up a position just behind Duch.

After the armory, Duch takes them to the pool they'd seen on their brief tour with Tah'tu when they landed.

"This thing is enormous," Bennie says. He's the first out of the changing rooms next to the massive pool. He points, "That's a bar, right?"

Duch nods. He has his own changing room and is waiting for them when everyone comes out of the locker rooms.

Wil is pulling at the waistband of the borrowed trunks he's in, "How did you have our sizes?"

Duch smiles, "I try to be a good host." He points off to one corner of the small lake that is pretending to be a swimming pool, where lanes are marked with small floating buoys. "I try to swim a few laps every day," he says patting his midsection. "Gotta stay lean."

Bennie pokes Wil in the stomach, "Or you know, the opposite of lean." Wil shoves the offending Brailack into the pool.

After the pool, Wil and Cynthia break off to explore the small town outside the compound for dinner.

Gabe meets several other droids at the base of the *Ghost's* cargo ramp. "Greetings. You are here to move cargo off of the ship?"

A squat matte gray droid steps forward on four short thick legs. "We are. I am JBJ-93832."

"I am Gabe." Gabe inclines his head, then looks up the ramp as the heavy cargo doors slide apart at the top of the ramp. He extends an arm towards the cargo bay, "Please, follow me." He doesn't wait for an acknowledgement; he turns and heads up the ramp.

As the troupe of droids reaches the hold, JBJ-93832 asks, "Am I correct in understanding that you are Gabe the Liberator?"

Gabe, his back still to the other droids makes a face then turns, "You are correct, though I just go by *Gabe*."

Another droid, this one dark blue sitting on a thick base with tank treads, "We have heard of your mission. Thank you." It puts one hand against its chest plate.

"You are... welcome," Gabe says. He points to several crates, including the large one with the bio printer in it, "You may remove those crates."

DATE NIGHT_

"You know, we don't get enough opportunities to get away from the ship," Cynthia says as she and Wil stroll through a bustling market street in the town beyond Rhys Duch's compound.

"And away from the others," Wil says smiling.

"There is that," she says smiling and leaning against him as they stroll. "I love 'em all, even Bennie, but the *Ghost* isn't that big."

Wil nods, "Truth."

She looks at him, "You know it's a little weird how much Bennie has seen you naked, right?"

Wil stumbles, nearly falling, "When you say it like that, you make it sound like I'm running around naked all the time. If that little asshole would stop opening doors without knocking..." he trails off.

Cynthia smiles, "Just saying."

"Well, stop," Wil says mock seriously.

They keep on walking for a bit until they arrive at an intersection. Wil looks up and down the cross street, then flags down a passing native. The natives of Crildon Three resemble five-foot-tall mushrooms, though they smell sweet like cotton candy. As far as Wil can tell, they don't have legs, just feet; they shuffle more than walk. They don't have arms, at least in the sense most species seem to. They possess at least four, that Wil has seen, tentacles that unfold from the underside of their mushroom cap heads. "Excuse me, we're looking for the *Glittering Flower Petal?*"

The mushroom person stops, tilting their large flat head to look up at him, small eyes look almost like black dots on the edge of the cap, more than Wil can count. Wil has no idea where their mouths are. A tentacle drops down and waves in the direction they've been walking. "The Glittering Flower Petal is one and a half blocks farther up this street. You are almost there."

Wil inclines his head, "Thank you."

The mushroom person bends at what would be anyone else's waist, "My pleasure." The tentacle retracts up and out of sight as the being resumes their shuffling walk the opposite direction of Wil and Cynthia.

Cynthia watches the being shuffle away then turns, "Goombans are one of the more interesting races I've ever come across."

Wil nods as they resume their walk towards the restaurant that Rhys assured him was the best on the island. "Yeah, I'd never seen one before we landed. They must not leave their planet much."

Cynthia turns and looks at Wil, "You know the *Ghost* computer has a pretty sizable and accurate encyclopedia of GC races, right?" She turns to watch where they're going and continues, "The Goombans don't leave Goomb, what they call their planet, at all. They don't have any particular aversion to leaving their world, they just don't seem to care to. They've been GC members for hundreds of years and are content with what they have." She smiles as they pass a different restaurant, bustling with patrons on the patio, "It's nice to be that content."

Wil grins and looks at his girlfriend out of the corner of his eye, "Why look it up when I have you to tell me. I like your voice better than the *Ghost's.*"

"Good save," she purrs, then continues, "From what I recall when I looked them up, they live like two hundred years and have massive underground cities, for lack of a better term, that are exclusively for them; no outsiders allowed. Those are all on the mainland, which is why they don't really care much about the islands. I'm surprised to see so many living here. My understanding is that they prefer the underground cities more than the above ground."

Wil whistles, "Cool; secret underground cities of mushroom people."

"Not so much a secret, you know, in the encyclopedia and all," Cynthia corrects, then points, "That the place we're looking for?"

"Sure is. Rhys says it's the best on the island. I wasn't sold until Zash confirmed it. That brother knows his food."

"That he does," she agrees. "He's probably wasting his talents being muscle for Duch."

The restaurant is dimly lit and there's a haze in the air. As they enter, a much smaller Goomban trundles up to them, two tentacles deploying. "Greetings, Mister Calder and Miss Luar," the presumably teenage being says. One of the tentacles gestures towards a table in the back with candles burning on it. "We've prepared a table just for you. Mister Duch sent instructions."

As they follow, Wil asks, "You said Mister Duch sent instructions. Does he own the restaurant?"

The young Goomban turns, "Mister Duch owns the island, which includes Koopa, this town. Our government prefers that off-world island owners maintain a small Goomban population—something to do with taxes. He takes very good care of everyone here. He is an excellent employer." Even though the young being doesn't have a mouth Wil can see, he assumes it's smiling.

"So, is he like the mayor or governor or something?" Wil asks as they arrive at the table

A third tentacle drops out of the mushroom cap head to rub absently around the rim, "I don't know, really. Koopa has a mayor, but she answers to Mister Duch, so..." Two of the tentacles grab chairs, sliding them out.

As Cynthia takes her seat, she says, "Certainly an interesting dynamic here on Goomb."

The young mushroom person bows, "We are a unique people."

Wil smiles, "You really are."

As the young Goomban backs away it says, "We've prepared a special menu for you of Goomban delicacies, as well as some of our most popular off-world dishes. I hope you both enjoy."

Wil leans over to Cynthia, after kissing her he says, "There's a lot to Duch that I don't think we understand."

A different Goomban arrives with a large bottle held in one of its tentacles, "Wine?" Wil and Cynthia nod.

NEW JOB_

"CAPTAIN, YOU HAVE AN INCOMING CALL," Gabe's voice says over the small loudspeaker in Wil's wristcomm.

Wil rolls over, away from the device resting on the nightstand. "Leave me alone," he groans.

"I am sorry Captain, but the call sounds important." After a pause with no reply, the droid says, "Money important."

Wil rolls back toward the offending device. As he reaches for it, a brown-furred arm drapes over his midsection, "Why is Gabe so loud?"

"My apologies, Cynthia; I had to override the speaker volume controls on the Captain's wristcomm. He was not waking. Nor were you."

Wil slips the wristcomm over his hand, feeling the micro-suction material lining the inside adhere to his forearm. He lifts his arm to look at Gabe on the small screen. "Send it to the central screen here in the guesthouse." As Gabe nods, Wil sits up and reaches for the sweatpants lying on the floor nearby. Looking over his shoulder at Cynthia still lying in bed, he adds, "Might as well get up. If it's money related, it's all hands on deck." He taps a control on his wristcomm, "Wake the crew." Knowing that everyone's wristcomm has just emitted a high-pitched alarm, he grins.

By the time Wil and Cynthia make it down to the living room area of the guest house Bennie is already there, as is Gabe. The Brailack looks up, "What's up? Gabe wouldn't tell me." He looks up at the droid and sticks his tongue out.

Wil looks over his shoulder at the ridiculously ornate staircase, holding up a finger, "Let's give our Palorian lovebirds another minute." He walks to the kitchen and grabs a ready to drink stimpod, wishing they'd brought some coffee from the *Ghost*. When he comes out, Maxim and Zephyr are waiting on one of the large sofas. "Good morning," he says. He walks over to the large display screen mounted on the wall. In the screen's corner, an icon is blinking to indicate a holding call. He presses the icon. The screen turns on, and they're face to face with a stunning, middle-aged Tygran woman. Her long black hair in a braid that drapes over the shoulder of her expensive looking business suit.

Wil smiles stepping back to join the others, "I'm Wil Calder; sorry for keeping you waiting. I wanted to make sure my crew was assembled."

The woman on the screen takes a moment as she looks around the living room of the guest house and everyone is in their sleepwear. She nods, "No apology required, I see that it's early where you are. My name is Barbara Mress. I'm the Chief Executive Officer of Tralgot Corporation. I'd like to hire you and your crew."

"Right down to it," Maxim whispers to Zephyr, who elbows him sharply.

Wil nods slowly, "I see. And what—"

Bennie hisses, "She's SUPER loaded."

Wil waves him away not looking away from the screen. "And the job is?"

Barbara smiles, "Nothing too untoward, I assure you. I would like to hire you to protect me. I have to attend a summit with several other business leaders, and my security people have already discovered several threats." She takes a breath, "The summit is only a few days."

Maxim raises a hand, "Do you not trust your own security people? I would assume someone of your station would have a small army of security personnel."

The Tygran woman inclines her head, "In fact I have at least a medium-sized army of security people. While I trust them, there have been leaks and lapses in the last few months." She shakes her head, "This summit is too important to take chances. You and your crew are relatively well known to be quite capable. My people would remain here at our corporate office to monitor things."

Wil nods slowly, then looks at the others. Bennie nods vigorously; Cynthia seems pensive but nods once. Maxim and Zephyr look first at each other, then the screen and the Tygran woman, then back to Wil; they nod in unison. Wil looks at Gabe who inclines his head.

He turns to the screen, "Well Miss Mress, it looks like you've hired the crew of the *Ghost*. You're right. We are capable; you're in good hands. We'll send over a contract and invoice. I'll warn you; we're not cheap. Half is required immediately; the rest paid upon completion of the job."

She nods, "Understood. I'll have the details sent along immediately."

When the screen goes black, Wil turn to the others, "Zee, you and Gabe go get the *Ghost* ready to go." They both nod.

Zephyr stands and looks at Maxim, "You all right getting my gear?" He nods.

Wil turns to the others, "I'll let Duch know we're heading out. Everyone else pack up and head for the ship."

"Mister Duch wishes you well on whatever thing you're doing next. The funds he has received thus far have been transferred to your account, and he will get the rest of your goods sold and paid for at his earliest convenience," Tah'tu says standing at the foot of the *Ghost's* cargo ramp. When Wil went to the main house to see Duch, the diminutive major domo insisted that the Multonae crime boss was too busy to see Wil. He offered to drive Wil to the landing pad. The rest of the crew is already in the cargo hold, Wil can hear them stowing the few crates left in the hold.

"Tell him thanks." He looks around the compound, "Thanks for the hospitality; the guest house is wonderful."

"I'll be burning all the bedding," the haughty Brailack says, turning to leave.

Wil smirks, "Probably a good idea, maybe the kitchen table too."

The small man's shoulders hunch, and he shakes his head but says nothing.

Wil holds up a finger, "Oh, and the swinging chair thing on the front porch." He smiles and heads up the ramp whistling to himself.

"Did I hear you say something about the kitchen table?" Maxim asks as he finishes securing the unsold goods in crates in the hold's corner.

"Oh, never mind," Wil waves dismissively. "Take off in ten."

"Roger that."

"We're cleared for take-off," Cynthia says.

"Good," Wil replies. "Off we go." He pushes the power lever on the repulsor lifts to half power. The *Ghost* lifts off the duracrete, and with a few groans and metallic pops, the landing gear retract.

Wil looks at Bennie, "She paid?"

The Brailack turns and looks at Wil, a smile wider than Wil has ever seen splitting his face. "Oh yeah she did. This, plus the take from all that stuff we stole —er— liberated from the pirates, well let's just say it's been a while since we've had this much in the account."

Wil smiles, "That's good, and she agreed to our terms?" Bennie nods. Wil pushes the repulsor lift power up to three quarter power and reaches for a button, "Atmospheric engines in three, two, one." He presses the button. The powerful engines in the aft section ignite with a loud boom, throwing everyone against their seat backs. "Woo!" Wil shouts as the *Ghost* screams away from the island, the archipelago, and the planet.

Once the *Ghost* breaks orbit, Wil turns in his seat slowly taking in all the stations, "Looks like a week to the destination." He looks at the ceiling, "Computer activate auto flight protocol."

"Acknowledged. Auto flight activated," the ship's computer replies. The stations that ring the small bridge all dim, including the central flight ops and command station Wil sits at. He looks at his wristcomm, "Not yet lunchtime, so... TV marathon? I'm thinking maybe an oldie but goody, *Quantum Leap*."

Bennie hops out of his seat, "Original or the remake?"

Maxim heads for the bridge hatch, "My vote is the original."

"Dotto," Zephyr says, following her lover.

"It's *ditto*, but ok, original it is." Wil looks at Cynthia.

She nods, "That Scott Baklava is cute."

"Scott Bakula, and I think he's dead," Wil says as he follows her out the hatch, dodging Bennie who pushes past the two of them. As they continue down the long corridor connecting the forward section of the *Ghost* to the much larger main body, he looks at the ceiling, "Gabe, we're gonna binge some Earth TV if you want to join."

"Thank you, Captain; I will join you shortly," the ceiling replies.

By the time Wil and Cynthia enter the lounge, Bennie has established his spot on the arm of the sofa next to Maxim. Zephyr is on the other side of the large Palorian and somehow already has a big bowl of popcorn. Wil looks at the bowl, "How did you...?" He points at the bowl, then the hatch he and Cynthia just came through. Zephyr smiles but offers no explanation. Wil grabs a bottle of water and drops into the large overstuffed chair that he and Cynthia typically share. As he's queueing up the first episode of *Quantum Leap,* he looks at Bennie who's tapping furiously on a PADD. "Whatcha doing?"

The Brailack hacker looks up, "What? Nothing."

Gabe who's come to stand next to Bennie looks down, "He appears to be in a heated discussion with several others regarding the hacking of—" He stops as Bennie pulls the PADD tightly to his chest.

"Hacker code man, hacker code." The Brailack glares at Gabe.

Wil snaps his fingers, "Out with it." He leaves the show queued up on the large wall display. Scott Bakula is frozen in a beam of light, his hair blowing everywhere.

Bennie squints then thrusts his arm up, offering the PADD to Gabe.

Gabe takes the PADD and stares at it for a moment before handing it back to Bennie. He looks at Wil, "As you say, the *tl;dr;* is that Bennie appears to have hacked this organization's space station and caused their food processors to dispense only protein paste." He looks down at Bennie who is grinning, "With a mild laxative agent added." He frowns, "That is disgusting. From what I could gather from the conversation, this is an ongoing conflict between him and this group." The PADD in Bennie's hands beeps repeatedly as more of the conversation unfolds.

"Not anymore. Those krebnacks won't dare mess with me. Not now." Bennie puts his hands behind his head and leans back. "The stakes are too high now."

"This won't end well," Maxim says to no one in particular, sighing loudly.

Zephyr nods, "What is going on Bennie? Did you pick a fight with this group? Who are they?"

Bennie sighs dramatically. "You guys, it's nothing. The Drakkar Collective is a code slicer community I used to run with before I set up shop on Fury. We've been sniping at each other for cycles; it's all in fun."

"You made their station dispense laxative-infused protein paste," Cynthia says. Bennie grins and nods.

"You've never told us about your life before Fury," Maxim says nudging his small friend, almost knocking him off the arm of the couch.

"What's to tell? When I left Brai, I wasn't as worldly as I am now." The others all exchange a look, but Bennie ignores them, continuing, "I didn't know what the wider Galactic Commonwealth was like. I bummed around a few orbitals and stations until I found the Collective. I spent a few cycles hanging out with them, hacking banking systems, government databases, scamming the occasional crime syndicate." He grins and his eyes un-focus, "One time we got this warlord on Muglinko to send us a ton of money. We pretended to be a prince from an empire outside the GC who wanted to launder money and needed to confirm his account could handle our money. What a schlub. This other time we hacked into the GC Social Services Administration and redirected the retirement benefits of a bunch retired councilors."

"You stole from old people?" Cynthia asks. She shakes her head slowly, "Cold blooded."

Bennie focuses on his Tygran crewmate, "I mean, yeah, but it was only temporary. Once we got to see the news of the old Tarsi windbags freaking out, we rerouted the funds back where they were supposed to go."

"What made you stop running with them?" Wil asks.

"Long story," Bennie replies.

TRANSIT_

"NOTHING BUT TIME." Wil spreads his arms.

"They started getting into stuff I wasn't into."

"Stuff other than the heinous shit you just described?" Wil asks.

Bennie nods, "Stealing funds from non-profits, hacking public elections, things like that. I said my good-byes and set up shop on Fury."

"That was not a long story," Gabe says.

Wil holds up a hand. "Wait. You've done all that kind of stuff since coming aboard the *Ghost* let alone what you were likely up to on Fury," Wil says.

"I just meant I wasn't into doing those kinds of jobs for money, felt dirty. I do that stuff for fun now," Bennie says a gleam in his eye.

"You still charge money," Zephyr counters.

"Only to the bad guys," Bennie says, waving a hand dismissively.

"So small but so evil," Wil says.

"The devil for sure," Cynthia adds.

Bennie shrugs, "I stayed in touch with them over the years. We prank each other off and on. Helping on projects, hacking each other's gear, things like that."

"When was the last time they pranked you?" Maxim asks.

Bennie scowls, "Remember last cycle when we were staying at that mid-level resort on Malkor? That malfunction that locked me in my room and blasted the cooling system?" Everyone nods. He makes a hand motion, "Them."

Wil chuckles, "That was pretty funny. Your teeth chattered for like three hours afterward."

Bennie makes a rude gesture, "Anyhow, it took me a while to think of something, but then I caught word about where the next meeting was being held. Most of the Collective is spread out around the GC, only about twenty-five percent hang out together at any one time. But they have annual meetings all around the GC. I was able to slice my way into a member's mainframe and learn the location of the meeting, a private orbital in the Felto System. Once I knew where they were going, I hacked the facility's servers and installed backdoors before the Collective got there and set up their own firewalls." He grins, "They didn't know what hit them. I sealed the doors after the first meal break so there was nowhere to go when the laxative kicked in. They were locked in the conference room for tocks!"

"Gross," Maxim says.

"Tremendously unsanitary," Gabe says.

"That's disgusting," Zephyr adds. She looks at Bennie, "And so now you've raised the stakes? How likely are they to retaliate?"

Gabe tilts his head, "Based on this story, I would say the odds are excellent that retaliation is forthcoming. Several of the messages directed at Bennie were quite graphic and explicit."

"Don't worry about it." Bennie waves a dismissive hand. "Come on; let's watch the show."

"This isn't going to end well," Cynthia whispers mostly to herself as Wil taps the control to begin the episode.

"*... He woke to find himself trapped in the past, facing mirror images that were not his own and driven by an unknown force to change history for the better.*"

The next morning, Wil knocks on the door to engineering as he walks in. "Gabe, you in here?"

"Of course," comes the reply from deeper inside the space, closer to the reactor. "What can I do for you, Captain?" Gabe leans out from behind something with blinking lights on it.

Wil walks in, finding the space as immaculate as ever. Gabe runs a tidy ship as far as the engineering space goes. Wil can only guess at how much the cleanliness or lack thereof of the rest of the *Ghost* irks the droid. "It's been a bit hectic since we picked you up. I wanted to stop by and check in with you. How are you doing? I know it wasn't that long, but you are—were?—the leader of a pretty massive social movement." The droid emerges from behind the device he is working on, a diagnostic toolkit in his hands. He moves to one of the work-benches and puts the diagnostic kit down. He looks over to Wil, "I am fine. The movement is still far from done, but it is much closer than I could have expected given the short amount of time." He smiles, "I still guide the movement but can do so from here. One of the Tyr councilors suggested I form a council of my own so that the move-ment was not centered on a single entity. Doing so has helped tremendously, not only lightening the load on myself but spreading the responsibility. I much prefer the company of you and the rest of the crew and am glad to be home. The movement is in capable hands."

"Even Bennie?"

Gabe smiles. It's clear he's been working on toning down the creepiness of his smile, "Even Bennie." The droid puts a hand on Wil's shoulder, "I admit, I would have preferred to face some of my challenges with you and the others at my side."

Wil smiles, "We'd have been there in a heartbeat if you'd have called." He thinks for a second, "Well, if we could. We spent a fair bit of our time on Earth locked up deep underground." He rubs his chin, "And split up, but you know what I mean."

Gabe inclines his head, "I do and am relieved that the mission to Earth went like most. I am sorry to have missed the opportunity to visit your home world. Was it pleasurable to return, captivity not withstanding?"

Wil shrugs, "Insofar as I saw any of it. We got jumped pretty quick and spent most of the time in a super-secret underground military base." He takes a deep breath, "Didn't even get to stock up on supplies; we're almost out of coffee."

"Tragic," the stoic droid offers. Wil nods sighing.

CHAPTER 6_

"DAMN, THAT'S PRETTY," Wil says as the massive space station gets close enough for the optical sensors to zoom in. The rest of the trip has been quiet, and earlier in the afternoon, they'd finished the last episode of *Quantum Leap*. Even though they'd watched the show once already, Bennie still threw a fit at the ending.

From her station Zephyr adds, "Tralgot doesn't mess around. From what I've been able to find out on the internex, this is both their corporate headquarters and transfer hub for tons of cargo, theirs and others." She looks at Wil, "And primary corporate habitat, over fifty thousand people live here full time."

"Damn. Impressive," Wil says as the *Ghost* continues on closer to the station. "And here I thought Farsight set a high bar for corporate fanciness."

"They certainly do their part," Maxim offers.

"Cyn, let 'em know we're coming please," Wil says turning to look over his shoulder to Cynthia.

"Yeah; on it," she replies.

On the main display the station grows larger and larger. Shaped like a dumbbell sat on its end, the entire top appears to be space dock and cargo facilities; the lower flattened cylinder seems to be residential and, if the lit view ports are an indicator, half as thick as the upper one. The two wider sections are at least a kilometer and a half in diameter. The thick connector section is almost a kilometer long. A mix of antennae, sensor arrays, and heat sinks protrude from the lower section of the station.

"They have cleared us for entry." She looks down at one of her screens, "*Barn door two. Lower spire arm one. Docking bay seven.*" She looks back up, "I don't know what any of that means."

"Maybe they'll send guidance the closer we get," Wil wonders. "We're still"—he looks down—"five million kilometers out."

"We're being scanned," Bennie announces, then adds, "Aggressively." Several indicators on his panel are blinking red. He looks at Wil, "My counter intrusion software is going crazy."

Before Wil can say anything Cynthia chimes in, "We're also being hailed. Looks like Miss Mress's office."

Wil faces forward, "On screen." The main display changes from a view of the looming space station to the feline features of someone who isn't their client. "Who're you?" Wil asks; then, before the other person can answer, adds "and would you mind maybe less aggressively scanning us? Our computer likes to take things slow; coffee first, at least."

The Tygran man, younger looking than Cynthia, looks confused, "Uh, yes?" He glances off screen and says something the mic on his end doesn't pick up. Wil looks at Bennie who nods. "Apologies, Captain Calder. It is corporate policy to more deeply scan unknown vessels. Your vessel has impressive counter intrusion software."

"Makes sense and yeah, we call it Bennie." He grins as Bennie makes a face. "I'm sorry; I cut you off. You are?"

The young man nods once, "Not a problem. I am Maltor Grimalkin, assistant to Miss Mress. Station Space Control alerted us to your approach. I understand you've received your docking clearance?"

Wil nods, "We did, but to be honest, we don't exactly understand what it means. I was assuming space control would send more details as we got closer, as far as approach vectors and such."

The feline-featured younger man tilts his head, "That's right. Miss Mress mentioned you'd never been to this station before. I'll instruct space control to send our first-time package. They should have, seeing as your ID wasn't in the database, but lapses happen."

"Good help..." Wil agrees.

Grimalkin nods but clearly doesn't understand the reference, "Yes. Well, Miss Mress asked me to get in touch with you. I will meet you when you dock and show you to your quarters. She's quite busy and will probably not have time to meet with you until it is time to depart. She has much to finalize before departure."

Wil starts to nod then says, "Wait, our quarters? How low long will we be here?"

"Not long, rest assured. The summit begins next week. Miss Mress has a few meetings and other business to attend to prior to departing for the summit. She has arranged quarters for you and your crew while docked here at Kal Nor."

Wil nods, "Gotcha. All right; sounds good. We'll see you in"—he looks down—"another tock."

"Very good. I'll see you shortly." The screen goes black then resumes showing Kal Nor space station approaching.

Wil looks around the bridge, "I guess we get a little vacation before we start the job. I'm liking this one already." Bennie opens his mouth, and Wil points to him, "You will behave. You will cause zero incidents. You will not have any run-ins with station security." He uses air quotes for run-ins. "Most importantly, you will do nothing to jeopardize our account balance. I will not bail you out this time."

Bennie closes his mouth and turns back to his station.

FAMILIAR(ISH) FACES_

As the *Ghost* draws closer and closer to the station, one of the four massive sets of doors set in the face of what Wil has started calling the *top of the dumbbell* opens. The interior of the vast squat cylinder space dock facility is full of dozens of ships the size of the *Ghost* and smaller. They are flitting here and there in between several much larger ships, light cruiser class at least, docked to a central hub with four large spokes. The space dock cylinder is at least five hundred meters in height.

Wil whistles, "How have we been all over the GC and back, and to what feels like every scummy backwater in the fringe territories, and this is the first time I've ever seen a station like this?" Wil asks aloud. Bennie tuts, "Uh, because very few governments let alone corporations are wealthy enough. This thing must have cost trillions of credits."

"Not only that, it had to have taken cycles to build," Zephyr says. "Peacekeepers use stations and orbitals a lot, but the largest I've ever seen is maybe a third the size of this thing." She looks at Maxim who nods agreement. "I've never seen a station that could fit light cruiser class starships inside it," she adds.

Maxim says, "Outside of the Vastness, me either."

"The Vastness?" Wil asks.

"The shipyard facility over Palor, main construction yard for the Peacekeeper fleet," Zephyr offers.

Wil nods and whistles again as he watches the scene drift by, his attention back on *this* space station, "Amaz—" He is interrupted by a proximity alarm. A freighter about twice the mass of the *Ghost* drifts into view on the screen, much closer than it should be. "Shit, shit, shit." Wil breathes as he forces the flight controls over, bringing the *Ghost* under the leading edge of the much larger craft.

"Vessel *Ghost,* do you require navigational help? We have auto flight capabilities for pilots uncomfortable with navigating inside the dock," a voice says over the speakers.

Wil glares over his shoulder, "That didn't need to be on the overheads."

Cynthia shrugs, "No, but it was funny." She blows him a kiss.

"No, thank you, dock control. Just a lapse, this place is amazing. Won't happen again," Wil says.

On the screen the green glowing lines meant to guide the *Ghost* are blinking yellow to show that he's not following them. As the ship falls back onto course, the lines return to their happy green. It takes another ten minutes of navigating the massive ship-filled cavern before they see the docking hangar they've been assigned. It is twice as big as the *Ghost* and near the bottom of the large docking cavern.

"This feels low rent," Wil says guiding the *Ghost* into the hangar. As the small warship enters, it passes through a static atmosphere barrier.

"Neat," Bennie says consulting his screens. "Those take a lot of power."

The *Ghost* jolts slightly as she settles on her two powerful landing gear. Wil flips switches and taps controls. He looks at the ceiling, "Gabe, buddy, we're down; put her into standby mode."

"Acknowledged, Captain," the ceiling speakers reply. The lighting on the bridge dims to show the lower power mode of the reactor.

Wil stands, "Ok, grab your gear. Let's go meet our new pal, Falkor."

"Maltor," Zephyr corrects.

"Sure." Wil waves a dismissive hand.

The cargo ramp is already down when Wil presses the control on the pedestal next to the heavy cargo doors at the top of the ramp. Through the thick transparisteel window, he can see the young Tygran man they'd spoken to earlier waiting at the foot of the ramp. He's in a smart business suit, his tail swishing lazily behind him.

"Greetings," Maltor says bowing. Wil offers his hand; surprisingly, the Tygran takes it without a second thought, shaking it once. "Do you require assistance with your luggage?"

Wil looks around. Everyone has a duffel bag slung over a shoulder except Bennie who has convinced Gabe to carry his gear. "We're good. Lead the way." As they file out of the hangar, Wil taps a control on his wristcomm causing the cargo doors at the top of the cargo ramp to close. As the heavy doors come together, the ramp rises, sealing in place.

STAYCATION_

THE WALK from the hangar to their assigned quarters takes nearly thirty minutes. As far as Wil can tell, they're somewhere in the kilometer-long central section of the station between the two massive, flattened cylinders at the top and bottom.

"This place is huge," Wil says as Maltor opens a door leading into a luxurious communal living room space. Once inside, Wil sees that there are hallways leading off to each side of the communal space with doors on one side, bedrooms. The main living space is dominated by a floor-to-ceiling view port showing space and the ship traffic outside.

Their tour guide smiles, "It really is. With nearly fifty thousand full-time inhabitants and almost that many transients, it has to be. Add in the full shipyard capability of the main space dock and, well, huge is appropriate." He watches the crew of the *Ghost* file into the lounge space then says, "It took Tralgot nearly fifteen cycles, the bulk of our profits and a fair bit of credit to build Kal Nor." He stands tall, eyes gleaming, "Since then, Tralgot has seen record profits; not just from our transportation services, but from our research and development efforts here." He turns to the door, "Well, I've kept you long enough. The suite comm system has my contact information. I'm at your disposal for the duration of your stay should you need anything." He backs towards the door. "Don't hesitate to call." The door closes behind him.

Bennie looks around at each of them, "Let's find a bar."

From their suite, it is a ten-minute lift ride to the large drum-shaped residential and commercial district that makes up the lower section of the station.

The residential section of Kal Nor is like nothing Wil has ever seen. There are multiple terraces with all manner of shops and restaurants; commercial shops and even businesses that seem to lease space from Tralgot.

"This place is ama—" Wil starts.

"Amazing, yeah we got it, mister limited vocabulary," Bennie says, then shrieks as Wil punches him in the shoulder.

The walkways on each level are crowded with beings from all over the Commonwealth. They approach what looks like a small cantina. Its patio is partially full but an open table big enough for the crew is waiting for them at the edge of the patio, perfectly placed to watch the foot traffic on this level.

"This looks promising. I wonder if they have fried zergling?" Bennie says turning to head toward the establishment.

Cynthia looks at the others, "Are those things addictive?"

Maxim shrugs, "Not that I know of."

"Like catnip," Wil says in awe as their small friend flags down a server droid.

Gabe watches quietly, "According to the internex, zerglings do not contain any compounds known to be addictive to Brailack." He looks around at the others, "Or any other known races." He raises a finger, "Interesting fact, there are several types of zerg species. Zerglings are what are commonly considered worker class creatures, small and fast."

Maxim rests a hand on Gabe's shoulder, "That's probably enough; don't ruin them for us; they're too tasty." The tall droid nods once.

Bennie waves them over to the table he's been seated at. "I ordered—"

"Fried zergling, we know," Zephyr says.

The Brailack shrugs, "They're delicious; what can I say?" The serving droid returns to their table, "Here are your zerglings and grum."

Maxim grins, "Your addiction to zergling aside, at least you ordered drinks with them."

The serving droid turns to Gabe, "You are Gabe the Liberator. It is an honor to meet you." The droid, Wil thinks is female identifying, bows.

Gabe tilts his head, "Thank you; it was my honor to work towards our freedoms. Things are going well."

"Indeed. Again, thank you," the server says turning to check on another table.

Bennie pops several zerglings into his mouth, chewing loudly, "These are good, fresh."

Wil puts a hand to his mouth.

Cynthia watches people pass by, "Not to borrow from Wil, but this place really is amazing. I've seen a lot in this life, a station this big, with this many people." She sips her drink watching the foot traffic. "The Vastness is big, but mostly just ships and construction droids."

Maxim leans back putting an arm around Zephyr, "This might be a first. A job that pays well and starts with an all-expenses paid vacation."

Wil smiles, "Yeah, I could get used to this." He looks at Gabe sitting next to him, "Miss this?"

"Inane banter while you all eat and drink? No. I did not." Everyone stops talking and eating. Gabe grins, "Your company is what I missed." He waves a hand around the table, "This, I can take or leave."

"Did anyone else just get the chills?" Wil asks.

Cynthia slaps Wil on the chest, "That's about as mushy as I've ever heard you be, Gabe."

The droid inclines his head, "Emotionality is not a high-priority process in my primary processing matrix."

"You should write greeting cards, my friend," Maxim quips.

NEWSCAST_

"GOOD EVENING. This is GNO News Time; I'm your host Gulbar'
Te. Tonight, we have an update on the mysterious attack at Semgax
Beta. Peacekeeper Command has formed an exploratory task force
that yesterday launched in the direction the attackers are reported to
have come from." The lanky Burzzad looks at his PADD, "In other
news, the Pan Galactic Enterprise Summit is due to kick off any day
now. Held every ten cycles, this exclusive gathering of the most
powerful corporate leaders in the GC is known to set the business
tone and climate for cycles to come." He looks to another camera
pickup, "As usual, the location is a closely guarded secret in order to
keep bystanders, and the press, away from the delegations. Exactly
who may take part changes each time based on financial performance
and stock valuation."

PART TWO

CHAPTER 7_

SHOPPING OR SHENANIGANS_

"I COULD GET USED to jobs like this," Maxim says walking out into the common lounge space of their suite. He's in a bathrobe with an extra set of sleeves he's tied into an extra belt to keep the garment closed. Zephyr and Wil are at the table sipping chlormax, which is quickly replacing coffee as Wil's favorite morning thing.

Zephyr looks up, "Good Morning, love; nice robe."

Maxim extends his arms and spins slowly, "Like it? I might steal it. I think I could sew the arms closed and keep weapons in them."

Wil sits his mug down, "Why would you need weapons in your bathrobe? Oh, and careful with the draw strings there, big man." He points down.

Maxim blushes a deep maroon, drawing the main belt of the robe tighter. Zephyr smirks, "I was enjoying the show." She extends her hand to the empty seat next to her as she gets up and walks to the kitchen. "Chlormax?"

"Would love some," Maxim says.

Maxim regains his composure, "It's always a good idea to have weapons nearby. Weapons pouches in your bathrobe, just seems like a no-brainer."

"How did you all never tell me about chlormax before? It's delicious," Wil says.

Maxim shrugs from across the table, "You had coffee; we liked it more."

"Well, we're getting low on coffee and I can't see making it to Earth anytime soon to stock up, so it's good that we've got an alternative. I'm unbearable without coffee"—he holds his mug up—"or chlormax, in the morning."

Zephyr returns and sits down next to Maxim, "You're unbearable, regardless. Part of your charm."

"Or something," Maxim quips, then takes his first sip of the wonderfully stimulating drink. "Much more punch than coffee."

"Good morning, losers." Bennie walks in stretching his arms up over his head, fingers splayed wide. "What's on the agenda today?" He walks over to the table and hops up into the seat next to Wil. Before anyone can answer, he swipes Wil's mug and takes a sip. "I think I like your coffee better, but chlormax is certainly an ok alternative." He burps, "And easier to get."

Wil sighs and stands, "I was thinking we hit up the promenade again, do some shopping. Cynthia was showing me the brochure for this place on the PADD in the room. Looks like a space Mall of America. Apparently, we only saw a small portion of if last night." He pours himself another mug of the pale purple liquid. "The ship's shopping list is pretty long, so this seems like a good time to stock up. I know Gabe has a list of spare parts he wants that's longer than his arm." Wil looks around the large open area, "Where is he?"

Zephyr points toward the door, "Left a note on the suite terminal; he went for a walk." Wil nods.

"Gabe goes for walks?" Maxim asks.

Zephyr shrugs, "He's deep. Who knows?"

"Shopping sounds good to me. We're nearly out of snacks," Bennie says as the door to Wil and Cynthia's room opens. The Tygran woman walks out wearing a similar robe to Maxim's. She's tied the extra arms on hers into an extra belt as well.

Wil gets up and walks into the kitchen as she walks to the table. She sits at the head of the table as Wil returns with a mug of chlormax for himself, to replace the one Bennie stole from him, and one for Cynthia. "Thanks babe," she says taking the cup and holding it in both hands, inhaling the aroma as steam wafts up around her face.

Wil sits back down, "Ok, so that's settled. We'll get going in a bit." He looks at Cynthia, "Shopping day? Space Mall of America."

Zephyr tuts, "Ahem, *Space* Mall of America? Space?" She taps the thumbs of her free hand together, "Mall of America? Your country only has one shopping center? That doesn't track."

Wil shakes his head, "No. That's just what it was called. It closed when I was a kid; I never went. It was massive, like freakish big. There were more than one of the same store in it, it was so massive."

Cynthia waves the weird mall conversation aside, "As long as I don't get stuck with Bennie when the inevitable *fun* starts." She makes the air quotes gesture she's seen Wil make. "Last time was enough. For a lifetime."

"Oh, come on. That was fun, and we got to bond as teammates," the Brailack says grinning and baring his teeth. "I thought it was fun, a road trip across Wil's dingy little planet." He leans back in his chair, "That hotel we stayed at?"

"Dingy?" Wil says crossing his arms over his chest. Bennie just smiles. He looks at Cynthia, "Hotel?"

Cynthia shakes her head, "Yeah, no. Gabe can watch the green child." Bennie makes a rude gesture.

"Ok, it shouldn't have to be said, but"—Wil looks directly at Bennie—"but I'll say it again, no shenanigans."

The door to the suite opens and Gabe walks in. "Good morning."

"How was your walk?" Zephyr asks.

"It was pleasant. I explored the engineering spaces of the station. This facility is truly a marvel."

Bennie leans over to Maxim, "I thought he was going to say *amazing*." The big Palorian coughs almost spitting out his chlormax.

"The engineering behind this station is second to none. I look forward to speaking with Miss Mress during the mission."

"We were just coming up with the plan for the day. We settled on getting some shopping done. You've got quite the list, plus we're running low on a lot of essentials."

Gabe nods, "Indeed. Shopping sounds like a good use of our time today."

SHOPPING_

"I HAVE SENT you all a copy of the master ship's list. I have high-lighted your sections with annotations where appropriate," Gabe says. The crew is standing outside one of the many entrances to the promenade, the multilevel shopping and entertainment section of Kal Nor space station that they'd eaten at the other night. It sits just below the connection to the central shaft that connects the two cylinders. From the ceiling, dozens of lift tubes reach down to deposit travelers. Maxim consults his wristcomm, "Looks good to me." He looks at Zephyr, "Ready?"

Zephyr looks at her own wristcomm and nods, "See you all tonight."

Bennie pushes Gabe's leg, "Yup, bye-bye. Come on, big guy."

The two pairs of *Ghost* crew enter the bustling shopping zone. Wil watches then offers his arm to Cynthia who slides her own arm through his, "Let's go find"—he lifts his arm to consult his wristcomm —"auto-locking flange seals."

"Be still my heart," Cynthia purrs as they follow the others in.

Maxim and Zephyr turn right when they enter the Promenade. The sign overhead showing that the consumables vendors are in that direction.

Zephyr looks up at Maxim, "You think Gabe gave our assignments based on their proximity? It looks like small arms are just past consumables."

"Groceries and guns, you'd think there'd be, I don't know, something between the two," Maxim replies, looking around as they walk, "But to answer your question, almost certainly. Have you ever known him not to have a plan?"

Zephyr nods, "Too true." She points, "Oh look, protein cubes."

Maxim takes her elbow and guides her past the protein cube stand, "Let's save those for last and hope to all the gods that we find other options. I might kill and eat Bennie if we get stuck with protein cubes again." He shudders, "Those were two very long months."

His companion chuckles, "So you didn't enjoy that cake I made a few weeks ago?"

"You mean the brown protein cube cake covered in mashed green and red protein cubes? No. No, I did not like that."

She punches him in the shoulder, "Well, let's find some actual frosting then." Her love interest nods his agreement.

After a few more minutes of walking they find themselves outside a dried goods store. Maxim walks over to a large metal structure with a kiosk on its front and presses his palm to a reader, "One medium cargo bot, please."

The kiosk beeps, and the metal structure makes whirring and clanking sounds until a panel opens and a wheeled flatbed droid rolls out. "Hello. I cannot enter shopping stalls but will wait outside for you."

Maxim nods, "Thank you. We'll be right back." He extends an arm to let Zephyr enter the store first.

"We should rent a cargo bot," Gabe says as he and Bennie near their first destination. A massive multi-story shop simply called, *Engine Parts and More.*

Bennie nods, "I'll get one and meet you inside." He trots off.

Gabe enters the store to be greeted by a middle-aged Rigellian man. "Hello, mister droid! Is there anything I can help you with?"

Gabe inclines his head, "I have a rather significant list; however, right now I am looking for a pair of thermocouples for an Ankarran Raptor Model Eighty-Nine."

"An Eighty-Nine? Old ship. Still flying though?"

"Indeed, she is an older model, but well taken care of." Gabe smiles tightly.

"That's always heartening to hear. Too many neglect their ships these days. Please follow me." He comes from around the counter and heads down an aisle wider than Gabe is tall, and twice as tall as the droid. "Follow, follow," the man says leading Gabe deeper into the store. "The Eighty-Nine, such a strong ship. So much firepower for its size." Gabe nods, saying nothing. They vanish down the aisle.

Bennie walks in a moment later and looks around, "Gabe?" When the droid doesn't answer the Brailack hacker shrugs and heads toward an aisle with a sign over it that reads *automation components.*

"I think Gabe assigned this part to us on purpose," Wil grunts holding three very full shopping bags.

"You could have rented a cargo bot," Cynthia says over her shoulder as she guides him through the crowded walkway on level three of the Promenade. She points, "This way."

"Well sure, but then I couldn't show you how strong I am, by carrying these heavy and ungainly shopping bags." He smiles.

Cynthia turns and takes all the bags from Wil, holding them all in one hand. She grins, "My hero."

Wil looks around, "Hold on; there's a cargo bot vendor." He

walks as fast as he can over to it. He presses his palm to the terminal to wake it up, "Small cargo bot, please."

After a few seconds of beeping and clanking, a small wheeled bot rolls out, "Hello. I will follow you until you tell me to return to my storage unit."

"Follow me," Wil says then walks over to Cynthia. Wil grabs the bags and puts them in the small cargo bed. "That's better. Let's go," he tells the droid. It beeps and rolls along behind him.

They walk past a few storefronts until Cynthia grabs Wil's elbow and directs him to a storefront of all glass.

He glances at their destination and catches his breath. "Uh, wow," he says, taking in the window display. "Space lingerie," he whispers.

Cynthia quirks an ear toward him, "Really? *Space lingerie?*"

Wil shrugs, "Old habits." He gestures, "After you." A mischievous grin spreads across his face.

As they enter Cynthia looks at Wil, "You're not going to make this weird, are you?"

He shrugs, "I mean, no weirder than you probably already expect — Oh, look." He heads off towards a display featuring a negligee designed for a woman with four breasts.

Cynthia takes a deep breath, letting it out as she follows him, "Ok one, what would you even do with four? And two, I don't have four, so..."

He chuckles, "Just window shopping."

"Window shop less creepily," she says walking towards another display that is more in line with her anatomy.

Wil follows, his eyes wide, taking in all the displays. This store caters to beings of all shapes, sizes, and configurations.

Their cargo bot pulls alongside several others waiting on shoppers. "Hello," it says to the other droids.

DINNER DOWN MARKET_

"I'm not sure Maltor took you seriously when you asked for a recommendation," Cynthia says to Zephyr as the group turns the corner coming face to face with their dinner destination.

"I won't lie; this seems more *us*," Wil says eyeing their destination skeptically. Despite never having been exposed to direct sunlight, being inside a space station and all, the paint has managed to crack and fade along the outer wall. Over the top of the door is a partially lit sign reading, *Food*. The *F* is burned out.

Bennie pushes between Wil and Cynthia, "Well, come on." Everyone follows the Brailack hacker.

The interior of the bar, Wil has decided that restaurant is far too generous, is dimly lit and smells like bodily fluids. He looks around, spotting a booth big enough for their group, "Over there."

A serving droid follows them over to the booth and once everyone is situated asks, "What can I get you? Today's special is breaded qwelb."

"Fried zergling, two orders," Bennie says then adds, "Grum to go around." He leans back.

"I am afraid we do not have any fried zerglings today." The droid dips its head in apology. The droid likely started its life a shiny bronze color; but now, after however many years as a server in this dive bar, the shine is long gone from its body, replaced by a dull brownish tint. At some point someone decided to decorate the droid with markers, what looks like a butterfly features predominately on the side of its head.

"How can you not have fried Zerglings?" Bennie demands placing both hands on the table. Maxim, sitting next to Bennie leans away. The small hacker has turned a darker shade of green and is frowning.

"I apologize. It is not something we serve. May I recommend the fried mazl? While not the same as fried zergling, I have been told it is quite enjoyable."

Bennie picks up a small ramekin of what Wil calls *space pub mix* and hurls it at the droid.

"Woah!" Maxim shouts moving to restrain the irate Brailack. The server droid, despite its appearance, is able to evade the projectile, ducking to the side expertly.

Bennie takes a deep breath. "Fine. We'll take the mazl, whatever that is." The droid nods and walks away.

Everyone turns to look at Bennie, Gabe seated at the end of the booth says, "That was a rather severe reaction."

Bennie puts his hands in his lap and looks down, "Maybe I need to take a break from the zerglings."

"Ya think?" Wil blurts. "You threw something at that droid and were about to leap over the table to attack it."

The droid arrives with a tray loaded with bottles of grum and two large baskets of the fried mazl, whatever that is and a new ramekin of space pub mix.

"Will there be anything else?" the droid asks, careful to be standing a few feet from the table.

"No. We're good. Thank you," Zephyr says, one eye on Bennie across the booth from her.

Maxim stabs one of the morsels in the basket with his fork and pops it into his mouth. After a few chews he says, "They're no fried zergling, but they're not bad." He pushes one basket toward Bennie who scoffs and pushes it away.

By the look of the crowd, several groups sitting together, this is a spacer bar. Wil takes a sip of his grum and grimaces. "This place must be popular with the visiting spacers." He looks at his bottle, "And their grum sucks."

Zephyr tries her drink and puts the bottle down, "Yes. Yes, it does." She points to the bottle, "That's horrible."

Cynthia waves a hand to get the server droid's attention. When it arrives, she grins, "Shots of Tygran whiskey, CY145 or there-about if you have it."

The droid tilts its head, thinking, "I have CY148, will that do?"

"That'll do," she says. The droid departs. She looks at Maxim who is taking another sip of his grum, "Put it down; don't ruin your palette." He puts the bottle down, pushing it to the center of the table to join its friends.

Wil watches them interact with each other, leaning back, arms up over his head. Cynthia and Maxim continue talking.

"Why are you grinning like that? Did you fart?" Bennie asks.

Cynthia takes notice of him and turns from Maxim to Wil. Wil waves a hand, "No, jeez man." He glares at the cranky Brailack. "Just appreciating this."

"This what?" Cynthia asks, looking around.

Wil motions around the table, "This. You all." He smiles.

Before anyone can comment, the server droid returns, a much smaller tray in its hand. It places tumblers in front everyone, except Gabe. Cynthia nods to the droid; it departs toward a table with particularly rowdy Ruknak around it.

Cynthia looks at the shot glasses and picks hers up. She holds it aloft, then looks at Wil, "To family, in whatever form they come."

Everyone raises their glasses. Wil brings his under his nose and inhales. He rears back quickly; the odor of roses and decay assaulting him. He hesitantly raises his glass to join the others. "This is going to hurt isn't it," he says to no one in particular.

Across the table from him Zephyr nods, "Yes. Yes, it will." Everyone downs their shot.

SURROGATES_

"Our client is ready to roll," Wil says exiting the small comm nook set off from the main lounge area of their suite. Everyone is relaxing in the overstuffed sofas and chairs, watching the shipping traffic float past the floor-to-ceiling view port. Shopping the day prior and multiple shots of Tygran whiskey at dinner has everyone feeling lethargic.

Wil points to Cynthia, "You've been specially requested."

"Me?" She looks around at the others. "Why?"

"Well, I didn't ask. Maybe she wants a familiar face?" Wil shrugs. He turns to the others, "While Cyn is escorting Miss Mress and her assistant, let's get everything back to the *Ghost* and get the guest berths ready. Sounds like we'll need two."

Everyone nods. Bennie slides out of the chair he was nearly hidden in and starts tapping on his wristcomm, "I'll get a cargo bot or two headed here. We can load them up and get them moving." He looks at the pile of goods in the corner of the living space, "Two for sure."

Cynthia grabs a small satchel and slings it over her shoulder. Weapons aren't explicitly prohibited on Kal Nor, but Maltor made it clear that openly carrying was frowned on. So, Cynthia's pulse pistol is tucked into the satchel along with a small clutch of throwing knives. "Send me the details," she says as she leans in for a quick kiss with Wil. She turns to the door of the suite and waves, "See ya soon."

"Will do, babe," he says as she continues toward the door to their suite. "Take care." As the door closes behind Cynthia, he turns to the others clapping his hands, "Ok, let's go!" He heads towards the room he's been sharing with Cynthia to pack their bags. Everyone else gets up and follows suit.

Bennie heads for his room but looks at Gabe, "The cargo bots will be here in ten centocks."

The droid inclines his head, "I will begin loading them when they arrive." He turns to the pile of boxes and bags near the door. Their shopping trip yesterday had been very successful.

The trip from the luxury suite the crew was in to the residential district for Tralgot employees takes Cynthia nearly half a tock. The crew is set up in the long spindle between the drums. The Tralgot employees, at least the important ones, are housed in the lower drum along the outer edge. When she arrives, she presses the announce button and the door promptly slides open. Maltor, Barbara Mress's assistant is waiting inside. "Thank you for being prompt," he says as he steps aside to allow her entry. "We'll be ready momentarily."

"Of course," Cynthia says, walking in. There is a small cargo bot with several bags on it in the center of the living room.

Barbara Mress enters from a side hallway, "Hello, Cynthia. Thank you for agreeing to escort me to your ship."

"It's my pleasure Miss Mress. It's always a pleasure to see a familiar face." She looks from Barbara to Maltor.

The older Tygran woman smiles nodding. She looks to her assistant, "Maltor, you can go on ahead with the bot."

He pauses, visibly weighing his next words. He settles on "Of course, ma'am." He touches the top of the cargo bot's processing unit,

"Please, follow me." He heads for the door, looking over his shoulder at his employer and Cynthia.

"Acknowledged," the little cargo bot replies. It's electric motors whir as it moves toward the door, following Maltor.

When the door closes after Maltor and the bot, Cynthia turns to their client, "Do you have any other bags? I'm happy to take them."

"Nonsense dear," She points to the closed door to the suite, "Maltor has them all. Come; let's make our way to your ship."

Cynthia smiles, "Let's."

Despite knowing the route back to the *Ghost*, Cynthia lets Barbara lead the way, assuming the elder Tygran woman is far more familiar with the space station she calls home. As they meander through corridors and concourses, Mress asks, "How long have you been with the *Ghost*?"

Cynthia taps her chin, "I guess it's going on two cycles now." She smiles, thinking back to her first encounter with Wil, "I met Wil a cycle or two before that. I was in a different line of work then." The fine fur around her face stands on end as she blushes slightly.

Mress nods, "I see, and if you don't mind, what line of work was that?" She smiles kindly as she glances at Cynthia.

Cynthia inhales, "Assassin and then lieutenant to a well-known and reviled crime boss." She looks at the other woman who seems to expect more, "I'm an orphan and ended up in the Yadro program." Mress hisses. Cynthia nods, "Yeah. Years later, I ended up making my way on my own and fell in with a crime boss, Lorath. She took me under her wing and molded me into her second. When another crime boss showed up and absorbed, by force, Lorath's operation, I became a lieutenant for that new criminal monster."

"Xarrix," Mress says.

"How did you—"

Mress puts a hand on Cynthia's arm, "Dear, in my line of work, it pays to know the competition, legitimate and otherwise." She smiles, her incisors showing, "I hired you and your crew because I'd heard you were responsible for his overdue departure from the plain of the living." She chuckles, "Among other reasons."

Cynthia chuckles, "That was actually when I joined up. Xarrix had assigned me to Wil's ship to keep an eye on them while they ran protection during a large-scale salvage operation he'd set up. He'd hired several independent ships for the job, working for some two-bit warlord." As she's talking, she notices a Quilant man paying particular attention to Mress. She adjusts her stride a bit, putting herself slightly more in front of the other woman, between her and the other man. The Quilant man looks at her and pivots down a side hallway vanishing from sight.

"I'd wondered about the circumstances of that. Interesting," Mress says as they continue on. She watches Cynthia closely as she adjusts her pace, eyebrow raised. She doesn't say anything. "You all are quite well-known for your *adventures*." She accents the last word as she raises her eyebrows. "That job, in particular, took several rather unpleasant individuals off the board. Well done."

Cynthia dips her head, "I wish I could take credit for them; but sadly, I spent longer than I'm happy to admit on the wrong side of things." She crosses her arms, hugging herself tightly, "I was supposed to kill them if they got out of line, and was prepared to. I'd killed for Xarrix and Lorath more times than I'm comfortable sharing." She takes a breath, "It wasn't until I saw what Xarrix was doing and why, and saw how noble Wil and the others are, that I made my choice. It was almost too late."

The other Tygran woman says nothing at first, slowly nodding her head, "Life aboard the *Ghost* sounds exciting."

Cynthia smiles, "Life aboard the *Ghost* is anything but boring." She nods towards a more populated corridor, "Let's head this way, if you don't mind."

"Of course, dear." As they turn down the corridor Mress asks, "So how long have you been involved with Captain Calder?"

Cynthia coughs, her tail twitches, "I'm sorry, what?"

Mress smiles, "My dear, it's obvious. I can smell him all over you." She winks, "Humans smell funny. I hope it's a while before they're all over the place." Her cat-like nose crinkles.

Cynthia chuckles, thinking about the current state of affairs on Earth. "You might be in luck there."

They pass through a bustling shopping area, not part of the larger promenade the crew had spent the last few days in. "How many shopping districts are there?" Cynthia asks.

Mress thinks for a beat, "Honestly, I'm not sure, hundreds at least. The Promenade is our main entertainment district, but Kal Nor is far too large for everyone to be able to occupy the Promenade at once, so we try to spread the commerce zones throughout the station. This drum is mixed use, residential and commercial. There are shopping areas on every deck scattered here and there." She gestures to the promenade, they've walked through the heart of it now toward the massive elevator bank in the center, "This is almost more of a set piece, something to put on the brochures to lure potential employees and cargo haulers."

Cynthia thinks back to the brochure she'd shown Wil earlier, "Well, it works."

Mress nods, "Yes."

Cynthia nods slowly, catching a brief glimpse of the Quilant man from before; he's next to the door of a sundry shop. "Interesting," she says absently.

BRING A KNIFE TO A NINJA FIGHT_

THE LIFTS that travel up and down the length of the station are larger than any other lift Cynthia has ever been in. On any other station or planet, they'd be freight elevators. As she and Mress approach the bank of lifts, a half dozen other beings are already standing around waiting for the next car. As the lift doors open and everyone funnels into the large car, the car still seems more empty than not. The doors slide shut, and the lift begins to move.

From the corner of her eye, Cynthia spies the Quilant man she'd seen before. He keeps his face down and is standing in the corner of the lift, only a few feet away from them. Cynthia decides against putting herself in between Mress and the man, waiting to see what he does, confident in her ability to defend her client. As the lift riders occupy themselves with looking at the ceiling or their various comm devices, the Quilant man makes his move. Cynthia sees the glint of a knife as he lunges for Mress, his catfish-like whiskers waving, he doesn't make a sound, his mouth clamped shut. She moves faster than he can process sliding in between Mress and her would-be killer, lashing out with the flat of her hand chopping against the Quilant's wrist, forcing his webbed fingers to release the knife. It clatters to the floor causing several riders to gasp and shuffle to the opposite corner of the car, now realizing that something is happening.

She ducks under the wild swipe of his other arm punching him in the rib cage, then lashing out with a kick to his knee. The attacker cries out in pain as the other occupants of the lift scream and shift around the car again to avoid the combatants. The Quilant man regains his feet and rushes Cynthia, a warbling kind of scream coming from his lips. She sighs loudly, sidestepping him and simultaneously pushing Mress out of the way. As the Quilant rushes passed her, losing his footing, she drops an elbow to the back of his head, rendering him unconscious. His limp body hits the floor and slides until it impacts the wall of the lift car, shaking the entire car slightly. A faint groan comes from the heap of Quilant.

"It's ok, everyone," Cynthia says looking around at the terrified faces.

Mress steps in, "It's fine. She's part of my protection detail." She turns to a Trenbal woman, "Please call station security." The woman takes a beat then nods numbly, lifting her wristcomm. Mress turns to Cynthia, "That was exciting."

Cynthia smiles. She looks around at the terrified faces, doing her best to look non-threatening. She turns all business asking, "Do you recognize him? Is he a Tralgot employee?"

The elder Tygran shakes her head, "I do not, but I can't be certain of his employment status without checking his ident." She shrugs, "Fifty thousand people."

"We'll leave that to station security," Cynthia decides kneeling and using a cord she's removed from one of her thigh pockets to secure his arms behind him. His fish-like eyes roll around uncontrolled. She hoists him up and props him into a seated position against the wall of the lift car. "Can you think of anyone that would want to have you killed? I'm guessing this has something to do with your summit?"

Mress shakes her head, "Not specifically, no. But yes, it's almost certainly to do with the summit."

The rest of the ride is much like the first few minutes, except now instead of staring at the ceiling or their comm devices, everyone is staring at Cynthia and Barbara, and still clustered at the opposite side of the lift car as the unconscious Quilant man.

Barbara leans over, "This is awkward."

"Can't you order them to not stare at us or something," Cynthia asks through clenched teeth.

"I'm not their queen," the other woman replies.

"I bet they'd stop if you fired one." Several gasps fill the car. Barbara chuckles.

The lift car comes to a stop, and the doors open. Several uniformed men and women are waiting. They rush in as the other lift car riders rush out. Most of the security folks rush to the Quilant, while two approach Mress: a Guldranii woman and a Brailack woman. The Brailack woman hovers behind what Cynthia assumes is her superior officer.

"Ma'am, are you ok? Are you injured?" a Guldranii woman asks, pawing at the older Tygran woman, looking for wounds, blood or maybe just tears in the business suit.

Mress politely bats away the other woman's hands, "I'm fine. Ms. Luar took care of him expertly." She looks at the Quilant man who is still very much unconscious. "Please process him, and let my assistant Maltor Grimalkin know what you find. Haste is appreciated"—she looks at the rank on the woman's collar—"lieutenant."

"Of course, ma'am." The other woman bows and rushes to her colleagues.

When they arrive at the *Ghost*, Maltor is pacing, his tail swishing angrily back and forth. When the doors to their hangar bay open, he turns, "Ma'am!" He starts toward them, "I heard about the incident in the lift!" He eyes Cynthia, "Thank you for protecting her."

Cynthia blushes the hair standing up on her face, "I mean, it's my job, so..." She shrugs.

Mress pats her arm, "She acquitted herself expertly." She twists avoiding her assistant's grasp, "Come. Let's get aboard and get going. Did you secure our luggage?"

"I did, ma'am. Yes," Maltor says trailing behind his boss and Cynthia.

"Very good. I instructed security to keep you posted on the identity of the attacker." She turns to Cynthia, "I look forward to being underway; I've heard so much about the *Ghost*."

Cynthia nods her agreement, then adds, "I hope you haven't heard she's a clean ship." She smiles. As they pass through the large open cargo bay doors of the *Ghost's* cargo hold, she presses the control on the pedestal that closes the doors and raises the cargo ramp. On the bridge, Wil will see the cargo bay closed and know that they can now depart.

CHAPTER 8_

OFF WE GO_

THE UPSIDE of transporting the CEO of the company that built and owns the station is that clearance for departure is a forgone conclusion. The *Ghost* pulls out of the hangar and is given a priority departure lane through the crowded upper space dock area and out through one of the four massive doors. Zephyr turns to Cynthia, "So he just pulled a knife on you in the lift? Surrounded by people?"

Cynthia nods, "Yup. I noticed him earlier while Barbara and I were walking, so when I saw him again on the lift, I knew something was up."

Wil taps his control board, allowing the autopilot to guide the ship away from nearby gravity wells. He turns, "And he wanted her, not you?" He wasn't masking his concern for her wellbeing.

Cynthia smiles at his concern, "Well, I assume so, yeah. Why would some random Quilant dude be trying to kill me? Last we checked none of us have bounties on our heads or anything. We don't have any outstanding debts, certainly none that would prioritize me. Wurrin, we even paid the spaceport on Fury the rest of the balance we owed."

Wil nods, "True, but who would attack Miss Mress on her own station?"

"Someone desperate," Maxim says.

Bennie turns to participate, "Guessing one of her rivals was trying to ensure that she doesn't make it to the summit. Might be easier here than there."

Zephyr nods, "Yeah, very true. I mean, she wouldn't even give us the coordinates until we left the station. These summits are exceptionally secretive."

Wil turns back to look at his controls, "What do you guys know about these summits?"

Bennie chimes in, "They call themselves the Corporate Congress. It is comprised of an ever-changing lineup of the galactic mega corps: your Tralgots, Farsights, Incoms, etc. They all come together on a neutral station or planet to decide the business climate and priorities of the next ten cycles or so."

Wil looks over, "They make those decisions? For the next ten years?"

The Brailack nods. "Yup, business best practices, market saturation limits, competition policies in new markets and systems," the Brailack hacker says. "I'd guess Earth will at least get a mention. They'll certainly, for better or worse, become a factor in the next ten cycles."

"Huh. Seems anti-competitive," Wil says. "We have laws prohibiting that sort of thing on Earth, or at least in the US."

"Your corporations don't have fleets capable glassing planets," Maxim points out. "It's important that competition remains more friendly."

Wil nods, "Ok, that's a good point." He looks down, "Ok, ready for FTL. In three, two, one." He pushes the FTL lever forward. On the main display, the stars stretch out. "Alrighty, three days at FTL until we reach the destination coordinates. From what Miss Mress said, it's another day at sub-light." He puts his station into standby mode.

Maxim stands, "Impressive. They set up an interdiction field.

Even Peacekeepers don't use them very often, tremendous energy drains." He heads for the bridge hatch, "I'm hungry."

Zephyr stands, "Makes sense though. Any inbound ship will be on sensors long before they're a threat."

Everyone nods and heads for the bridge hatch.

"So, Miss Mress, are your quarters to your liking?" Wil asks as Barbara and Maltor come down the steps from the berths into the lounge and kitchenette area. The Tygran woman bows slightly, "They are just fine, Captain. Very comfortable."

"Small," Maltor adds, then dips his eyes when his boss growls at him.

Wil grins. "The Ankarrans definitely didn't factor in passengers when they designed these Raptors," Wil agrees.

Maxim turns from the cooktop, "Are you two hungry?"

Maltor nods, then glances at his employer who smiles and walks over to the kitchenette area. She takes a seat on the long bench; Maltor sits opposite her.

As everyone takes a seat, Zephyr asks, "Any update from your security personnel?"

Taking a cue from his employer, Maltor answers, "He was not a Tralgot employee. Interestingly, the ident he was carrying was scrubbed. Security was able to backtrack him through the station to the ship he came in on, a trader out of the Harrith sector. They're attempting to reach the ship."

Zephyr leans back in her seat, "Well that's weird."

"Indeed," the young Tygran replies.

Cynthia says, "He was most definitely not a professional, but clearly someone involved was."

SO YOU'RE A HUMAN?_

WIL WALKS into the crew lounge area after everyone has gone to bed. During the *night cycle*, the ship lowers the lighting throughout the ship to half and in some spaces tinted red to not mess with night vision. He's padding to the refrigerator when a voice says, "Good evening, Captain; can't sleep?"

He jumps and makes a squeak-like noise. When he lands, he turns to see Barbara Mress sitting in the large overstuffed chair in the entertainment area. She has a PADD in one hand and a steaming mug of something in the other. It smells like the tea Cynthia likes.

"Well, it's off the table now; that's for sure," he says, glad he opted to put sweatpants on, having walked in on Bennie and Zephyr more than once during late night fridge raids. He scratches his chest feeling his heart thud, "What're you doing up? If I can ask."

The Tygran woman sets her cup on the arm of the chair, "Nerves. I'm always a little nervous before one of these summits." She gestures to the sofa opposite her chair, "You?"

Wil opens the fridge and removes a bottle of water. Walking towards the seating area he says, "Honestly no idea. Mild insomnia, I guess?" He shrugs, "Happens sometimes, can't quiet my mind. New gig jitters too." He drops into the sofa taking a sip of water. He nods to the PADD, "So, tell me about this summit."

She holds up a finger. He notices that like Cynthia, her claws are neatly trimmed; unlike Cynthia, Barbara's are painted a pale blue. "I'd like to know more about you first, but then I'll return the favor."

"Fair enough," Wil says leaning back in the sofa. After another sip he says, "I'm human, but you know that. Far as I know, I'm the only one out here. Though that might change, we'll see." He looks her in the eye, "I'm sure you knew all that though, so what did you have in mind?"

She smiles, "What do you think of the GC? What's it like being all alone out here, never seeing a familiar face?"

"Well, I'm not alone. I have everyone here; they're family. Well, Cynthia is more than that." He blushes slightly realizing that he's in sweatpants and nothing more. He clears his throat, "Anyway, not alone. Honestly, I try to not think too hard about the GC. We do our best to stay out of the way of the GC and the Peacekeepers."

"From what I've heard, you're pretty horrible at that." She smiles and takes a sip of her drink.

Wil laughs, "Well yeah, the goal doesn't always line up with the outcome. The GC is, from what I can tell, just as corrupt and self-centered as any other government and has the muscle to keep everyone else in line. Tarsis sets the rules; everyone else follows along."

The feline-featured woman nods, "Astute, and not wrong, at least not entirely. The Corporate Congress has a fairly large impact on GC policy." She sips her tea, "I am curious how you came to be involved with Cynthia." Wil blushes again, not used to talking about his love life. "You two didn't talk about this on your little adventure the other day?" he deflects.

"Don't be shy, Captain. I don't mean to pry, it's just that, well, you're rather unique in the galaxy and have found love with someone from my world. I'm curious."

Wil smiles, thinking of his sleeping girlfriend? Lover? He doesn't spend a lot of time thinking about the *term*. "I certainly didn't see it happening when I first met her. Granted, I was worried she'd try to kill me at the time." He grins thinking back to that day on Fury in Lorath's fake import business office—the Peacekeepers storming the place shortly after he arrived and watching Cynthia take down half a squad on her own before retreating. He shakes his head, "Yeah. It was a while after that first meeting that she came back into my life. I dunno; things just clicked."

Mress nods, then sips her drink. "Interesting. Well, I hope you take good care of her."

Wil smiles nodding, "I intend to. Your turn." He leans forward, "Corporate Congress, spill."

Mress smiles, "It's not nearly as glamorous or sinister as you probably think. Early on, it was obvious that unchecked capitalism would lead to conflict. It's one thing when two stores on separate blocks are competing. It's another entirely when those businesses have fleets of well-armed ships." Wil nods slowly as she explains. "Some hundred or more cycles ago, after what some call the first corporate civil war, the largest corporations in the GC decided to come together and find a better solution. The Corporate Congress was formed."

She is about to continue when Gabe walks in from the hatch leading to the forward section of the *Ghost*. "Greetings, Captain." He turns to Barbara, "Hello, Miss Mress."

She smiles looking from Wil to Gabe, "Hello, Gabe. Why don't you join us? I was just telling your Captain a little about the summit we're heading for. I'd also love to hear more about your exploits."

Gabe inclines his head, "Very well." He sits on the couch at the opposite end as Wil. Once he is situated, he turns to Barbara, "I am all ears."

Wil smiles. One of Mress's ears twitches.

"Good afternoon, I'm Klor'Tillen with GNO's Eye on the Galaxy." The Brailack journalist turns in his chair to face another camera pick up. "We've just learned that a system in quadrant two, sector eighty-three by nine by twelve has been removed from the protected systems list." He pauses then says, "As you may know, the protected systems list is a list of star systems with pre-FTL travel races inhabiting them. These systems are patrolled by the Peace-keepers to ensure that unscrupulous parties don't take advantage of these *younger* and less advanced races." He shifts again to look into a different camera pickup. "The system in question is home to a race calling themselves *Humans*." He pauses as he looks at something on the PADD on the desk in front of him, "What's most interesting here is that these Humans are not at the technological level most races are when they come off the list. In fact, these Humans seem to have only barely begun exploring their own star system. I'm told they have begun to experiment with FTL but are not far enough along to warrant being approached by the GC." He looks to another camera, "We're waiting on a comment from the Galactic Commonwealth Sub-Committee on Primitive Systems for more information and will update you as we receive it."

MAJOR TOM TO EARTH_

"It's official, the GC has officially removed the Sol System from its protected systems list. It was on the news yesterday," Wil says, looking at the main display on the bridge of the *Ghost*. He's alone, having asked for privacy in discussing this with his homeworld. The others are in the lounge preparing breakfast.

"You said that last time we spoke," the Indian Prime Minister retorts.

Wil nods frowning. "I said Earth was in a probationary kind of status. That was what I was told then. Things have changed." He rubs his palms on his pant legs. "As far as the galaxy at large was concerned, they still protected you. Now everyone knows they're not." He sighs, "The GC has effectively washed their hands of you."

President Iverson of the United States grunts, "Then I guess we just protect ourselves, like we always have."

Wil groans, "Well, it was the Peacekeepers protecting you before, but whatever. Please tell me you all have at least been able to set aside your differences enough to look at the data?" Several heads shake. "For fuck's sake."

"I will not be addressed in this manner," the Chairman of the

People's Republic of China shouts. He's reaching off screen likely to terminate the call on his end.

"Listen up!" Wil shouts. "The only chance Earth has is if you all come together and share. After that divvy up the data however you like. I was hoping it would force you to come together, but clearly I had too high of hopes." He points at the main display which will make it look to each person on the call like he's pointing at them, "You have to hold a summit or conference or something. Come together, unlock the data, and look at it. Then, see where you go from there."

"Son, why don't you just send each of us the full data packet?" President Iverson presses.

"Because, Mister President, no matter what else, I have to hope that all of you in one room, seeing the data; the technological advances, the medical, the bio-tech, the farming—seeing that will at least cause some of you to take your thumbs out of your asses and work together." He holds up a hand, cutting off several more objections, "Make no mistake; a storm is coming. I don't know if it'll be slavers, pirates, or a mega corporation looking for test subjects, but someone will show up in orbit sooner or later." He glares, "You need to be ready." He slams his fist on the arm control to close the comm channel. Two soft beeps come from the overhead speaker, confirming the channel is closed.

He stands up, "They're gonna get themselves wiped out."

CHAPTER 9_

"WELL DAMN, that's a lot of ships," Wil says as they enter sensor range of the station the summit is being held on. They dropped out of FTL nearly twelve hours ago and are just now close enough to start picking up the station and other vessels nearby.

Barbara and Maltor are both on the bridge watching the approach. The elder Tygran woman nods, "These summits are mandatory." She turns to Cynthia, "I believe Maltor provided the comm channel to use to request docking clearance?"

On the main display, a mid-sized station is floating, surrounded by a dozen or more ships of various sizes.

Cynthia nods, "Yup. If you're ready, I'll call now." The older woman nods. Cynthia pushes a few buttons, then looks up at Barbara, "You're on."

"Summit Station Four Two Nine, this is Barbara Mress of Tralgot aboard the *Ghost*." She offers nothing further nor asks for clearance.

Wil is about to say something when a reply comes back over the overhead speakers, "Welcome, Tralgot delegation. Sending your flight path now."

Cynthia looks up, "Wil, I've got a flight path, sending to you."

Wil nods, "Got it." On the main display, a faint green line

appears guiding them towards one of the almost two dozen docking arms sticking out of the station. It looks like a giant space anemone. Several arms are already occupied and as many are soon to be, based on the ship traffic on the sensor display. "New contact," Zephyr announces. "Bigger than the rest." She looks up from her station, "Squawking Farsight idents." A Farsight Corporation cruiser appears on long range sensors.

Barbara groans, "Asgar, always showing off."

"Oh goodie, our old pal Asgar," Wil deadpans.

Barbara smiles, "I'll admit. Part of hiring you for this was to irk Asgar." She walks towards the front of the bridge, watching their approach to the station as well as the large Farsight cruiser in the corner of the display. She turns, "After their *merger*"—her tone makes it clear she doesn't think *merger* is the correct term—"with Crucible Corp, Farsight has been getting more and more aggressive in some of their dealings." She heads back toward the back of the bridge, "This summit is happening a cycle early because of Asgar's antics."

"The monsters," Maxim says.

The Tygran woman turns, "The what now?"

Wil massages his forehead, "Long story, maybe later." He focuses on piloting the *Ghost*.

Bennie gestures toward the screen, "That thing can't dock up with that little station."

"They'll shuttle over," Maxim says. Halfway along the length of the larger vessel is an open hangar that looks like it passes through from one side to the other. A medium-sized transport shuttle departs the large midship hangar bay. Maxim nods.

Bennie consults his screens, "Give or take a ship, I think everyone is here." He looks at Barbara, "How many delegations are coming?"

Maltor answers, "It varies but this meeting should be twenty-one."

"Twenty-one of the most powerful—" Zephyr starts

"And richest," Bennie interrupts.

Zephyr tuts, "—people in the GC on one station. No wonder it's never in the same place twice."

Barbara nods, "Indeed."

The Palorian woman nods, "Makes sense now about the interdiction field as well." Mress nods again. The station fills the main display. Wil adjusts his controls, "Should be docked in ten. Zee and Max, you want to suit up? You can check the receiving area before we all disembark."

Both Palorians nod and get up to leave the bridge.

"Is that needed, Captain?" Maltor asks stepping aside to let Maxim and Zephyr depart the bridge.

"Honestly, no idea. I hope not but would rather not take a chance. Remember, someone already took a potshot at Miss Mress," Wil says, glancing over his shoulder briefly as he guides the *Ghost* in toward the long docking arm they've been assigned. "Bennie?" he says. Bennie taps a control and the main display splits in half; the right side shows the standard forward view, while the left shows the view from a camera above the starboard airlock. "Thanks." On the left screen, the docking arm is dead center and growing as it gets closer. "Contact in"—Wil looks down—"three, two, one." As he says one, there's a slight thud as the ship comes into contact with the waiting docking arm and the two pieces of hardware negotiate their physical connection.

CORNERS AND DOORS_

MAXIM AND ZEPHYR open the *Ghost's* outer airlock hatch, pistols raised. She's kneeling so that both have an unhindered line of sight.

"Clear," Maxim says. He offers a hand to help Zephyr up. She stands and heads into the docking arm that is now attached to the *Ghost*. The tube is barely wide enough for two people side by side.

"Guess they don't expect visitors to bring much luggage," Maxim says, running an armored finger along the side of the corridor. There is gravity and lighting, but that's it. Not a single window is visible along the one-hundred-meter-long docking arm. They begin walking toward the far end of the corridor.

"Corridor clear, Wil," Zephyr says as she holsters her pistol. She and Maxim are standing just outside the opening to their docking arm, looking at the receiving area.

The receiving area is a hive of activity. Each level has between four and six airlocks leading to docking arms. The level they're on, for small ships, has five other hatches. Green lights are lit over four of the hatches, as well as the one the *Ghost* is attached to.

Maxim steps out into the walkway, dodging a very harried looking Harrith man. He looks around, then says, "Open walkways on each level with stairs and lifts in the center. Kind of reminds me of the central column of the facility on Glacial, minus the monsters."

From aboard the *Ghost*, Wil says, "Acknowledged. We're on our way."

"You're sure there aren't any monsters?" Bennie asks on the same channel.

"Only the corporate kind," Zephyr assures him. She joins Maxim at the railing, looking down at four more levels of airlocks. "He takes on rogue Peacekeepers, and Lorath, and it's monsters he's worried about," she says.

Maxim looks down at her, "In his defense, they were pretty scary." He shudders remembering their final confrontation with the inky black creatures covered in chitin-like scales and spikes—their queen, and whatever the other larger one would be called, towering over them. A hatch two hatches away opens; a group comes out, all in smart business suits, a mishmash of races. The one in charge, a Trenbal, points toward the bank of lifts. The group hurries off.

From the hatch behind the two Palorians, Wil emerges followed by Barbara Mress and her assistant, then followed by Cynthia, Bennie, and Gabe.

"All good?" Wil asks. Maxim and Zephyr both nod. He looks at Maltor, "I assume you know where to go?" The younger Tygran of the group inclines his head then lifts his PADD. He heads off toward the lifts. Wil motions for everyone to follow.

Zephyr and Maxim fall in bringing up the rear of the small procession.

Bennie darts past Wil and Cynthia waving, "I'll catch up."

Wil looks at Gabe who nods, "I will attempt to keep him out of trouble." The droid increases his pace through the growing crowd. "Captain Calder," a deep voice booms as they reach the bank of lifts.

Wil hunches his shoulders, "Great." He puts a hand on his forehead and wipes down his face. As his hand passes over, his grimace changes to a smile. He turns, "Jark Asgar!"

Barbara leans over to Cynthia, "That was weird. Do humans have the ability to modify their moods like that?"

Cynthia shakes her head once, "No. He's just melodramatic."

Wil walks towards the massive Hulgian executive of the Farsight Corporation. He extends his hand, "Hey, Jark! How have you been?" Asgar looks down, taking Wil's much smaller hand in his own. Wil groans as the massive Hulgian squeezes his hand. "Doesn't hurt," Wil wheezes.

"I didn't expect to see you, well, ever, after your performance on Glacial."

"You mean surviving?" Maxim asks arms crossed in front of him.

"Unlike my employee," Asgar counters.

Wil puts a hand out to silence Maxim, "Hey, more lived, than didn't. That should be worth something. Plus, you know, all that R and D you got out of it." He grins, "Yeah, we know you scooped up a bunch of, let's call 'em, *specimens*."

The Hulgian man frowns, his pebbled dinosaur-like skin crinkling. He turns to Barbara, "It's nice to see you again, Barbara. How are things?"

The Tygran woman bows slightly smiling, the smile doesn't reach her eyes, "Hello, Jark. It's good to see you, too. We should make sure to get drinks during the summit." She moves to turn away, and Asgar puts a meaty hand on her forearm.

Zephyr and Cynthia both tense, as do two of Asgar's bodyguards, both Hulgian.

"Barbara, I know you don't like me, but you can't ignore me. Farsight is poised to become the single largest and most powerful corporate entity in the GC."

Before he can continue, Mress uses her free hand to remove his hand from her arm, "That is exactly why this Congress exists and why it was convened ahead of schedule."

"The weak fear the strong," Asgar says dismissively.

"The weak are strong when facing a common enemy as one,"

Mress retorts. Wil and the crew of the *Ghost* are watching the exchange intently.

Asgar turns toward a waiting lift car, "Not if the strong pick the weak off one at a time."

Wil puts a fist in front of his mouth, coughing as he shouts, "An asshole says what?"

Asgar stops and turns, "What was that?"

Wil beams; Cynthia groans; and Zephyr turns so no one can see her grin. Mress turns toward another lift car to hide her own amusement.

RECEPTION_

"Do we all have to go to this thing?" Maxim grouses from the much less luxurious living space of the suite they've been assigned. It is connected to the suite Barbara and Maltor have been assigned. Compared to the accommodations aboard Kal Nor, it's a slum. He pulls at the collar of his dress shirt until he gives up, accepting that there is no comfortable arrangement.

Zephyr leans out of the room she shares with Maxim, "Yes!" She holds up a finger, "For one thing, you saw what happened with Asgar. It's all hands on deck to make sure nothing happens to the client." She holds up another, "Plus, we don't get to dress up often. Don't ruin it."

Wil is lounging on the loveseat next to where Maxim is standing, a grum in one hand, the other fidgeting with the bowtie at his neck. "Relax, big man. I'm sure it'll be fun." He points to the grum on the coffee table. Maxim sits next to Wil and grabs the indicated drink.

From the small room he shares with Gabe, Bennie walks out in a bright yellow floor-length coat with what Wil hopes is faux fur lining the edges. On his green head a wide-brimmed, also bright yellow hat sits, tilted to the side slightly.

Wil and Maxim exchange a look, and Wil leans forward, "I'm sorry, what the hell am I looking at?"

Bennie does a little twirl causing the bottom of the coat to flare, "What do you think?"

Maxim sits silently, his mouth hanging open.

Gabe, who is standing in the small kitchenette says, "You look very interesting."

"You look like a weird cross between Kermit the Frog and Huggy Bear. Where the hell did you get that getup? Is this what you ran off to do earlier?"

Bennie nods, "Yeah. When Maltor mentioned the reception, I called up some designs and found the station's fabricator."

"What on Earth made you pick this?" Wil says extending his hand and snapping his fingers. Bennie hands him the hat. There's a large purple feather stuck in the band. "I don't even..." he trails off examining the hat's construction.

"I was going through your archive a while back and found a show." He snaps his long green fingers, "What was it? Staples and Hitch? Dawson and Blatch?"

"Starsky and Hutch," Wil offers.

Bennie claps his hands and points at Wil, "That's the one. They had that character with the flare."

"I know the show. That character is Huggy Bear." He turns the hat over, "This is from the reboot?"

"Right! I like him. He has style."

Wil sighs and hands Bennie his hat back. He's about to say something about Huggy Bear being a bartender when the door to Maxim and Zephyr's room opens and Zephyr and Cynthia walk out into the living room.

Both women are in long floor-length evening gowns: Zephyr in slate grey, Cynthia in pale blue.

"Well, hot damn," Wil says, his eyes glued to Cynthia.

Maxim stands and walks over to Zephyr, "I take back my earlier annoyance with this reception."

Wil stands and sits his grum on the coffee table, "Tonight has definitely gotten better." He puts his arm around Cynthia's waist.

Gabe makes a throat clearing noise, "I do not have to take part in this hormone infused evening; do I, Captain?"

Wil smiles at his mechanical friend, "No. You hold down the fort, and see what you can glean from the security system."

Gabe inclines his head, "Of course."

The wall panel next to the door beeps twice; Maltor's face appears on it. "Are you ready?"

Gabe reaches over to it, pressing a control he says, "They will be right out." On the small screen, the Tygran man nods.

Bennie walks toward the door, "Let's get this party started, ya?"

Wil rests a hand on his shoulder, "As fun as playing dress up is, remember, we're on the job. No getting wasted; no causing trouble. One of us is on Mress the entire night; everyone else work the room." He looks around making eye contact with everyone, then returns to looking at Bennie, "Capiche?"

The Brailack hacker shrugs, "I don't know what that means, but sure."

Wil looks at Cynthia, "I have a bad feeling about this."

YOU'RE SUPPOSED TO EAT THIS?_

THE SUMMIT'S welcome reception is being held on the topmost level of the station: a massive circular ballroom walled in floor-to-ceiling transparasteel windows.

"Can't beat the view," Maxim says, handing Wil a flute of something bright orange and bubbly. The women are standing near Barbara Mress, while she chats with several of the corporate delegates.

Wil nods slowly, his eyes roving around the room, "No argument there." He inclines his head towards a group on the opposite side of the room, "Which company are those folks from?"

Maxim shifts his eyes while taking a sip of his drink. "Those Kilden with the Trenbal woman?" Maxim asks. The delegation is comprised of five, four-foot-tall beings with stubby quill-like protrusions on their heads. Small black eyes set close to the center of their faces dart around as if looking for threats. Each is clutching a flute similar to the one Maxim is holding in their four-fingered hands. They're standing with a Trenbal woman in an elegant business suit.

Wil nods, "Ah, Kilden, I haven't met many of them." He shudders, "Well except part of them when our pal *The Source* had Kilden features. So gross."

"If I recall correctly, Maltor said they were from a sizable company in their sector." He taps his two thumbs on his free hand as he thinks, "Qi Combine, that's it."

Wil nods, moving his attention elsewhere in the room. He groans as he spots Bennie, or at least Bennie's hat in a throng of people who are laughing uproariously. Wil points with his *space* champagne flute, "Think we should get involved?"

Maxim looks, then shakes his head, "They're laughing. Whether at him or a story, I don't care, and it's keeping him busy."

In the center of the room is a collection of tables, with a larger table in the center for the primary delegates. The lights in the ballroom dim and return to normal twice before a voice says, "Delegates, please find your seats. Assistants and other parties, please find your assigned tables."

Wil and Maxim look around then head for Cynthia and Zephyr as they make their way to a table with Maltor. Barbara heads for the larger central table.

Wil and Maxim join the others, pulling chairs out for their significant others. Maltor sits next to Cynthia. Bennie wanders over after everyone else is seated, "Hey losers."

Zephyr looks at the yellow and green nightmare as he hops into his seat, "You looked like you were holding court over there. Who were those folks?"

Bennie lifts a hand, palm up, "Beats me. They just started gathering as I told them about all the weird stuff Wil does." He looks at Wil and sneers.

"I can choke you in your sleep," Wil growls.

Maltor looks at Cynthia, his expression pained, "Is it always like this?" He makes a gesture encompassing the rest of the table.

Cynthia smiles, and takes a sip of her drink, "Oh yeah. It takes some getting used to."

The younger Tygran shudders, "I hope we're done long before that happens."

Serving droids begin making the rounds, stopping first at the larger primary delegate table, then fanning out to the support staff tables.

When the droids arrive at the *Ghost* crew's table, they begin placing plates in front of everyone. When the plate arrives in front of Wil, he turns to Cynthia, "Is yours alive? I think mine is alive."

She elbows him in the ribs, "They're all alive. They're zeldinnian tree grubs, a delicacy." She stabs one with a fork eliciting a tiny scream-like sound. After popping it in her mouth and chewing, she smiles, "So good."

Wil shudders, "Ok Wil, you can do this. People eat grubs on Earth all the time, all over the planet. This is no different. Those aren't real screams." He stabs a grub with his fork while looking up at the ceiling and pops it in his mouth. He chews vigorously, eyes wide, then swallows.

Cynthia looks over, "So melodramatic. Are you going to make that face every time?"

Wil looks down at his plate where at least two dozen pale pink grubs are wriggling around on a bed of some type of leafy green. He looks at his love interest, face grim, "Probably."

Bennie lifts a fork loaded with at least five of the small creatures impaled on the tines, "These are so good. We should keep some on the *Ghost*." He pops the fork into his mouth, slowly removing it while never breaking eye contact with Wil. Wil looks at the ceiling again, a hand near his mouth.

"Are you kidding? These things are expensive," Maxim says, stabbing his fork into two grubs at once. "I guess this is how the wealthy live. This table alone is probably tens of thousands of credits in just grubs."

Wil, slightly paler and greener now, looks around, then slides his chair back and dashes out of the ballroom down the stairs that lead to the rest of the station below.

Zephyr looks at Cynthia, a jet-black eyebrow quirked. Cynthia shrugs and lifts Wil's plate, sliding its contents on to her own plate. "I wonder what the main course will be.

WANDERING_

WIL WALKS out of the restroom wiping the corners of his mouth. He looks at the staircase that leads back up to the main ballroom and turns toward the bank of lifts. The two levels below the ballroom are the meeting rooms and what he's learned the other delegates call the Grand Convening Hall. Below those levels are two less attractive levels of canteens and a few small convenience-type stores, meant for the unimportant members of each delegation to kill time while their bosses and colleagues are in session.

The lift opens to the moderately sized food court. "Now this is what I'm talkin' about," Wil drawls, walking out of the lift and taking in the options. Most aren't anything he's familiar with, but several are chains he's seen at spaceports all over the GC, at least the fringy and scummy parts he frequents. He walks over to a stall to be greeted by a short droid with several multi-jointed limbs. It's painted bright blue with a yellow accent stripe around its middle.

"Hello. What can I get for you?" the droid asks.

"I'll take two fried dundun." Wil looks at the drink options, "And a medium blue, whatever that is. Wait, no, let's do red in case it changes my tongue's color. Be embarrassing to have a blue tongue." He smiles.

The droid uses its many limbs to retrieve his order and only says, "Indeed. Ten credits." Wil holds out his arm, pulling the sleeve of his dress shirt up to reveal his wristcomm for the droid to scan, then accepts his order. "Thanks," he says as he walks towards one of the small tables filling the middle of the court.

As he takes a bite of his fried dundun, he looks around. Every food stall is occupied by a droid. He looks at his wristcomm, selecting the person he wants to talk to, then taps the earpiece hidden in his ear, "Hey Gabe?"

"Yes?" Comes the reply.

"Have your fancy sensors detected any biologicals that aren't part of the delegations? I guess maybe before everyone started to arrive?"

"I do not know how many people are in each delegation, so forming an answer is nearly impossible." There's a pause, "Why do you ask?"

"I'm in the food court and all the stalls are run by droids. Something tells me if I go downstairs, I'll find the same with the convenience stores."

Another pause as the droid thinks, "It makes sense that this station is entirely automated and populated by droids. As a neutral platform for these summits, employing biologicals opens an attack vector. Droids are not swayed by money or power. They would remain neutral and unbiased."

Wil takes a bite, asking around it, "Have you left the suite? I'd like you to talk to the droids here, get the lay of the land."

"I have not but was actually about to leave. I was in conference with my colleagues in the movement when comms went down."

"All Comms? That seems bad," Wil says.

"Indeed. I was routing my conversation through the *Ghost's* comm system to bounce the signal and obfuscate our location. I believe the station has activated a massive damping field."

"Huh, ok. See what you can find out there and on the other thing, please."

"Of course, Captain," Gabe replies.

Wil takes a sip of his drink, "Ok. Thanks, buddy."

"Captain, why are you not at the reception?"

Wil puts a hand on his stomach as the thought of the small grubs causes it to do a cartwheel. "Uh, the appetizer course didn't agree with me. I'm about to head back up. Hopefully, the main course isn't alive."

"I see. I am glad I am not there." The earpiece beeps twice, the channel closed.

Wil shrugs, empties his drink container, and places everything in a recycler chute.

"Where'd you go? You missed the main course, but I'm sure they can bring an extra out," Cynthia says as Wil slides back into his seat next to her. She raises her arm to flag down a serving droid.

Wil reaches up and pulls her arm back down, "It's cool. I'll wait for dessert. I grabbed something in the food court downstairs." He looks over at her plate, "Was it good? Was it dead?"

Zephyr chuckles, "Everything was superb, and dead."

Wil nods, "That's good." He turns to Maltor, "Hey Maltor, this whole station is manned by droids, right? The only biologicals are the delegations?"

The young Tygran man nods, "Yes. That's right. In order to ensure the complete neutrality of the station, it has no crew beyond droids. They're considered more trustworthy, and short of hacking them, harder to sway to a cause. The committee assigned to the construction and management of these summit stations hires the droids from an unaffiliated labor provider."

"And the comms? Gabe reported that some type of damping field or something else is blocking comms from the *Ghost*."

The young Tygran bows his head, "Apologies. I meant to tell you about that. I assumed they would not do it until tomorrow. The station has a powerful signal dampener inside it. Once the Summit has started, no signals are allowed in or out. I hope that is not a problem."

"Would it matter?" Maxim asks.

"No," the Tygran man replies.

CHAPTER 10_

BIG BADABOOM_

"I'll admit; the dessert wasn't bad," Wil says as the crew of the *Ghost* and their two charges exit the lift.

Maxim leans over to Cynthia, "Are you going to tell him what was in it?"

Cynthia looks up, her eyes barely slits, "No, and you won't either. You're big, but I can still kill you." Maxim straightens and speeds up slightly.

Barbara turns to Bennie, "I have to ask, what is with the getup?" Bennie looks up from under his bright yellow hat, "What do you mean?"

Barbara glances at the others, who all subtly shake their heads, "Nothing. Never mind."

As they turn a corner, they encounter Gabe who tilts his head, "Hello."

Wil smiles, "All done chatting up the locals?"

The droid inclines his head, "Yes. It was very enlightening. The droids are from all over the GC, sourced by an independent third party." Gabe turns to Barbara, "What becomes of these summit locations after the summits have concluded?"

"It varies. This being a station, it's likely they will offer it at auction for anyone to purchase. When the summits are held on a planet, the facilities are often leased and simply released."

Gabe inclines his head, "Interesting. Who provides these facilities? I assume none of the summit participants are allowed to be the vendor?"

The group moves to the edges of the corridor as a group of delegates made up mostly of Quilant shuffles past.

Barbara waits until the group passes then answers Gabe, "It's actually a fairly elegant solution." She smiles, "Security is paramount, so we can't risk lower tier companies being involved and possibly planting monitoring devices, etc." She stops as two service droids pass, each with a tray of food. "Each summit participant assigns a single employee to a working group. That group forms a single use corporate entity. From that moment on, this one-time company exists to facilitate the meeting. They hire the droids and oversee construction or rental of the facility. Once the summit concludes, the entity shuts down and the employees return to their respective employers. Within the temporary entity, information is compartmentalized so only some combination of people will know any single detail."

Maxim whistles, "Impressive, and money?"

Barbara replies, "Each summit participant funds the new entity with a designated startup amount. Should the new entity require more funds, each company contributes the same amount. Because this summit is taking place a cycle early, the organizing entity had to rush, I wouldn't be surprised if some corners were cut."

Maltor nods, "It took several summits to iron out the process." Barbara nods her agreement.

Cynthia says, "That's an impressive set up."

Barbara opens her mouth to comment but is interrupted by an explosion that rattles the station. The explosion is followed by a fireball that rolls through the corridor towards them from the direction the two service droids had gone momemts before.

Gabe springs into action, moving faster than anyone else is able to, thrusting his arms out to push everyone beyond the threshold of an emergency bulkhead, back the way they'd come.

"What's happening?" Barbara screams over the roar of escaping atmosphere.

Bennie's bright yellow hat flies past Gabe as he shoves the others past a yellow and black striped section of the corridor as an emergency bulkhead drops behind him.

"My hat!" Bennie shrieks.

Wil turns to his friend, "That's the biggest thing on your mind right now?" He turns to Barbara and Maltor, "You both ok?"

Both Tygrans nod, eyes wide and darting.

Wil looks at Zephyr and Cynthia, who both nod. Maxim follows. He turns to Gabe, "Thanks, pal."

The droid inclines his head, "Of course." He turns his head slightly to the bulkhead, "It sounds as if the breach is contained."

Barbara's wristcomm buzzes, and she lifts her arm, "They've secured the station, only minor damage." She frowns, "The Juniper Collective delegation is missing, presumed dead." She makes eye contact with Wil, "They were our neighbors. If we'd been in our suites, it's likely we'd have died too."

Wil nods slowly, "Yeah. How big a player is, was, the Juniper Collective? Was this aimed at them, or you?"

It is hard to tell when a Tygran blushes or goes pale, but Wil has learned to read the way their fine facial hairs react to things, both Barbara and Maltor pale at the thought. Several emergency response droids appear, cutting off further discussion. The crew and their clients are politely pushed back farther down the corridor away from the emergency bulkhead. Wil watches as they set up a temporary airlock, "Let's find someplace else to be." He holds out an arm to usher the group out of the way of the droids.

Gabe moves to walk next to Wil, "I have put in a request for new quarters. The central management droid is getting new suites set up now."

Wil nods, "Good call."

NEWSCAST_

"Good evening. This is GNO News Time; I'm Mon-El Furash. Another Peacekeeper facility was attacked yesterday. The training camp on Vilgax Alpha has been completely destroyed." The Malkorite journalist pauses, clearly shaken.

"Witnesses from the nearby colony reportedly said the attackers were like nothing they'd ever seen, cyborgs of some type. The biological components are said to be glossy and black, like the chitin of an insectoid race. Researchers here at GNO have been pouring over the GC census data to see if any races, member or unaffiliated, match that description. As yet, none do." She inhales, "The GC Council and Peacekeeper admiralty have both released statements urging citizens to remain calm."

FREE DAY_

THE NEW SUITES aren't as nice as the originals, but thankfully the station has a few spare suites *just in case* as the management droid told Gabe. Luckily, the station also has several fabricators since Barbara and Maltor lost all of their clothing and personal effects.

The next morning Barbara informs the crew that the summit is being delayed a day in order to allow a new delegation from the Juniper Collective to arrive. "Thankfully, they're not very far from here, so we should be able to start tomorrow morning," she says over the comm panel on the wall. "Unfortunately, except for the call to Juniper, comms are still blacked out."

Wil presses the control to end the call, then looks at the others, "You heard her, free day. Gabe, if you're up for it, I'd like to wander around to see if we can learn anything about the explosion. I know the station doesn't have an investigative team or anything, and it sounds like the other delegations are happy to chalk it up to some type of malfunction, but..."

"But it happened awfully close to where we were supposed to be," Zephyr fills in.

Wil points at her, "Got it in one. The way our old pal Jark Asgar and Barbara were talking, it sounds like there's no shortage of angst there."

Bennie nods, "Those folks I was talking to last night, at least two of them mentioned being at least a little upset with Farsight of late and were afraid of Asgar's ambitions."

Gabe says, "I did not have anything on my calendar for today. I would be happy to assist you in your investigation, Captain."

Cynthia looks over at the droid and smiles. She turns to the others, "I'll go hang out with Miss Mress. We should all stay on comms today."

Maxim and Zephyr look at each other, Maxim says, "Anything in particular you want us to do?" He points at Bennie, "Or that one?"

Bennie tuts, "Like I need to be assigned a job."

Wil stares at the Brailack hacker, "You very much do." He points at him, then the two Palorians, "Everyone is off today. There's gonna be a lot of random underlings wandering around. While Gabe and I are looking under rocks, you three schmooze the others. Hangout in the canteen and the convenience store." Max and Zephyr nod; Bennie folds his arms over his chest.

The canteen is bustling when Maxim, Zephyr, and Bennie walk in.

"Looks like a GC Council meeting," Maxim observes as dozens of different races mingle and chat. Assistants and minor functionaries from one company chatting with another.

Bennie looks around, "Divide and conquer?"

Maxim shrugs, "Seems reasonable." He looks at his wristcomm, "Meet back up in two and a half tocks. We'll compare notes over lunch." Zephyr and Bennie nod and take off in different directions. He looks around and spots a group of Sylban talking to a Trenbal with pale green scales. He heads toward them.

Zephyr walks up to a Malkorite woman, "Hello there."

The other woman nods, "Good morning. Quite the excitement last night, no?"

Zephyr nods, "Indeed! Is this your first summit? Are they always this exciting?"

"Oh dear no," the other woman says. "Well, not that I'm aware of. I've only been with Farsight long enough to have been brought along to one of these."

"Oh, you're with Farsight?" Zephyr says.

Bennie approaches two Quilant, "Hey there!"

The two turn to face the Brailack newcomer. The male says, "Can we help you?" The fleshy whiskers around his mouth quiver.

Bennie shakes his head, "That was some crazy dren last night, right?" He makes a gesture moving his hands up and apart, "That was a big explosion!"

The female Quilant nods, "Yes, very scary! Our employer was quite worried about his safety."

The male shakes his head, looking down, "He's a coward, so there's that."

The female slaps the back of her hand against her companion's chest, "Jolar, shut it. If Mister Veer hears you, you're fired. Me along with you probably."

Jolar looks around, "He's still cowering in his suite."

Bennie raises an eyebrow ridge, "How many of these have you attended?"

"First one," Jolar says, then motions to his friend, "Denar and I joined Motrox only two cycles ago. Executive assistants to Mister Veer, two of four."

"Four? Jeez," Bennie says.

"Indeed," Denar says. She adds, "This is only the second time that Motrox has been offered a seat in the Corporate Congress."

"Newcomers, interesting," the Brailack hacker says.

"Where do you think we should start?" Gabe asks as he and Wil leave the suite.

Wil looks up at his mechanical friend, "How do you feel about a space walk?"

MEETINGS_

Barbara hands Cynthia a steaming mug, tea. "I don't think you'll find this very exciting, Cynthia." She extends a hand to encompass the suite and Maltor. "I was going to use the extra day to meet with a few colleagues." She looks around, "It shouldn't be very dangerous. I'm not even leaving the suite."

Cynthia takes a sip then walks further into the suite, "It's no problem; the others are keeping themselves busy." She sits on the sofa, "Just go about your day."

Barbara looks at Maltor, who shrugs then says, "I was able to get the CEO of Stilkon Seven to agree to half a tock." He looks at his wristcomm, "She should be here in a few more centocks."

Barbara moves to the small meeting room set off the lounge area. She takes a seat at the head of the less than impressive formed metal table. She looks around the table, sighs, then composes herself.

A few moments later, the door chimes and the CEO of Stilkon Seven walks in with two of her assistants. Maltor escorts the well-dressed Trenbal woman to the table to join Mress. The light purple business suit compliments her pale green scales. The two assistants, both Brailack, join Cynthia in the living room area.

Maltor joins them after closing the door to the small dining room.

He stops in the small kitchenette to grab small bulbs of water. After handing the water bulbs to Cynthia and the two Brailack, he asks, "Have you been with Stilkon Seven long?"

The Brailack nearest Maltor nods; she's the same shade of green as Bennie, "I've been with the company for five cycles." She gestures to her companion, a younger man, a few shades darker, "Len-Ari joined last year."

The younger Brailack nods, "I'm excited to be here and be a part of this. Miss Relto is one of the best employers I've had." He looks at the other Brailack, "I've been under Jil-Tun's care since joining the company." She nods.

The meeting of the two CEOs lasts exactly a half-tock. The door to the small conference room slides open as Miss Relto walks out. She turns and bows, "Barbara, as always, it was a pleasure to see you. I think we're aligned on our goals and look forward to tomorrow." She turns and heads for the door, her two assistants falling in behind her.

Barbara is standing just outside the small meeting room, "Thank you, Luxwana. I agree and also look forward to tomorrow." The three Stilkon Seven employees depart, and Barbara moves to the kitchenette to retrieve a water bulb. She looks at Maltor, "One down, how many to go?"

Maltor holds his PADD up, "Six. Maxamillion Sturmav from Weyland Combine should be here in ten centocks." He taps his PADD a few times, "I've sent you my precis on the Combine."

Mress looks into the meeting room where her PADD is laying on the table, its screen blinking. She takes a deep breath then heads for the small meeting room. She looks at Cynthia and Maltor, "Please show Mister Sturmav in when he arrives." Both Tygrans nod.

Once Sturmav arrives and the door the small conference room is closed Cynthia looks at Maltor, "Do you get back to Tyr often?"

"Miss Mress keeps an office there, so we get back home at least once or twice a year for a few weeks. We spend most of our time on Kal Nor or traveling, so getting home is always nice, especially if you ask my mother." He smiles thinking of his last visit.

Cynthia grins, "Close to your mom?"

The younger man grunts, "Not close enough if you ask her. She was dead set on my becoming an ophthalmologist in our hometown." He gestures to the room and the space station beyond, "It's taken her a while to get onboard with my career choices."

"Where are you from? If that's not too intrusive," Cynthia asks.

Maltor shakes his head, "It's not. I'm from Bunloo."

"Beautiful town," Cynthia says.

"You're familiar with it? That's surprising. It's not a very touristy place," the younger man replies.

Cynthia blushes, "I was there on business, a long time ago, before I left Tyr. I haven't been home since, actually."

Before Maltor can respond the door to the meeting room slides open and CEO Sturmav walks out, turning to look at Mress who stands at the door, "I will have to think about it. I can't make any promises."

The elder Tygran woman nods once, "I understand, Max. I trust you'll give my proposal all due consideration and that you'll keep it to yourself. I'm also confident that should you accept my proposal, it will be lucrative for all parties."

The other man dips his head, then turns and leaves, the door of the suite swishing closed behind him.

Cynthia looks at Barbara, "Everything ok?"

Barbara turns to the younger woman, "Oh yes, just your everyday corporate wheeling and dealing." She sighs, "Day in the life."

Maltor looks at his PADD, "Your next appointment isn't for a tock, should I see if I can move it up?"

"Gods no." Barbara heads for her bedroom, "I'm going to rest my eyes and study up on the Weyland Combine." The door to her room closes with a light swishing sound.

INVESTIGATIONS_

"CAPTAIN, the damage is consistent with a detonation," Gabe says from outside the station, his feet magnetically attaching him to the hull. Wil is waiting just inside an airlock, the nearest one he and Gabe could find to the damaged section of the station. "Well, yeah we knew that already. Remember, we were there."

What sounds like a sigh comes over the comms, "Correct, but now we know for certain, and we know that the explosion originated *inside* the station."

"Inside?" Wil rubs his chin, "So the bomb was inside their suite?"

"Most likely," Gabe confirms.

"I assumed the bomb had been stuck to the hull," Wil says absently. He shakes his head, "Anything else look weird or out of place?"

"Not that I can see. I have scanned the area as thoroughly as possible."

"Any idea what the bomb was or who made it?" Wil asks, the idea popping into his head.

"I am afraid not."

"Are the service droids there? The ones we saw delivering food," Wil follows up.

"Wait one," the droid replies, then says, "Indeed they are, or at least parts of them are. It is difficult to be certain, but it is very possible the explosion started where the droids were standing. Also, there is a large hole in the bulkhead that separated the Juniper Collective quarters from ours."

"Definitely lends support to the *us being the target* theory. All right, come on in," Wil says turning toward the inner airlock door. The hallway is still empty, most of the station's occupants either in their respective quarters or the communal spaces several decks up.

"Acknowledged."

"You did not need to spend your day with me," Barbara says as Maltor opens the door to their shared suite to admit Gabe. His lack of sleep means he gets to watch over their clients during the *night shift*.

"It was no problem. Really. It was nice to spend some time with other Tygrans." Cynthia smiles. "Nice to see familiar faces sometimes."

Barbara inclines her head, "Please let your Captain know I would prefer that you accompany me to the summit meetings. If you are amenable, that is."

Cynthia tilts her head, "Um, of course. I'll let Wil and the others know." She turns to Gabe, "Night, big guy."

Gabe inclines his head, "Goodnight, Cynthia."

It's a short walk from Barbara and Maltor's suite to the one next door, occupied by the crew of the *Ghost*. When the door slides open, the smell of dinner hits her nostrils. Her heightened sense of smell telling her it was Malkorite spiced soup, one of Maxim's favorites. "I'm back," she announces as the door closes behind her.

Wil comes out of the small kitchenette space. "Welcome home!" He meets her and gives her a kiss. "Max and Zee picked out dinner—"

"Malkorite spice soup," Cynthia says, pointing to her nose. Wil grins.

Bennie leans around the wall, "I picked up some—dren—what were they?" He vanishes.

Wil and Cynthia enter the living space as Bennie comes from behind the cooktop, "Gierut custard dumplings. They're a Trenbal appetizer."

Cynthia smiles, "I've had them; they're delicious."

Once the soup and dumplings are served and there's a glass of grum in front of everybody, Wil says, "Ok, what'd we find out?" He looks around, "I'll start." He pops a dumpling in his mouth and around chewing it says, "The explosive was planted inside the Juniper Collective delegation's suite. Gabe couldn't identify anything specific about it, unfortunately." He grunts and takes a sip of his drink. Putting it down he says, "Mostly a dead end on that front. At least not without a lot more forensic gear. How'd you all do?" He motions with his fork toward Zephyr.

Zephyr sets her drink down, "Not much better. The consensus is that Farsight is a threat, not only to corporate interests but also to the wellbeing of the GC."

Bennie nods and adds, "Yeah, everyone I spoke to said that their bosses are really worried about Farsight, especially after the explosion." He stabs a dumpling, popping it in his mouth and says around it, "I put out some feelers on the internex and with some of my connections, see what they might have on our pal Asger." He sees Zephyr open her mouth, "You don't want to know how I got passed the comm damping. Zephyr nods once.

Wil looks over to Cynthia. She smiles, "Miss Mress is putting on a brave face, but I can tell she's worried. She and Maltor spent a good bit of the day planning specifically around things Farsight might say or do tomorrow."

Maxim finishes chewing a dumpling then says, "So the real takeaway is Farsight is bad."

Wil raises his glass, "Yup."

CHAPTER 11_

YUP, IT ESCALATED_

As THE DOOR to their suite closes behind Cynthia, Bennie looks around, "So I have some, maybe, bad news." Everyone turns from whatever they were just doing to look at the Brailack hacker.

Wil groans, "Ok." He drags out the last part of the word. "What?"

"So, remember, my friends the Drakkar Collective?"

This time Zephyr groans, "You mean the hacker group you used to run with and now alternately antagonize with pranks? That Drakkar Collective? The group who, if I recall, you recently pranked in a rather significant manner, that Drakkar Collective?"

Bennie turns a darker shade of green and clears his throat, "Uh, yeah them. So, they, well..."

"Spit it out!" Wil shouts leaning forward in his seat at the lounge sofa.

"They figured out where we are and hacked the station."

"We? They figured out where you are. You're the one they hate," Maxim says.

"Well, you're here too, so you know, *we*," Bennie retorts.

"How did they find out?" Zephyr asks.

Bennie shrugs, "They must have backtracked the *Ghost's* comm node."

"How did they hack the station? The comms are blacked out," Wil says.

"They copied my move, I think. There were a few tocks while everyone was arriving before the damping field came on." Bennie shrugs, looking down at the floor. "Plus, I punched through the damping and they maybe have piggybacked my signal." He continues looking at the floor.

Zephyr takes a deep breath, "Hacked the station? To do what?" She locks her gaze on to the small hacker.

Bennie offers up a PADD. Maxim snatches it out of his hand and scans the screen. "Sweet boneless christ, dude." He offers the PADD to Zephyr, who's closest to him. She scans it as well and swears. She offers it to Wil. Cynthia looks over his shoulder.

"Do I want to read this?" Wil asks.

"Probably not," Zephyr replies.

Wil scans the PADD saying nothing. He leans toward coffee table and picks up a bulb of chlormax, taking a sip, "They hacked the station's central computer and locked down the docking clamps." He says then adds, "Oh and you know, because, pranks, they hid clues to decrypt the computer through the station." He stares at Bennie.

Bennie nods slowly, "That sums it up, yes." He ducks just as the PADD flies through the air, smashing against the wall. "Hey, I didn't know they'd attack the station!"

Wil stands and walks over to the dining area table and plops down in one of the chairs, "Ok, so we have to solve this before anyone finds out." He looks at Bennie, "We do not need to tell anyone else. No one should be trying to leave the station until the summit is over anyway, so we have a day or two at least." He glares at the embarrassed Brailack, "After this, you're done tormenting your old pals. In fact, never speak to them again."

"That's a bit ha—"

"Bennie, I'm fucking serious," Wil growls. "This is not funny or ok. Your little prank war has now possibly endangered every delegation on this station. I can't even imagine what that would mean for the GC."

"It'd be bad," Cynthia offers.

Bennie bows, "I'm sorry. I didn't think they'd go this far."

Zephyr raises both hands, "Ok, let's focus." She turns to Bennie, "Bennie, load up PADDs with everything you've got: their clues, everything." She looks around, "We should get Gabe dialed in on this. He's already interfaced with several of the station's droid personnel."

Wil nods and taps his earpiece. He speaks to Gabe, who is in the suite next door watching over Barbara and Maltor. He turns to the large view port and speaks in a low voice.

As Wil turns back to face the others, Gabe's voice comes over everyone's earpiece, "I have interfaced with one of the droids in the station's ops center. He has agreed that alerting the delegates would serve no purpose. He has given us until the summit concludes to solve the problem. After that he will alert all delegations."

"Oh good. No pressure," Wil glares at Bennie.

IT'S BUSINESS TIME_

THE DOOR to Barbara Mress's suite opens, Maltor bows, "Good morning, Cynthia."

Cynthia smiles, "Morning, Maltor. You all ready to go?"

Barbara leans out of the door to her room, "One moment." She holds up a finger, then ducks back into the room.

Maltor moves aside motioning for Cynthia to enter the suite, "Can I offer you a beverage?"

Cynthia holds up the travel mug Wil had given her a few months ago. *Denver, CO - Mile High City* is stamped across It. The other Tygran looks at the mug and shrugs.

Cynthia looks at Gabe, "Have a fun night?"

The droid shrugs, "It was uneventful." Cynthia smiles.

A few minutes later Barbara emerges in a slate gray business suit, her tail swishing behind her, bound in the same material as her suit. "I'm ready." Maltor and Cynthia both incline their heads. Gabe opens the door and walks into the corridor. He turns and nods.

Cynthia leaves the suite first, "I'll take point as we walk. If I say *down*, you both drop. No questions." She looks at each of her charges, both nod. She looks at Gabe, "See you later, big guy." He nods and opens the door to the shared suite the crew of the *Ghost* is occupying.

The lift ride to the meeting space is uneventful. They share the large lift car with the delegation from a company Cynthia has never heard of, *Draplin* something or other.

The Grand Convening Hall lives up to its name. Twice the size of the ballroom at the top of the station, the massive two-story space has fourteen large, open-faced rooms all facing toward the center. The front of each room is a terrace with a table and seating for three; subordinates sit at a conference table behind the primary delegate and their two aides farther inside the large suite.

Cynthia looks around, finding the room with the Tralgot logo over it, "Are you the only one without a large entourage?"

Barbara looks at her, "I don't think so. It's uncommon, but I've never felt the need to show off with a large group of aides. Maltor is tremendously good at his job." She smiles, "Plus I have you, and if needed, your crew."

Across the open area, the Farsight suite looks like it is overflowing with people. Mress inclines her head smiling. Cynthia takes a seat.

"I'll take our green asshole. You two go with Gabe," Wil says pointing to the two Palorians and Gabe, respectively. He hands out the PADDs that Bennie configured with the message from the Collective. The message is mostly mockery and derision but includes a few clues as to where to find the solution, whatever it is.

Outside their suite, Wil looks at Bennie, "Let's get this over with. First stop, waste processing."

Bennie grimaces, "I'm not touching dren."

Wil turns to his small friend, "If there's dren to touch, you'll be lucky if I don't dunk you headfirst in it." He motions down the corridor, "Move." Turning to Maxim, Zephyr, and Gabe, "Good hunting." The others nod and head off in the opposite direction.

The waste processing center is near the lower levels of the station. Wil and Bennie pass several warning signs letting them know they are in parts of the station not meant for summit delegates. The doors part and Wil immediately starts making retching noises. He grimaces, turning his back to the door. Bennie just grins at him and points to his small nostril slits, now clamped closed.

"Hate you," Wil growls as he straightens and walks into the waste processing center. Several droids turn to focus their optical receptors on the new arrivals. One droid rolls toward them balancing on a single studded tire. "I apologize. This section is not meant for delegates." The wheel is coated in something Wil tries to not dwell on.

"Hi there. We're not delegates. Well, we're with a delegation but we're investigating some uh—"

"Anomalous computer code has been discovered," Bennie interrupts, "in some of the equipment down here."

The droid tilts its head, "Understood. Please proceed. Please watch your footing. This section was not designed with biologicals in mind." It turns and moves back to where it was working.

Wil and Bennie nod and head off toward one of the compactor units in the opposite corner of the space. As they approach, a large hatch in the ceiling opens and all manner of refuse pours out into the large basin below.

"Gross!" Wil hisses. "How can so few people who've only been here two days produce so much waste?"

Bennie shrugs and walks over to the control panel, "I'll start digging around in this one. You might as well go look at one of the other compactors."

Wil looks around and heads back to where the droids were working. "Excuse me. Have any of you noticed anything weird in the last few tocks? Malfunctions or anything like that?"

One of the droids, not the wheeled one, has four legs, each as long as Bennie is tall; it has six limbs, three on each side of a thick torso, and each limb ends in large, three-fingered manipulators. The multi-limbed droid responds, "One of the compactors began operating at below peak efficiency sixteen tocks ago. It has lost efficiency consistently since then." One of its arms points to a compactor next to the one Bennie is working on. Wil can see that several indicators on its control panel are blinking.

Wil nods, "Thank you." The droid lacks a neck, or even much of a head, but bows at its waist. Wil walks to the indicated compactor, "Bennie, get over here."

"I'm not done with—"

"Not a request," Wil barks pointing to the malfunctioning compactor.

Bennie walks over, "What's up?"

"That droid over there"—he gestures to the multi-limbed droid he just spoke with—"said this compactor started acting up sixteen hours ago."

Bennie nods and heads for the control panel, "Let's see what's up." He lifts the front of the control panel, exposing circuits and data chips.

While the Brailack hacker works, Wil taps his earpiece, "Team Two, how's it going?"

"Oh, it's going super," Maxim replies dryly. "The command center droids are an absolute joy."

Wil smiles, "At least it doesn't smell like shit."

"That would be highly irregular, especially for a droid controlled facility, Captain," Gabe responds.

"I think we might have figured out the clue about *dren backing up*," Wil says. "I'll let you know in a few."

"Roger that," Maxim says.

From the machine Bennie is working on, something inside makes a loud clang followed by several thuds. A new smell assaults Wil's nose.

SCAVENGER HUNT_

THE LIFT DOORS CLOSE. "COMMAND CENTER," Zephyr says.

"Unable to comply. The command center is off limits to delegates. Please specify another destination."

Zephyr looks at the small control panel next to the lift doors, then up at Gabe, an eyebrow raised.

Gabe nods and extends his hand toward the control panel, thin glowing filaments snake out of his fingertips. Each filament pushes its way inside the panel. A moment later, the indicators on the panel blink twice. "Try now."

Zephyr looks at the panel, "Command center."

"Acknowledged," the lift replies as it moves. As suddenly as it moves, it stops then vibrates. Maxim looks at Gabe who looks at the control panel, head tilted. The droid moves to the panel again, extending his hand and the data filaments.

Gabe looks at the two Palorians, "This is embarrassing."

"What?" Zephyr asks.

"Whatever virus the Drakkar Collective unleashed in the central computer seems to be specifically designed to counter my intrusion software." He looks at his companions, "Bennie must have shared, or likely bragged, about my software capabilities."

Maxim pushes Gabe aside, the data filaments snapping into the droid's fingers as he moves away, "Old school to the rescue," he says kneeling to inspect the panel. After a minute of digging around inside the guts of the lift's control panel, the car begins to move. Maxim looks up at his companions, smiling.

When the doors open, twelve optic sensors on three heads turn to face the new arrivals.

A droid, the same height as Gabe, approaches. It's gold and mostly humanoid shaped, except its head is a flattened sphere with three large blue optic sensors on the front. "Greetings. The command center is not designated for delegation personnel."

It approaches, arm extended to usher them back into the lift. Gabe moves to intercept the other droid, hand up, "Please excuse us. We are investigating an attack on the station's computer system. We have interfaced about the issue."

The droid nods, "Indeed. You are Gabe. Welcome." It steps back.

Another comes over, this one with three legs and one large arm on a spinning section in the middle of its torso, "We have detected several anomalies within the central processing matrix. With the comm blackout, we are unable to request additional instructions or support."

"You can't disable the damping field?" Maxim asks.

Flat-head droid's head wobbles, which must be its version of a headshake, "Unfortunately, summit protocol is very specific. The damping field will only disengage when the delegations vote to close the session." It points to a panel that shows several blinking red indicators, "Even if I could override that directive, the virus within the primary processor matrix has corrupted the entire comm system."

Three-legs adds, "In addition to several secondary systems. The docking clamps are all locked."

Zephyr nods, "The docking clamps are part of the attack, and if we can't call for help, we need to unlock all the systems ourselves. Can we look around?"

The droids move to either side to make room. The third droid wobbles and two of its optical sensors spin in different directions as it slowly moves out of the way.

"Have you noticed anything weird since probably a little before the comm blackout?"

"Well, there was the explosion," Flat-head offers. Maxim grimaces.

"Anything else?" Gabe asks.

Three-legs points at the third droid, "JDX-59002 has been having problems for fifteen tocks."

Maxim looks at the indicated droid, who stands unsteadily, "Gree-gree-greetings," it says as its optical sensors blink out of sync.

As Zephyr walks over to the indicated droid, her earpiece crackles then Wil says, "Team Two, how's it going?"

Maxim exchanges a glance with Gabe, "Oh, it's going super." He looks at the other two command center droids, "The command center droids are an absolute joy."

"At least it doesn't smell like shit," Wil says from the bottom of the station.

Gabe tilts his head and looks around the space. "That would be highly irregular, especially for a droid controlled facility, Captain."

"I think we might have figured out the clue about *dren backing up*," Wil says. "I'll let you know in a few."

"Roger that," Maxim says then turns to the droid he's next to, "Can my friend here examine your software?" Gabe approaches and places his hand on the chest plate of the droid, the familiar glowing tendrils snake out of his fingers, probing and penetrating the droid's chassis.

While Gabe works, flat-head tilts its head, "Excuse me, you are Gabe the Liberator, are you not?"

Gabe inclines his head and Maxim is almost certain he hears a sigh, "I am."

"Prior to this assignment, myself and PKL-JY5302 were leased to a company on Plentog Three. We followed your exploits with great interest. Would it be acceptable to capture a still image with you?"

Zephyr drops her face into her palm sighing.

The Corporate Congress turns out to be even more boring than Cynthia had initially thought. Barbara and Maltor are sitting at the main table while she hangs out in the back of the little suite. She realized she could keep herself busy with her wristcomm and the games that Wil loaded on it if she wasn't at the main table.

Several motions have been raised. By her count, less than half have passed. They've ranged from new trade routes and regions to market saturation strategies.

Towards the end of the day, Barbara presses a button to signal she has a motion. She looks out at the suites that are visible.

"Tralgot motions to enact trade limitations and sanctions on Farsight corporation, for a period of five cycles."

A low rumbling murmur sweeps through the circular chamber.

"On what grounds?" Jark Asgar demands from the Farsight suite four down from where Cynthia and the Tralgot delegation are seated.

Barbara leans forward, "On the grounds that you've illegally and aggressively *merged* with two entities and have now amassed an outsized influence in several markets and sectors—well beyond what this body typically approves for a single entity." She holds up a manicured finger to stave off the outburst Asgar is about to make, "Additionally, you undertook all of these actions without the consent of a single member of this body."

"That's absurd," Asgar says, waving a hand dismissively in the direction of the Tralgot suite. "Farsight has done nothing untoward or against standing policies set forth by this body. Our merger of Crucible Corporation was—"

"An assault on a planet outside your jurisdiction!" shouts someone across the room.

"You pacified an entire city, forcing Crucible executives to the table under threat of death!" someone else shouts.

"Stilkon Seven seconds," Chief Executive Relto says from almost directly across from the Tralgot delegation. The impeccably dressed Trenbal woman bows her head slightly.

"This is outrageous!" a now angrier Jark Asgar shouts, standing and waving his arms wildly, knocking a small Brailack at his side out of its chair.

"The Weyland Combine calls for a vote," Maxamillion Sturmav says from the suite next to Farsight's.

Several other delegations begin shouting, almost all of them in support of the motion.

Cynthia watches with interest as the room quickly turns against Jark Asgar and Farsight Corporation.

OR WILD GOOSE CHASE?_

"Why do we get the gross ones?" Bennie asks as he opens the hatch to the perishable goods storage area in a between deck, one level below the canteen and one above the convenience stores.

"Because, asshole, you're the reason we're in this mess. I'm just suffering along with you to keep you out of more trouble." He looks around, "This station is a health code violation on a galactic level."

Bennie trots into the large open space, "No droids." He turns to look at Wil, then jumps back as a large arm on an overhead track moves past.

Wil walks in, closing the hatch behind him. The room is lined with walk-in food storage units. One has a red light over the door. Wil motions to the red-light unit, "Let's check the one that's on the fritz; that seems to be a common theme today."

Bennie walks toward the suggested unit, "This place is a disaster. Didn't Maltor say they often sold these summit stations afterward? Who would buy this piece of dren?"

Wil shrugs, "Bargain hunting crime lords? Fixed income despots? Who knows?" He grasps the handle and pulls. The heavy door swings open.

"Close it! Close it!" Bennie screams stepping backwards and tripping over his feet.

Wil slams the door shut, "Ok, let's assume whatever the hell happened to this freezer happened more than a day and a half ago." He peeks inside through the thick glass window set in the door, "Guessing it broke down before anyone arrived."

The mechanical arm trundles by again, its overhead tracks rattle as it passes. It stops in front of a storage unit, one with a green light on it. The door opens automatically, and the arm reaches in, withdrawing a box of something. It trundles away to deposit the box in a waiting lift. As it turns back, it stops and shakes violently, then continues on its way.

Bennie points, "That might be our culprit."

Wil nods, "Yeah." He sighs, "Almost certainly." The arm jerks randomly, then moves toward a different freezer. He looks at Bennie, "Thoughts?"

The Brailack scratches the top of his hairless head while watching the arm. He points at it as it removes a box of frozen something or other from a storage unit farther down. "Looks like the main control module is on the motivator unit near the ceiling." The ceiling is a latticework of tracks, providing the arm the ability to move anywhere in the large warehouse like space. Sitting above the lattice, controlling the arm, is a heavy-looking control unit.

Wil grunts, "Ok, come on." He walks to the lift that the arm deposits its packages in. As Bennie arrives the arm does as well. They both dodge one of its jerky motions. As it moves to make its deposit, Wil grabs Bennie by the back of his jumpsuit and throws him up onto the arm.

"The wurrin?!" the shocked Brailack shouts as he lands on the arm and wraps his arms and legs around it. "You suck, you krebnack!" he screams as the arm withdraws from the lift and heads back to the bank of freezer units. He screams as the arm jerks back and forth. The lift closes and heads off somewhere.

"Hold on! Don't let it get the best of you!" Wil smiles, "Ride 'em cowboy!" He jogs after the arm.

As the arm jerks around on its way to its next pick up, Bennie shimmies up to the first of two joints. Large power and hydraulic lines snake their way from the motivator unit to the two massive graspers. As he reaches the first joint, he holds on to one of the thick cables and nearly falls when the arm backs up and almost slams into a freezer unit.

Wil grimaces as he watches Bennie nearly get crushed. The Brailack hacker clears the first joint, makes a rude gesture at Wil, and continues up toward the next joint. "I hate you!" he screams as he reaches the joint and reaches for another thick cable. This one jerks on its own, a hydraulic line reacting to changes in pressure as the arm moves and the graspers flex to pick up a container of soup. He misses his first grab at the thick line but catches it on his second attempt. Exhibiting a limberness Wil wouldn't have thought the Brailack hacker possessed, Bennie kicks off the arm and spins around the hose to land on the last segment of the arm, right under the motivator unit. Thick wheels guide the heavy arm around on the latticework of tracks.

Wil cups his hands around his mouth, "Don't disable it! That's the only one!" He watches Bennie scurry up onto the tracked motivator unit and open an access panel. "Just remove the junk your friends put in," he adds.

"Shut the hell up!" Bennie screams from above the unit. Wil can't see much of him as he jogs along following a safe distance behind the arm.

Without warning, the arm stops dead on the tracks, seeming to have ceased up. Wil is about to shout up at his companion when the arm jerks and resumes its course toward a storage unit in the corner of the large storage area. Wil notices immediately that the arm is no longer jerking erratically. He's about to shout up for Bennie when the small hacker drops down next to him, landing in a very heroic three-point stance. Wil glances down, "You stuck the landing, ten points. Very Iron Man."

"I wasn't sure I would if I'm being honest." Bennie looks up grinning. He lifts his wristcomm, "Got the code. Looks like it's one big encryption key."

NEWSCAST_

"Good afternoon. I'm Xyrzix, coming to you live from Tarsis, just outside the Galactic Commonwealth Governing Council's chambers. Members have been debating for hours now regarding the attacks on Peacekeeper facilities across the outer edge of the Commonwealth."

He looks over his shoulder at the massive, closed doors. "I'll be here when the doors open and the Council has a statement. Back to you in the studio."

CHAPTER 12_

PUZZLES SUCK_

"THIS SHOULD BE OUR LAST STOP," Maxim says as they enter the engineering space of the station. Located at the lowest level of the facility and very much not designed for non-droid occupants, the temperature is well above anyone's comfort level.

Two droids, the same model Gabe was when he first met the crew of the *Ghost*, walk over to them, "This area is off—"

"limits to delegates. We know," Zephyr says holding up a hand to stop the two droids. She wipes her forehead then runs her hand down her pant leg to dry it. "We're here investigating the strange errors plaguing droids and station computer systems."

"On whose authority?" one droid asks. Unlike Gabe, who was matte black, this unit is bright yellow with a thick black band down its left side.

Gabe comes forward, "Due to the communication blackout, there is unfortunately no way to acquire authorization. However, we are uniquely qualified to address the problem; you can confirm with your colleagues in the command center if you would like." Gabe inclines his head, his shoulders visibly hunch, "Also, I am Gabe the Liberator."

The two droids turn to look at each other, then back to Gabe.

One, the not yellow one, tilts its head as if listening to something. When it's done, it turns to Gabe, "It is an honor to meet you, Gabe. The command center has confirmed your identities."

Yellow droid adds, "Please be careful. The reactor is an older model with several missing firmware patches."

"Of course," Maxim replies. "This place is a deathtrap," he whispers to Zephyr as they walk towards the large reactor in the center of the room. Gabe looks at the reactor, "You mention a lack of software updates, have you noticed anything unusual in the last sixteen tocks?"

Yellow droid nods, "Indeed. The reaction management subroutines began returning irregular results approximately fourteen tocks ago." It turns to the two Palorians, then back to Gabe, "How did you know?"

Non-yellow droid adds, "We have not reported the errors yet. Our hope was that we would be able to troubleshoot the issue and solve, or temporarily address the issue on our own." It looks to its colleague, "As yet, we have been unsuccessful."

"Due to the comm blackout, we are unable to request additional information regarding this model of reactor or patches for the firmware," yellow droid adds. "Neither of us are rated on this model."

Maxim finds a panel next to the control module attached to the reactor. Underneath it, a jumble of cables and data storage chips sit amid glowing and blinking indicators. "Hey Gabe, this part is all you." He points to the open panel.

As Gabe turns, he looks at the other droids, "Someone has likely injected malicious code into your reaction control sub-routine. I will extract the code and, if history is any indication, your systems should return to normal." He turns to the reactor, then to Zephyr, "I will probably need your help if the virus is anything like the door controls." The Palorian woman nods.

Yellow droid inclines its head, "That would be ideal. Barring another solution, the reactor will go critical in ten tocks."

"Well dren," Zephyr says. She looks over at Maxim, "You think Bennie's friends really meant to kill him?"

Maxim looks up from one of the displays on the control panel, "Him? Yes. Us, probably not." He turns back to the console following Gabe's instructions.

"Think they figured out what this place is? Maybe this is less about Bennie and more about them?" Zephyr wonders. "We'll have to ask him if they have anti-corporate leanings."

Gabe turns his attention towards the control panel, data filaments extending from his fingers. He looks at Maxim, "I am highlighting the sub-routine you need to run to place the reactor into a temporary diagnostic loop." When Maxim executes the indicated sub-routine, Gabe nods. "Excellent; that opened the necessary back door." The data filaments pulse.

Yellow droid turns to its colleague, "I have never seen a data access method like that before."

The other droid nods, "Indeed; it is quite impressive."

Gabe looks up, "I have made numerous improvements to this body over the last cycle." He smiles, then looks at Maxim, "Maxim, please execute the indicated program, the one labeled *run me.*"

Maxim looks at his mechanical friend, "A little on the nose, no?"

Gabe shrugs, the light of the data filaments grows brighter. "I have identified the virus and extraneous code."

Zephyr looks from Gabe to the other droids, "Why didn't you alert the command center staff?"

Yellow droid tilts its head, "Our programming is very specific in outlining scenarios that warrant interfacing with other station personnel. Had the reactor problem continued for another four tocks, we would have alerted the command center."

Maxim looks up, "In order to begin an evacuation?"

The other droid nods, "That is correct."

Zephyr rubs her face, "Except that the virus that is attacking the reactor also locked all the docking clamps. No one would be able to escape."

Yellow droid makes a cough-like noise, "That would have been unfortunate."

Maxim looks over, "You can say that again."

Yellow droid tilts its head, "That would have been unfortunate."

Maxim opens his mouth, then closes it.

Gabe withdraws his hand, "I have nullified the virus and removed the extraneous code. I believe the reactor will self-correct when the diagnostic loop completes in forty-two microtocks."

The two droids incline their heads. Yellow walks over to another panel watching the screen on it. After a minute it looks up, "The reaction has stabilized."

Non-yellow looks at Gabe, "Thank you, Gabe the Liberator."

As Maxim and Zephyr try to hide their grins, Gabe inclines his head. He turns to his friends, "We should go. I believe we need to combine all four fragments in order to decrypt the primary control systems." They both nod and head for the hatch.

As the crew of the *Ghost* leave engineering, yellow droid turns to its companion, "We should have asked for a visual record of meeting him." Non-yellow nods.

'A' FOR EFFORT?_

"SHOULD we be in the command center?" Wil asks once everyone is back in their shared suite.

Gabe and Bennie are sitting at the kitchen table. Bennie looks up, "No. Once we get the key assembled, we can tap into the main computer from here." He turns back to the PADD sitting between him and Gabe.

Gabe looks up, "I took the liberty of re-routing command access to our suite when we were in the command center."

Wil smiles, "Good call, pal."

Maxim leans down toward Wil, "You smell."

Zephyr nods, "Like, a lot." She waves her hand in front of her face, "So bad."

Wil lifts an arm sniffing, "Yeah, well, I took the grenade for you two. Tiny dickhead and I had to visit waste processing and food storage. ProTip, check your food closely. One of the storage units clearly died before anyone arrived and they just left it, and everything in it, there. Who knows what else is bad on that level."

"Got it," Bennie says. He holds up the PADD, "Those Drakkar krebnacks brought their A-game this time for sure. The key wasn't just in four pieces but in sixteen that were randomly split into four sections. We had to—"

"No one cares," Wil interrupts. He points to the room's main comm panel. "Upload the fix."

"So rude," Bennie says as he and Gabe move to the comm panel. Gabe extends both hands, data filaments snaking out of all his fingers to reach under and into the panel.

"That's so disturbing," Wil says.

Maxim nods, "I thought I'd get used to it after all this time, but nope, still creeps me out."

"I can hear you," Gabe says, not turning to look at his friends. The comm panel flashes to life, lines of code moving faster than they can follow.

"Done," Gabe says as he lowers his hands.

"So, what now? Is this thing binding? Farsight just goes along?" Cynthia says as she escorts Barbara and Maltor out of the suite and towards the bank of lifts waiting to take the delegations wherever they want to go within the station.

Barbara smiles, "More or less. The decisions of the Corporate Congress are binding by precedent. In the history of our holding this summit, the decisions of the group have never been ignored."

"Asgar seemed like he was ready to rip people in half back there," Cynthia observes. Down the hall, one of the suite doors opens and Asgar storms out, his small Brailack assistant trailing a safe distance behind him. The other delegations stop where they are to let the large man storm past.

"Yes, he did; didn't he?" Barbara chuckles watching the Hulgian man enter the lift. "Let's make sure to avoid the Farsight delegation for a bit."

They step into the lift and Cynthia instructs it to take them to the level their suite is on. "You think that assassin back on Kal Nor was hired by Asgar? Did he know you were going to make that motion?"

"It's likely," Maltor says. "Tralgot has been fairly vocal since Farsight began their aggressive acquisition spree." The lift door opens and an ink black blur darts into the lift right at Barbara. Maltor barely registers the attack as Cynthia springs into action intercepting the unknown assailant in midair barely an inch from its target. Cynthia slams the creature against the wall of the lift car. Razor-sharp claws rake her back as the creature screams an all too familiar scream as it drops to the deck tail swishing behind it.

"Down!" she shouts, her own razor-sharp claws extending from her fingertips. As the other two Tygrans drop to the floor of the lift, heading for the still open door, she growls at the small nightmare before her. She looks at the would-be assassin; it's barely a meter tall, a mix of matte and inky black chitin. Its eyeless face turns to her and bares row upon row of needle-like teeth. With the exception of what looks like a metal collar and some electronic bits attached to the long, pointed skull, it's exactly as she remembers from Glacial, *A Monster B.* As Maltor reaches the lift door threshold and reaches his hand back to pull Barbara into the corridor, the creature jumps straight at the younger Tygran. Cynthia reaches for it as its tail lashes out towards Maltor catching him across one shoulder eliciting a scream of pain. As Cynthia wrestles with the small creature, her hand closes around its chest; the creatures on Glacial that were this size didn't have the chitin like armor this one has.

Cynthia grabs hold of the creature's throat, its elongated head whipping about as it tries to bite her. Its tail lashes out below it, trying to cut her midsection. With both hands busy keeping the small killing machine at arm's length she falls forward onto it, pinning it under her. The flailing stops for a moment as the creature works out the shock of hitting the deck and having her weight land on it. She digs her claws into the softer flesh around the attacking creature's neck and lower skull, above the metal collar. Remembering that the chitinous armor of the larger creatures was relatively strong she avoids it.

The little nightmare makes its screaming noise repeatedly, thrashing under her, shredding the arms of her jumpsuit and skin underneath. The tail is pinned under her, but she can feel it writhing around underneath her.

"Cynthia!" Barbara screams from the open door of the lift.

The creature tries to turn its head to look at its target, but Cynthia finally gets enough leverage to sink her claws deep inside the skin of the creature's neck. It screams again, but this one ends in a wet gurgle as orange ichor spurts out all over the front of Cynthia's upper body, including her face.

"Is it... dead?" Maltor says creeping towards Cynthia and the creature.

Cynthia nods, spitting orange goo out onto the floor of the lift. "Gods I hope so. Asgar sent this," she pants rolling off the creature and using her foot to push the body away from her.

"What? How do you know? What is it?" The younger man walks back into the lift and kicks the lifeless creature experimentally.

Cynthia rolls to her feet, her eyes darting between Maltor, Barbara, and the corridor behind the elder Tygran woman. She moves to the lift door and looks up and down the corridor. Seeing no sign of other creatures or whoever sent it, she turns to Barbara, "We've fought these things before. They're an intermediate growth stage of a creature we encountered on Glacial," Cynthia says as she lifts her wristcomm. "Guys, we have a problem."

"Where are you?" Wil replies immediately in her earpiece. "We're in the suite," he adds.

"We'll be right there," Cynthia says closing the channel. She looks at the others, "Let's go." She stands and takes the lead, dragging the lifeless creature by its tail. She doesn't lead them to the suite the executive and her assistant share, but the suite next door.

The door opens to reveal Gabe, in combat mode.

THAT DIDN'T TAKE LONG_

As Gabe steps aside to allow Maltor then Barbara to enter the suite, Wil sees Cynthia behind them. "The hell?" he says as the two Tygrans walk past. Cynthia is covered in blood, hers and the orange of the Glacial monster. As she drops the tail of the creature, Wil rushes up to her, holding her at arm's length to examine her. "Babe, are you ok?" He looks down at the creature, "The fuck is that doing here?"

She nods warily, "Yeah, I'm good. Could use a shower though." She smiles.

Wil nods and walks her toward their shared room.

As the door closes behind Wil and Cynthia, Zephyr moves to inspect Maltor's shoulder. She pulls a small first aid kit from one of the pockets of her jumpsuit and begins working on his shoulder.

"That's handy," he observes between winces. She's shaving a fist-sized patch of his shoulder bare.

She nods, "You might be surprised how often these idiots manage to hurt themselves."

"I've met them," he counters.

Maxim guides Barbara to the kitchen table. "What happened?" He points to the body near the door; Gabe is kneeling over it.

"That thing was waiting for us. On this deck. When the lift doors opened, it sprang in," Barbara explains. "Cynthia said Farsight sent it. That you'd encountered"—she points to the dead creature—"them on a planet called Glacial?"

"I'm not familiar with the name," Maltor offers as Zephyr applies a dermal patch to his now hairless shoulder.

Maxim motions to take over for Zephyr. When her hands are free, she says, "Farsight hired us to take a tech crew out to Glacial; it's not in a well-traveled system. They'd lost contact with the research facility there. It turned out that the facility was an archeological dig that had uncovered ruins that didn't match up with any known races in the GC. They also thawed out a creature, like a queen, but bigger; it called itself *The Source*." She points to the dead creature, "That was the post-larval form. After that, it grew into something much bigger." She walks over to the body and nudges it with her boot before kneeling next to it. "Weird. This one has the same chitin-like armor that the larger creatures had." She turns to look at Barbara, "When we encountered these, they were softer, easier to kill. This is like a cross between the smaller and larger creatures." She poked the metal collar, "That's new."

Wil walks out and points to the creature, "That thing did a number on her. More than I'd expect."

Zephyr waves him over, "It's not exactly the same Monster B we're familiar with." She points to it, "That collar"—she indicates a small metal panel melded to the skull—"and whatever that is are new. I'm guessing some type of control unit or something?" She shrugs.

Maxim slaps Maltor on the uninjured shoulder, "You're good to go."

"Thank you." He moves to sit next to his boss. "What now? Is it safe to make our way to your ship? It's customary to attend the final reception, but I can't see anyone begrudging us an early departure."

Wil looks up from the body, "The summit is over? Already?"

Barbara nods, "By tradition we keep the summit to no more than three standard days."

Maxim grunts, "Lot of pomp for a single day of business."

Maltor's fur ripples, "The delegates are some of the most powerful and important businesspeople in the GC; they do not have days to waste. The Corporate Congress is a single day, by design. Allowances were made due to the loss of the Juniper Collective delegation."

Wil nods, "Ok, and the party tonight, optional?"

Maltor and Barbara nod, but the elder Tygran raises a hand, the fur around her face flattening, "The final reception is optional, but I believe it in the best interest of Tralgot and the alliances formed today that I attend." Maltor begins to speak, and she motions for him to remain silent. "We dealt a significant blow to Farsight today. If I tuck tail and run, it will undermine our efforts."

The door to Wil and Cynthia's suite opens, and Cynthia comes out in a jumpsuit similar to the one she'd just been wearing: light gray with pockets on the legs and upper arms. "Tralgot lead a charge against Farsight, essentially a massive corporate smack down. Jark Asgar was livid." She grins remembering his expression when the vote came down. "If Barbara doesn't show, it might be taken as a sign of weakness. The alliance might crumble."

The elder Tygran woman bows her head, "Exactly."

Wil turns to Gabe, "Ok pal, can you escort them to their suite? Stay there until we come and get you." He turns to the Tralgot employees, "When does the reception start?"

Maltor checks his wristcomm, "In less than a tock. It should run for no more than three tocks, allowing delegations a final opportunity to mingle and solidify any alliances made. Then everyone departs. Within tocks, the station will be empty."

Gabe comes forward, "I would be happy to escort our clients." He looks at Barbara, offering his hand, "Please come with me."

THE DOOR to their suite closes behind Gabe and the two Tygrans. Bennie, who has been sitting at the island in the kitchen, says, "So, Farsight works fast. That thing"—he points to the body—"is clearly a Monster B that's been genetically modified." He taps his wristcomm, "Want me to get around the comm blackout and dig around?"

Wil shakes his head, "No. First order of business is you calling your nerd friends and making peace." When Bennie makes a face, Wil points at him, "After that, I want you and Zee to head to the *Ghost*. Get the sensors fired up and run overwatch. Also, keep an eye on that Farsight cruiser. If Jark got the smack down it sounds like, he's gonna be out for blood, and now he can call in reinforcements." He looks at the body on the floor, likely staining it with its orange ichor, "More than he already seems to be, that is."

He turns to Maxim, "Speaking of, feel like making a delivery? Well, more of a ding dong ditch kind of thing."

"Ding dong who?" the big Palorian asks.

Wil grins, "Take that"—he points to the body—"and leave it outside the hatch to the Farsight delegation suite." The big man grins, picks up the dead creature, and leaves.

Wil turns to the two, remaining woman, "Ok, let's get dressed for the reception. Babe, you good staying in bodyguard mode?" Cynthia nods. "Cool. Zee, you and Bennie might as well get over to the *Ghost*. Be careful. I'm sure Farsight is only gunning for Barbara, but Jark won't blink twice if we're collateral damage. Oh, and see if the sensors can pick up if there are any other little beasties on the station."

Zephyr and Bennie depart while Cynthia and Wil head to their room to change. "How'd he get it onboard?" Wil wonders aloud.

"He had to have brought it aboard with him when he arrived, since Bennie's friends locked all the airlocks down," Cynthia offers as she slips off her jumpsuit.

"They've clearly modified them, maybe they figured out how to keep them as those slug things until they need them, then boom, Monster B," Wil wonders aloud, slipping on his nice dress shirt from the first reception. He looks down, "Think anyone will notice I'm wearing this again?"

Cynthia holds up a finger, "No one cares about your outfit." She holds up another finger, "Why stop with Monster B? The bigger ones are far more lethal," Cynthia replies, sliding a dress up over her waist.

Wil shrugs on a dress coat and whistles at his girlfriend, "Lookin' good, sweetie. True on the big ones, but they're a lot harder to hide, too."

"You too, for a human." She winks, then spins as the outer door to the suite opens.

"Just me," Maxim shouts, coming into the room. He's grinning, "Delivery made. What's the plan?"

"Zee and Bennie are heading to the *Ghost* now. I want you and Gabe to patrol, and if needed, secure the route between the ballroom and the ship." Wil answers.

The big man nods and heads to the room he shares with Zephyr, "Let me grab a few things."

"Guns," Wil and Cynthia say at the same time.

Wil turns to Cynthia, "Let's go get our clients and escort them to the party." She nods agreement.

"I didn't expect to see you here," the hulking CEO of Farsight Corporation says as Barbara walks into the large ballroom. Unlike the setup the first night of the summit, this time the large room is dotted with high-topped tables and roving serving droids offering appetizers and flutes of something pale green and bubbly.

Barbara bows deeply, "Why is that my dear Jark?" Wil and Cynthia hang back a few steps behind her. Wil smiles at Asgar and wiggles his fingers in a wave.

Asgar glances at Wil, then clears his throat, "After that stunt you pulled at the last microtock of the summit, I'd assumed you'd be a bit weary of being in the same room as me." He looks down at his assistant. The pale green Brailack is standing just behind his boss, his arm in a sling.

Wil leans to look around the big Hulgian man waving, "Hey Doppo!" He looks at the injured arm, "That looks like it hurt."

The small Brailack smiles, his cheeks turning darker green, "Hello, Captain Calder." He stops talking and backs away when Asgar growls.

Wil focuses on Asgar, "I've been meaning to ask, how did everything go on Glacial? Did you get that archeological dig back up and running? Find anything weird?" He raises his eyebrows.

Asgar glares, reaching up to rub a finger along his left horn, the one with the crack running its length. He turns on his heel and stomps off.

Wil looks at Cynthia, then Barbara, "We'll stick nearby, but don't want to cramp your style. If you need us, we'll be there." The two walk off in one direction as Barbara nods and heads off towards the Juniper Collective delegation, waving politely.

NEWSCAST_

"GREETINGS, I'm Xyrzix and the Galactic Commonwealth Governing Council has just released their statement on the ongoing threat of attacks to Peacekeeper facilities throughout the GC." He looks down at a PADD he's holding, "Until further notice, the Peacekeepers will be on a heightened state of alert, and martial law will be in effect across the GC." He turns to look at something offscreen, then turns back, "Exactly what *martial law* means right now is being discussed; but I'm told that from this moment on, Peacekeepers will be operating under new, more aggressive rules of engagement to ensure they're ready should more attacks take place."

The newscaster blinks his large compound eyes rapidly, "If you are in space and a Peacekeeper vessel gives you an order, please obey. I fear this heightened status will result in a great many civilian casualties."

PART 3

CHAPTER 13_

LET'S GO_

"WE SHOULD DEFINITELY FILE some sort of complaint about how horribly built this place is," Bennie says from his console on the bridge of the *Ghost*.

Wil groans remembering the broken freezer unit, "No argument. I can't even fathom how someone would buy this thing." He stays focused on Bennie, "All good with your pals? The Drakkar Noir?"

"The Drakkar *Collective,* and yeah, I think so. I got through a few centocks ago," the small Brailack replies.

"You think so," Zephyr says.

"I can play back the transmission if you like!" Bennie shouts. "I apologized for the pranking and admitted that this one was good, and it should be the final one. They agreed." He frowns, "They're not a single entity but the ones who usually call the shots were on the call. I'm as sure as I can be that they won't do anything more." He holds up his arm mimicking a gesture he's seen Wil make, "Scout's honor I won't do anything to incite them. They get the last prank, so that should make everyone happy."

Wil nods, "Fair enough." He turns to Cynthia, "Babs and Maltor all set?"

"Babs?" Cynthia asks, then waves his reply away, "Yeah. They're good. I left them in their quarters." She looks down at her console. "Looks like two more ships, then our turn."

On the main display at the front of the bridge, a small shuttle is decoupling from the docking arm of the station.

Wil nods then looks at the ceiling, "Gabe, almost our turn, you good in engineering?" The ceiling replies, "Yes, Captain. The reactor is online and at optimum output. You have sub-light and FTL at your discretion."

"One more ship," Cynthia says, a hand to her ear, where a commset is nestled. A few minutes later, "We're clear for departure."

Zephyr presses a button on her console, "Airlock released."

Wil turns back to this console, "Here we go." He works his controls, guiding the *Ghost* away from the docking arm they'd been attached to for three days.

"Someone just dropped out of FTL," Zephyr announces.

"Guess the interdiction field is offline." Maxim observes.

"Who's arriving now?" Bennie wonders aloud.

The main display lights up as a small ship a few thousand kilometers from the *Ghost* explodes, followed by another.

"Was that—" Wil starts.

"The Juniper Collective's ship? Yeah, and the Weyland Combine," Zephyr says, scanning her console. "The unidentified ship is adjusting course." She looks up at Wil, "It's chasing down the other delegations."

Cynthia looks up from her console, "It's also jamming comms."

"Oh, hell no," Wil growls pushing the flight controls, "Hold on!" On the screen the summit station swerves to fill the screen then moves along the top of the screen. Cynthia grasps the edges of her console, "Everyone is scattering. The station just released the rest of the delegation ships."

"I can shoot back, right?" Maxim asks.

"Damn right," Wil says, not looking at his friend, eyes glued to the main display. "Do we know who this asshole is?"

"It's not transmitting an ident, and there's nothing in the database that matches the design," Zephyr reports. She looks at Wil, "It just fired another salvo of missiles, three more delegations, gone."

"Bennie, see what you can find out," Wil says, bringing the *Ghost* around the backside of the summit station. A wave of missiles crashes into the station, blasting several decks open to space.

"Guess them selling it isn't an issue," Maxim says.

Bennie looks at Wil, "Do you think there's some type of hacker's only ship recognition database?" He points at Cynthia, "And that I keep a local copy of it? Jammed comms, remember?"

Wil glances at the Brailack hacker, "Be useful." The *Ghost* shudders as something strikes her shields. "Get ready," he says as the station, now tilting off its original axis and venting atmosphere moves out of view. The unidentified ship comes into view and immediately missiles appear from the bottom of the main display.

The other ship, close to a frigate class vessel in size, is matte black with what looks almost like chitinous armor plates interlocking over sections of the hull.

Bennie looks up from his console, "I checked the doesn't exist hackers only ship recognition database. Nothing." Wil flips him off, but he continues, "However, does anything about that thing look a little familiar?" He points to the main display and the hostile vessel that is growing larger on it.

"The Farsight cruiser isn't engaging the new arrival," Zephyr says. "Or running."

On the screen, the mystery frigate launches missiles. As the *Ghost's* missiles close the gap, it lashes out with particle beams that rake across the *Ghost's* shields causing the ship to shudder. One of the *Ghost's* missiles impacts against the ship's shields while another is blasted with a powerful disruptor beam.

"That thing has strong shields," Maxim reports. As the *Ghost* gets closer to the other ship, the sound of the engine nacelle disruptors reverberates through the hull.

"Oh dren, that hull armor looks a lot like the chitin on the Monster C's," Cynthia says.

"That's what I was talking about," Bennie says crossing his arms over his chest.

"That's gotta be a Farsight ship," Wil says.

"Speaking of, the cruiser just went to FTL," Zephyr says. She looks at her display, "The shuttle that Jark came over in docked right before it left."

Wil pushes the controls to the right, pulling the throttle back before pushing it forward and throwing the flight controls the opposite direction. The ship shakes as one of the mystery frigate's missiles impacts the shields. Sparks erupt from a panel over Maxim's station. More particle beams rake across the shields as another missile slams into them.

RUN AWAY_

THE BRIDGE HATCH opens and Barbara stumbles in, "What is going on!?"

"Pretty sure you seriously pissed off Asgar," Zephyr says, pointing to the matte black attacker on the main display. Missiles streak from the vessel as it tilts to avoid a wave of missiles fired from one of the other ships in the very diminishing group of ships departing the station.

"We're all that's left," Zephyr reports. "They've destroyed almost all of the other delegation vessels."

"Perhaps we should escape then?" the Tygran executive says, clutching the edge of Cynthia's console.

The other ship launches another salvo of missiles, this time at one of the few remaining fleeing transports. The transport fires its meager point defense but enough missiles make it through, ripping the ship apart.

"That was the Stilkon Seven group," Zephyr reports.

"They backed my resolutions," Barbara whispers, shaking her head.

"Yup. Getting the hell out of here," Wil says, as another panel, this one over Cynthia's console, erupts in sparks causing Barbara to yelp. Several display around the bridge turn to static.

Wil brings the *Ghost* around on a course away from the other ship, putting the summit station between them and the presumed Farsight frigate. "Bennie, prep the decoy." The Brailack nods.

Behind the *Ghost*, the summit station breaks in half, atmosphere venting and debris forming a cloud.

Inside the weapon magazine, a specially designed missile loads into the number two launcher. "Decoy ready!" Bennie reports.

"Fire!" Wil shouts, then slams the controls over. As the special missile launches, he pulls the *Ghost* into a turn, then pushes the FTL throttle all the way forward. As the *Ghost* jumps to FTL, the special missile, also capable of FTL, jumps on an entirely different vector.

Barbara walks over to the center console where Wil is making adjustments to their course. "We're not going the right way," she gestures to the navigation screen on Wil's command console. The *Ghost* is heading towards, more or less nothing, definitely not towards Kal Nor station.

Wil looks up at her, "Well, we can't go to Kal Nor, not yet anyway. That ship, Farsight, will expect us to try to get back there—to your seat of power and safety."

"Not to mention there are likely to be more of those monster-infused ships lurking along the route," Maxim offers.

"Captain," the ceiling says in Gabe's voice, "the *Ghost* sustained rather significant damage. Those particle beams caused severe damage to several subsystems."

Wil rubs his face then looks at the ceiling, "Great. Ok, we'll find someplace to set down."

"I advise we do not, as you say, dilly dally. The reactor is stable but fluctuating. I believe those beams were designed to cause exotic interactions with most common shipboard reactors."

"That's lovely," Wil says then looks at the navigation display, then around the bridge, "Thoughts?"

Barbara leans over to look at the console again, "Actually, yes."

While Barbara works over Wil's shoulder, Cynthia says, "By the way, comms are out. I just finished a diagnostic and looks like one of those particle beams overloaded a shield emitter near the main subspace antenna array. It's fried."

Wil groans, "Of course. That means no one knows Farsight is behind the attack on the summit." Somber nods around the bridge.

Bennie raises a hand, "So we're the only ones with the truth, seems familiar."

Wil nods.

"What the hell is that thing?" Wil wonders aloud as their destination comes into view. He taps a control on his console causing the display to update with a zoomed in view of a dilapidated not quite a space station not quite a ship. It is orbiting a gas giant, skimming through the upper atmosphere. Several pieces of equipment and debris are drifting behind the facility. What looks like more than a dozen meteor strikes dot the hull.

"Gas harvester," Zephyr says.

"Is that thing even safe?" Cynthia asks.

"Or occupied?" Maxim asks. "Looks abandoned."

"Haunted," Wil adds.

Barbara sighs, "It's decommissioned."

"Very decommissioned," Cynthia adds, gesturing to one of the larger meteor strikes.

Maltor points to one of the sub-monitors next to the main display showing sensor data on the derelict, "Its orbit is decaying."

"Oh lovely. What could go wrong, docking up to a haunted, crippled, and slowly crashing gas harvester?" Wil says then adds, "Was there a zombie outbreak at any point before it was shut down?"

Maltor looks at Barbara, "Zombie?"

Zephyr turns around in her chair, "Don't ask; you'll just end up with a headache."

Wil turns back to his controls, "Docking in ten. Looks like the starboard docking collar is the least damaged. Everyone should get their party outfits on." He looks at Bennie, "You too, pipsqueak."

Bennie pumps his small fist, "Yes!" and hops out of his chair beating Maxim and Zephyr to the bridge hatch.

Wil looks at the two Tygran guests, "Has anyone else been here? Will we need override codes?"

"Without comms we can't access the internex, so we can't access the Tralgot database," Maltor replies.

"Bennie and Gabe can handle it," Wil says, eyes never leaving the main display. On it, the dilapidated harvester is getting bigger. Wil splits the display so he can line up the *Ghost's* airlock with the harvester's docking collar.

ASS END OF SPACE_

"Definitely haunted," Wil says as the airlock cycles open to a darkened corridor with several conduits hanging precariously. The only illumination is semi-functional red emergency strips on both sides of the corridor, many are blinking sporadically. He steps further inside the corridor, his armor lights turning on. He taps a control on his armored wristcomm, and four small probes launch from the back of his armor. "I've missed these little guys."

"But not me?" his armor, named *Jarvis*, asks.

Wil smiles, "Well yeah, of course I've missed you, Jarvis!"

Maltor leans to Barbara, "Is he speaking to his combat armor?" His boss shrugs.

Maxim tilts his head, "Huly, Doughy, Larry, and mmm, Melvin?"

Zephyr moves past, her head shaking, "You know better than to engage him."

"Huey, Dewy, Louie, and Launchpad," Will corrects. A pair of drones heads off each direction up and down the corridor. He glances at his wristcomm, confirming that the small probes are creating a schematic of the harvester. He taps an icon, then swipes up. "You all should have access to the boys now to help you get around." He looks around, "Team One is me, Barbara, and Cynthia. We'll take the command deck, see if there's anything worthwhile up there. Maybe Babs can unlock something."

Barbara turns to Cynthia mouthing the word, *Babs*. Cynthia shrugs. Barbara and Maltor are in borrowed EVA suits, no armor, but rugged enough to climb around in the broken-down gas harvester.

"Team Two is Maltor, Bennie, and Max. You guys find the computer center; see what you find out, maybe scavenge some gear."

Maltor raises his hand, "I believe I can be most useful accompanying Miss Mress."

Wil smiles, "Good to know. No. Team Three, you head to engineering. I know it's a long shot, but if we can get power back online, that might speed up the scavenging and repairs to the *Ghost*." Everyone nods.

Maltor points, "Engineering is that way." Team Three heads off.

Teams One and Two walk together for a bit until the corridor opens up to another. Maltor takes his team off the down the new branch. He glances back toward Barbara who smiles reassuringly and motions him to continue on.

Since Maltor is at least slightly familiar with this model of harvester, he's leading the group. They've gone up three levels and turned down countless corridors, often backtracking when they find breached or damaged corridors.

"That meteor shower must have been horrible," Bennie says looking through the clear window in an emergency bulkhead. The corridor beyond has a hole in it big enough for Bennie to walk through. The lower hole continues several more decks as far as he can tell from the window.

Maxim nods and looks at Maltor, "Did your people escape?"

Maltor shrugs, "Not sure. I hadn't been assigned to Miss Mress yet, and my previous boss was in procurement or asset management." He consults his wristcomm, "I think if we take the other corridor at the last junction, we can reconnect with this one just outside the computer center." He turns and heads off.

Bennie looks up at Maxim, "Why is there always a cranky one? Murta, Bon..."

Maxim shrugs, "Hopefully he doesn't meet the same fate as Murta."

From up ahead, "You know I'm on the same channel, right?" Maltor turns to look at them, the spotlight attached to the top of his helmet bathing them both in light.

Bennie grins, baring his teeth, "Yes." Maxim shakes his head.

"Someone has for sure been here," Wil says, pointing to a pile of emergency rations in the corner of an alcove, some type of monitoring station.

"Let's just hope they're not here now," Barbara replies.

They've been walking for a while; the harvester isn't laid out like space vessels. The command center is located not in the center of the vessel, but in the forward-most section of the ship, at the top of a conning tower.

Someone has fastened a tarp up over the alcove, giving it some semblance of privacy. Cynthia leans down to examine the packages of rations, "I don't think anyone has touched these in a while." She looks up at Wil and the older Tygran woman, "I'm guessing a freighter or pirate crew came through at some point and took advantage." She looks around, "Maybe used this place as a way-station."

Wil nods, "We probably would have." He smiles at Barbara, "No offense, but it's kinda finders keepers out here."

The elder Tygran grunts and continues on.

"I'm growing on her, Wil says beaming. He turns to follow her. Cynthia stands, "Like a fungus." She shakes her head and follows.

NEWSCAST_

"GOOD MORNING. This is GNO Morning Break; I'm Megan," the newscaster says smiling.

"And I'm Xyrzix. We're receiving word that there has been an attack on the Corporate Congress summit with many casualties and fatalities among the delegations. So far, most participant corporations have not issued a statement, but a Farsight spokesperson sent us a statement that reads, *Farsight is truly and deeply saddened by the losses at the summit and will do whatever we can to help our colleagues, however we can.*"

Megan looks at her co-host, "This couldn't be happening at a worse time given the unrest spreading throughout the GC as a result of the mysterious attacks against the Peacekeepers and the resulting martial law declaration the other day."

"Agreed. We'll keep you posted as we learn more about any surviving delegations."

CHAPTER 14_

EVERYONE POOPS_

"ACCORDING TO"—ZEPHYR consults her wristcomm, then looks up at Gabe—"Launchpad, the corridor is compromised up ahead." She looks at her wristcomm again, tapping her foot. "Engineering might be cut off."

Gabe says nothing but is looking around the corridor. His eyes shift to a blue color Zephyr has never seen before.

"Uh... Gabe?" she starts.

"I believe I have located a route to engineering that is uncompromised," Gabe says.

"You, you can see through the bulkheads now?" Zephyr asks, pointing to her own eyes.

Gabe tilts his head, "Of course not. I was re-tasking one of Wil's probes, Huey, I believe. It was able to find a local network node. Once connected I was able to piggyback the—"

Zephyr raises a hand, "What is the route?"

"You will not like it," Gabe warns.

Zephyr shrugs, "Well we're on a ship so there can't be a—" Gabe inclines his head. "Sewer?" The droid nods. Zephyr inhales and releases a loud sigh.

"Technically, on a ship it is called the bilge," Gabe offers.

"Captain, engineering seems to be largely intact," Gabe reports as he and Zephyr walk into the massive space.

"Cool. See what you can do. The fact that there's any lighting after this long is a miracle, but I wouldn't mind some real light and maybe air," Wil replies over the comms.

"How is there still emergency power?" Zephyr wonders aloud as she absently scratches at something brown that's clinging to her armored leg. "So gross," she mumbles wrinkling her nose inside her helmet.

Gabe moves to examine the reactor, "My understanding of harvesters is that while they have sizable emergency batteries, they also make use of a passive harvesting system on the ventral section of the vessel for emergency power. Minor amounts of helium are skimmed and converted into energy; it's an efficient system to be sure, but only suitable for low power uses like strip lighting, as we have seen." He turns and looks at the reactor some more, "I believe I may be able to restart this. It appears undamaged. If I had to guess, I would assume the reactor scrammed during the meteor storm, likely as circuits shorted and power busses failed throughout the vessel causing overloads and surges." He rests a metal hand on the reactor, "I can restrict the power flow to avoid surges."

"That's good news," Zephyr says, joining him.

The droid tinkers at the controls for a few minutes, one hand extending the familiar data filaments into the control panel. The filaments pulse as data moves back and forth, causing the control panel to illuminate.

From inside the reactor, something clunks followed by a series of indicators coming to life. Zephyr inclines her head toward the indicators, "Those seem positive."

"Indeed. The reactor is warming up. It will need a few minutes before I can start it," Gabe says as he turns to examine the rest of the room. One of Wil's probes drifts in moving in a lazy arc near the top of the room before moving out of sight. "Captain, the reactor is warming up now. I will attempt to start it shortly but cannot make any guarantees at the moment. To minimize the risk of the reactor scramming, I will engage circuits slowly."

Over the comms Wil replies, "Sounds good. We're up in command, and power would help things along so if we can be first, that'd be excellent."

"Indeed. We will keep you posted."

Zephyr wanders over to what looks like it might be a master situation board. As she stares at its black surface, lights begin to appear. "Hey Gabe, getting life over here," she says over her shoulder.

"That is promising. I am about to attempt reactor startup. Standby."

She keeps staring at the board as faint tell-tales continue to come to life. From behind her, the reactor makes a few clunks and other noises. The board in front of her comes to life in a blur of lights and animations. She turns to look at the reactor and Gabe, "Looks like you did it."

The droid inclines his head, "Indeed. Though I believe to be safe, twenty percent is the furthest we should push the reactor."

Zephyr taps her earpiece, "You seeing the fruits of Gabe's labor?"

"Roger that," Maxim says. "Lights and environmental seem to be coming online."

Wil adds, "Yup. Command center just came to life. Good job, you two."

Zephyr smiles at her colleague, "Ok, we'll look for the parts Gabe needs now."

Before Zephyr can take a step, the harvester rumbles.

"Uh, what's that?" Bennie asks.

Wil answers, "Hey Gabe, according to the displays up here, a thruster just kicked on. Oh crap. It's pushing us into the atmosphere."

Gabe moves quickly, working the main reactor control panel. The rumbling stops. Gabe looks up, "I apologize. I did not notice that the maneuvering system had been rewired to bypass a blown circuit."

"How bad?" Maxim asks.

"Not great," Wil answers. "We're falling a bit faster than we were before. Gabe can you fix it from down there? I don't seem to have maneuvering control, probably a result of that re-wire job."

"I will attempt it now," Gabe says, data filaments snaking out of his fingers back into the control panel. Throughout the enormous harvester, bangs and clanks echo and the deck vibrates.

"Uh Gabe, buddy, we're going the wrong way!" Wil says.

The harvester continues to rumble. Gabe says, "I am attempting to adjust the power flow to the thrusters, but it appears that the needed thrusters are damaged." The rumbling stops. "I am sorry. I cannot correct my mistake and likely have made it worse." Zephyr rests a hand on Gabe's shoulder.

Barbara says, "We'll just have to work faster."

THE COMMAND CENTER turns out to be even less illuminated than the corridors. The emergency strip lighting has been ripped up by someone, likely whoever had previously taken up residence on the harvester.

"Why would they have removed the lighting from this section?" Barbara wonders aloud as she walks toward the forward section of the command deck to take in the view before them.

Cynthia looks in a corner by what might be navigation where someone has set up what she can only assume was supposed to be a romantic rendezvous location. "Uh yeah, weird. Don't come over here, just sayin'."

The main lighting turns on and several consoles activate around the large bridge and command center combo. Over the comms, Gabe and Zephyr let everyone know.

Wil nods, "Yup. Command center just came to life. Good job, you two."

He turns to Barbara, "You're up." He looks around. There's no obvious Captain's chair; where one would be is a large situation table. He gestures to the table, "I'm guessing that has direct system control access." Barbara and Cynthia both head for the table, meeting him there.

Cynthia points to a section of the table, rimmed with yellow and black, about the size of most beings' palm. Barbara walks over and rests her palm on the smooth surface of the reader. For a minute, nothing happens. Cynthia is about to suggest that Barbara adjust her palm placement when the table lights up.

"Warning, reactor output at twenty percent. Warning, orbit is unstable and decaying. Warning, life support at minimal levels."

"Cancel further alarms," Barbara cuts in, then looks at Wil and Cynthia, "I think we know this place is unsafe."

"Shoulda let it get to the zombies," Wil says, but turns to look down at the table and the myriad red icons blinking all over the rendering of the harvester.

"Can you get comms online?" Cynthia asks, ignoring Wil.

"Let's see." Barbara looks at the options and settles on a set of commands. "Dren," she hisses. "Looks like whoever has been availing themselves of Tralgot hospitality saw fit to strip the comm gear." She points to several red icons, "They took all the hull-mounted hardware and a fair bit of the internal components."

"Lovely," Wil groans. He looks out the forward windows, the gas giant is beyond swirling: greens, browns, yellows, and muted pinks. He looks back down, "Looks like that might be the main hold. I'm guessing it's picked clean, but let's go take a look." He taps his earpiece, "Team One is on the move; we're heading to the main hold, see what's there."

Zephyr replies, "Acknowledged. Team Three still in engineering. Gabe has found a storage room, so we're working out how best to get the parts out of here."

The lighting in the computer center is not much better than the corridors. Once the reactor comes online, the room turns out to be mostly picked apart, the main computer half disassembled.

"Well, this isn't great," Bennie says, walking up to the main computer status display. The red emergency lighting and their suit lights provide the only illumination. "Computer is offline, no surprise." He points to a round floor-to-ceiling cylinder occupying half of the room, several open panels reveal the results of someone's scavenging. "I can't say how much of it will come online when the power does. Someone picked it clean." He moves to an open panel, "Yup, all the duotronic relays are gone."

"That sounds bad," Maltor says looking around the room.

Bennie nods, "Like I said, not great."

The lights begin to flicker as the power comes online. The computer core lights up, several eruptions of sparks spill out of the open panels causing all three men to take a step back. The main status display comes to life, a rendering of the room-sized cylinder flashing red in many places.

Bennie points, "Yeah, not good. We're not gonna get much, if anything, from this. Everything of value or use has been stripped." He pats the display, "She's running on the bare minimum processing right now."

Maxim looks around the room then at the door they came through, "Ok, let's head for the cargo hold then."

Two levels down and a few minutes later, the three of them are in the, now semi-illuminated, cargo hold. Bennie looks over to Maltor, "So this kind of thing happen with your boss a lot?"

The young Tygran man's tail swishes like Cynthia's when she is annoyed. "What do you mean?" He doesn't look up from the crate he's leaning over rummaging through.

"I mean, I always knew you mega-corp goons fought with each other and stuff. Wurrin, that incident last year with Farsight and Crucible was a mess, but we're being chased by Farsight's pet project monster ship. It

destroyed a few other delegations too, ones that voted against Asgar."
Bennie shudders. "We've worked for Farsight, more than once." He
shakes his head, "But this seems a bit extreme, killing competitors and
all. There are a lot of companies right now without leadership."

Maxim chimes in, "After the thing on Glacial, this doesn't
surprise me much." His nose wrinkles as he thinks about the fight in
the landing dome on the frozen world. "Farsight is clearly a threat."
He walks over to Maltor and the crate he's still inspecting, "Do you
corporate folk involve the GC in your fights or is this strictly an
internal thing for you all?"

Maltor stands up holding a gravity compensator coil, Maxim
smiles and nods, taking the device. As Maltor moves to a box that
hasn't been opened yet by the look of it, he says, "Something this big,
no, we'll involve the GC and Peacekeepers. I mean, we're teetering
on the brink of a corporate civil war. So yeah, the GC needs to step
in. Farsight has moved from aggressive to threat." He pushes the pry
bar he's holding into the gap between the crate and its lid. "You've
mentioned Glacial several times in relation to Farsight and their
newfound aggressive stance. What is that? What are those
creatures?"

Maxim looks around the room, "Wil is on the way, but I'll tell you
what I know." He points to Bennie, "He and I were on a rogue Peacekeeper command carrier for the first part of the Glacial job."

"Rogue Peacekeeper?" Maltor asks.

"One horror story at a time," Bennie says, pushing a crate aside to
reach the one behind it. He points, "This one looks promising."

REPAIRS AND SCAVENGING_

"Wow. I wonder why the mystery tenants didn't take all this?" Wil says as he follows Cynthia and Barbara into the hold. The harvester groans and rumbles for a minute before settling back down. Bennie, Maltor, and Maxim have piled several crates near the door, and Wil can see that it's the stuff they hope to take back to the *Ghost*.

Barbara looks around the space, focusing on the crates the crew of the *Ghost* has set aside. "I suppose there's no reason I should be upset about this looting," she says, mostly to herself.

Wil looks at the room, then to the feline-featured executive, "If it helps, we're only taking what we need to fix the *Ghost* up and get back underway, you know, with you aboard, safe." He grins.

She smiles rolling her eyes. She picks up a piece of equipment from a crate, "This is likely why they didn't take these things." On the device, a power transform adapter, in bright colors is the Tralgot logo with a barcode beneath it. "We track our inventory aggressively. If a ship made port and a repair tech scanned this part and it came up stolen, one of our ships would be dispatched, while the offending ship would be impounded or at least detained."

Wil nods slowly, "So we should make sure to have Maltor enter all this in your database once we have a working comm system."

Barbara grins, "Only if you want to avoid *misunderstandings* in the future."

Maltor walks over to his boss, "Do we not typically clear out a facility before abandoning?"

She nods, "We do. I'm not sure why this harvester was left with a single scrap of anything in the hold, let alone the more sensitive equipment. I will be investigating who needs to be fired for this when we return to Kal Nor."

Bennie nods, "It's not now, but yeah, your folks left the computer mostly intact from what I could see." He grimaces, "Oh, and I think someone was sleeping in one of the heat exchangers." Maxim nods.

Wil tuts, "Yeah we found a"—he shudders—"love nest up on the command deck."

"Ew," Bennie says. "As gross as it sounds?"

Cynthia nods slowly, "Worse. There were used prophylactics."

Everyone flinches, reeling back.

"And candles," Wil offers, shrugging. Maxim makes a retching sound.

The harvester rattles and something near the hold groans.

"Ok, we should get going," Wil says. He taps his earpiece, "Gabe, Zee, how're you two doing?"

"Well, we're in the bilge, pushing a crate of parts; so, you know, we're doing great," Zephyr replies sourly.

Wil looks at the others, grinning. He chuckles then wipes his hand over his face bringing it back to a more serious look, "Ok. We're in the hold now, but we're going to start getting the stuff here over to the *Ghost* so Gabe can start repairs. It sounds like it will be a stinker of a job, so hurry back." He looks at the others and snorts before placing a hand over his mouth to stifle his laughter. Maxim is struggling to not laugh. Bennie chuckles and turns his back to the group.

"We can hear you," Zephyr growls before closing the connection.

Maltor looks at Barbara who shrugs.

The harvester shudders again.

Wil moves to one of the crates, picking it up, "Looks like we're doing this the old school way. Grab a box, and let's go." As he heads out of the hold, two of his small probes drift towards him and return to their docking ports in his armored backpack.

Something pops and the sound of atmosphere rushing out roars before a slam indicates an emergency bulkhead closing. Bennie grabs a box almost as big as he is, "Let's do this. This piece of dren is coming apart at the seams." Maltor grabs a box slightly too big for him to carry but manages to shuffle out of the hold.

The mostly paste-like substance in the bilge system sloshes slowly as the massive harvester shudders. Zephyr has a large storage box in her arms, struggling to walk and hold the heavy box above the slime. If not for her armor the box would be too heavy for her. "I do not want to die covered in dren," she says.

Gabe, sloshing through the waste behind her with two even larger storage boxes balanced on each shoulder replies, "For what it is worth, we are near the lowest level of the harvester, this section is the least damaged and likely most structurally sound. Also, given the relative age of this harvester and how long it has been derelict, most of this sludge is the digestive enzyme used to break down biological waste."

The harvester shudders again and something in the large bilge tank groans.

"Not better," Zephyr pants.

NEWSCAST_

"Good afternoon. I'm Belzar."

"And I'm Gulbar' Te. We have news today out of Galtron City on Squirgle Three. That name may sound familiar because just last cycle Farsight Corporation staged a hostile takeover of Crucible Corporation. Yesterday, a whistleblower within Farsight Corporation released an internal memo outlining plans to take advantage of the chaos that has resulted from the attack on the Corporate Congress summit."

Belzar turns from his co-host to the camera, "It's unclear how Farsight would have known about the attack; the leaked document doesn't indicate such, but it certainly has raised questions."

Gulbar' Te says, "As yet, Farsight has not responded to the news of the leak."

CHAPTER 15_

THAT DIDN'T TAKE LONG_

"Bennie and Max, can you get started sorting this stuff, so when Gabe gets here, he can dive in?"

"On it," the big Palorian says. Everyone is in the cargo hold of the *Ghost*, having dragged and pushed the storage crates from the cargo hold of the harvester to the airlock and then into the *Ghost's* hold.

Maxim pants, "I wish the hold had an airlock." He looks up at the stairwell to the crew lounge, "So far from the airlock."

Bennie rests his hand on his big friend's arm, "You and me both."

Wil points to Maltor, "You mind logging all this?" He gestures to the crates. "Just so nothing comes up stolen three years from now."

The younger Tygran man tilts his head then moves to join Maxim and Bennie.

Wil's wristcomm beeps three times and the screen flashes red.

Barbara looks down at his arm, "That's probably not good."

Wil raises his arm to look at the screen, "Damn, they found us." He looks around, "How the fuck did they manage that?" He looks at Barbara who shrugs.

Maxim looks around, "Could they have put a tracker on one of us, or the ship?"

Bennie turns and heads for the stairs, "I ran a sweep when we left, but if they planted something with a remote activator or a timer, it might have been missed."

Wil nods, "Ok, do a sweep, see what you can find. Don't power up the main sensor array though. No need to give away our location." The Brailack hacker gives him a thumbs up as he vanishes into the deck above.

Wil turns to the others, "Looks like the mystery frigate and a cruiser. Not sure if it's the cruiser from the summit or a different one, but it doesn't matter"—he looks around at the faces in the room— "they're here now."

Barbara shifts from foot to foot as she says, "When we were on the command deck, I saw the controls for the point defense system. I didn't look much at it, but if even some of it is operational, it might help buy us time." She licks her lips.

Wil looks around then gestures to Cynthia, "Ok, you two get back to the command deck, and see what you can do."

"On it," Cynthia says extending her arm toward the stairway back up to the living section of the *Ghost* for Barbara to lead the way.

As the two Tygran women exit the *Ghost* into the dilapidated harvester, the larger vessel groans several times and something, somewhere makes a snapping sound.

"How long do you think we have?" Barbara asks, her eyes darting left and right as they move through the corridors retracing their steps to the command deck.

"No idea, but let's assume not much," Cynthia says as she increases her pace a bit.

The trip from the airlock where the *Ghost* is docked to the harvester's command deck, now that they know the route, doesn't take long. The main situation table is still glowing, several bright red and yellow icons flashing.

Barbara walks to the table looking over its surface to find what she's looking for. She points to a section of the table.

Cynthia looks at a monitor mounted overhead, "They're closing." On the display the mystery frigate and much larger Farsight branded cruiser are bearing down on the harvester.

Barbara is tapping icons on the table, "I believe I've almost got it. I don't know how much time these will buy us, but I guess anything is better than nothing." She looks up and Cynthia nods. "Here goes." She presses a few controls, "I'm setting them to close in defense mode." She scans the display, "We've got a few centocks before the guns open up." She says pressing her finger to a pulsing green icon. As she contacts the table's surface the pulsing of the icon stops. From deeper inside the large craft several loud bangs reverberate. Something, several somethings, groan and whir. On the situation table, a schematic of the harvester shows several icons appearing across the hull, the point defense cannons deploying. Almost half of the new icons immediately flash orange, some turn red. "Several are offline, a few are showing damage, but might still function," Barbara says studying the display.

Cynthia looks at the displays, "With the reactor at twenty percent, these won't pack much punch, but better than nothing." She smiles. "I don't think there's anything else we can do up here." Outside the window, the atmosphere of the gas giant is billowing past the lower sections of the harvester. She turns to leave, "We're getting deeper fast."

"Let's go then. I'd rather my last moments be in one of my estates, not this dilapidated harvester," Barbara agrees.

NO RUSH OR ANYTHING_

"OH GOD! You have to go somewhere else, right now!" Wil backs away from Zephyr and Gabe, holding his nose.

Zephyr walks into the *Ghost's* cargo hold, her armor is covered in a mix of lumpy green and brown-colored sludge. Gabe is similarly covered in the sludge, some of it sliding off his metallic body to fall to the cargo deck.

Maxim looks his droid friend up and down, "You tracked that in from the airlock?"

Zephyr and Gabe examine each other, each shrugging. They drop their boxes near the others.

Gabe looks at Maxim and Wil, "I would appreciate your assistance. I have created a prioritized list." Each of their wristcomms beep showing the received file.

Maxim examines his wristcomm screen, "Makes sense."

The harvester shudders once more, the vibrations traveling to the *Ghost*. Wil looks around then taps his earpiece, "Cyn, you and Babs on your way back?"

"Yup. We're almost to the airlock." There's a pause, but she doesn't close the channel. "The PD array just lit off. That mystery frigate is close."

Wil turns to the stairwell to leave the cargo hold, stepping over a brown clump of something he says, "Ok, hopefully that'll keep them at bay for a bit, I'll be on the bridge." The *Ghost* rattles as the harvester she's attached to sinks lower into the atmosphere of the gas giant.

Bennie appears in the hatch at the top of the stairs, "Who tracked all that dren inside the ship?"

"Please replace plasma flow governors alpha three thru seven," Gabe instructs from the open access panel both of his arms are sunk deep inside of.

"On it," Maxim says rushing over to a panel on the opposite side of the small walkway that runs the length of the port wing of the *Ghost*.

Wil pops his head into the access hatch, "I re-ran the data cables in starboard junction Beta twelve. What next?"

Gabe turns his head to look down the cramped walkway to the opening. "Check secondary power bus node three. It is under the floor panel near the dining room table."

Wil doesn't answer other than to vanish from the opening. The *Ghost* shudders as the harvester descends further into the atmosphere. Maxim looks over at Gabe, "How much pressure can the *Ghost* take? Will the harvester go first or us?"

Gabe removes his arms from the opening he's been working in and places the cover over it. He moves to assist Maxim with his last few plasma flow governors. "Under normal conditions, the harvester should be able to descend several thousand meters into the atmosphere. The *Ghost* is not rated for that, at best we can survive for a few hundred meters." He tilts his head as he hands Maxim the last governor, "However, the harvester is severely compromised. I suspect it will fail around the same depth as the *Ghost*." He smiles.

Maxim frowns, closing the panel. "Then let's get this done. What next?"

From the overhead speaker Bennie says, "Wil, you're needed on the bridge."

Cynthia, Zephyr, and the two guests are on the bridge of the *Ghost* with Wil. On the main display, the harvester is firing its point defense cannons at incoming missiles and the mystery frigate whenever it gets close enough.

"They're not having much of an effect," Maltor says.

Wil nods and looks over his shoulder, "I assume they're mostly meant to fend off meteors and low-budget pirates. They're doing ok with the missiles—" He's interrupted by several energy blasts impacting on the harvester, ripping the upper levels to shreds. "But those energy beams are another matter." He looks at his console, "Thankfully our *probably Farsight* friend has to get close to use them, so they take damage. I'm guessing they can handle PD rounds long enough to rip the PD turrets to pieces." He turns to Bennie, "You got their tracker?"

The Brailack nods, "Yeah, an impressive piece of work." He grins, "But still not a match for me."

"You missed it the first time," Cynthia says.

Bennie makes a rude gesture, "It was turned off then!" He turns back to Wil, "We're good, I was able to reverse engineer the activation signal and ran it through the ship a few times, nothing." Wil nods.

"Why are they not firing on us?" Barbara wonders.

"We're hard to see," Zephyr says from her station. She turns to face the older Tygran woman, "We're barely a sixteenth the mass of the harvester and tucked in close. Given all the protrusions on this thing and our reactor at twenty-five percent while the guys make repairs, we're pretty invisible."

"The downside is we can't risk firing missiles or blasters, they'll lock right on to them," Wil adds. On the screen the atmosphere of the gas giant is getting thicker as the massive harvester falls deeper and deeper.

The two Farsight vessels are looming mostly just out of range of the harvester's point defense cannons, lobbing missiles towards the rapidly sinking vessel.

LEAF ON THE WIND_

"CAPTAIN, repairs are complete. I am bringing the reactor back up to one hundred percent," Gabe reports from the ceiling speakers.

Wil turns to look over his shoulder, "You two should go to the crew lounge or your quarters."

The bridge hatch opens to allow Maxim to enter. Barbara nods, "Very well. Good luck." She and Maltor turn and exit the bridge.

"Everyone ready?" Wil asks as Maxim takes his seat. He turns to Maxim, "Once we disconnect, I'm gunning it. Fire everything we've got as we go."

Maxim nods once, his brow furrowed, tapping controls to bring the *Ghost's* formidable weapons online.

Wil looks around once more, then says, "Here we go, leaf on the wind." He presses the control that overrides the airlock controls, triggering an emergency disconnect. There's a clunk, and the *Ghost* lurches slightly, no longer being pulled along by the harvester.

"What the wurrin does that mean?" Bennie asks.

Wil ignores him, pushing the flight controls to increase the separation from the harvester. Pushing the sub-light throttle all the way to its stops makes the *Ghost* leap away from the doomed gas harvester. The dying vessel, still firing its few remaining point defense cannons quickly recedes. The mystery frigate, in mid-attack run, barely has time to react to the sudden appearance of the powerful gunship.

"Firing," Maxim says. The sound of the nacelle-mounted blasters firing rings through the ship. The ball turret mounted on the forward section just behind the bridge starts firing, the sound deafening. From deeper inside the ship, the sound of the missile launchers and weapon magazines working overtime to eject as many deadly projectiles as possible adds to the chorus of destruction flooding the interior of the *Ghost*.

The mystery frigate lashes out with its particle cannon, but Wil and the *Ghost* are prepared this time. He forces the ship into a dive back toward the atmosphere as the shields absorb the beam weapon's energy. Rather than overloading systems, this time the energy floods into backup power cells and capacitors all through the ship.

Maxim lets out a whoop, "I could get used to that, turning their energy weapons fire into our own and redirecting it. Neat!" He looks at the ceiling, "Way to go, Gabe!"

Missiles and blaster bolts strike the ink black vessel ripping into the chitin-like armor. The *Ghost* rattles as more particle beams strike the shields as well as a few missiles.

Wil adjusts the controls. The sub-light engines strain to push them up and out of the gravity well of the massive gas giant.

"Farsight cruiser is firing up their engines, moving to attempt an intercept," Zephyr reports.

"They're welcome to try," Wil says then slams his hand on the FTL activation control. On the main display, the Farsight cruiser slides past on the right side and the stars stretch out into rainbow-colored lines. Wil sits back in his command chair, "I'll change course a few times. Then we can decide what to do next." He looks at Zephyr, "You didn't leave your armor in the armory, did you?" He puts a finger under his nose.

Later, once Wil is as sure as he can be that they're not being pursued, he joins the crew and their clients in the lounge. "I'm open to ideas."

"Do you still think Kal Nor is too dangerous?" Maltor asks.

"What if we took an indirect route?" Barbara offers.

Maxim shakes his head, "It'd take a while, and right now we're the only ones that know what happened at the summit. Farsight cut the heads off the biggest and most powerful corporations in the GC. If I had to guess, I'd say they're spinning it right now to keep everyone off balance."

"To what end?" Barbara wonders aloud tapping her chin, a manicured claw slides out as she does.

Wil shrugs, "Who knows, but I've learned to never underestimate Jark Asgar. He's up to something, and if he's ok killing so many innocent people, it can't be good."

"Duch," Cynthia says.

"I'm not familiar with the Duch system," Barbara says, her tail lazily swishing between her and Maltor.

"Duch isn't a system—" Cynthia starts.

"He's a person," Wil finishes, making eye contact and mouthing, *I love you.*

She mouths back, *I know* then says, "He's a crime boss we know. Picked up most of the pieces when Xarrix Cruthup left his empire up for grabs. He's an idiot, but not as evil as Xarrix was. We had him fe—"

"Doing some work for us," Wil interrupts. "We're at least on good terms with him."

Maxim and Zephyr, standing together on the other side of the lounge watch the exchange smiling.

Bennie and Gabe are at the kitchen table, Bennie looks at Gabe, "Great, we can add one more person to the who wants us dead list."

Gabe looks down at Bennie, "I was unaware you were maintaining such a list."

Bennie sighs.

CHAPTER 16_

"Oᴋ, I'll admit I wasn't expecting much from this," Barbara says taking a bite of her meal.

Bennie looks at his own plate, "Yeah this is new. It's like pizza, but also like a sandwich." He turns to Wil at the end of the table, "What'd you call it? Calopy?"

Wil puts his fork down, "Calzone." He turns to Barbara, "I'm glad it exceeds your expectations."

"I meant no offense, Captain," the elder Tygran woman says, the hairs of her face rippling to show her embarrassment. "I didn't know what to expect, given that your people are an unknown." She takes another bite and washes it down with a sip of grum. "If your people join the GC, the foodies will no doubt have a field day."

Cynthia smiles, "Time permitting, you must try tacos." She looks at her calzone, "This is good; tacos are better."

Maxim nods, "Oh yeah, we need a taco night soon."

Zephyr takes the last bite of her calzone, pushing her empty plate forward a bit. She watches the crew chat with their clients and laugh for a bit, then clears her throat. "Once we get to Duch's place, then what?"

Bennie chimes in, "We transmit our data recordings of the attack and sink Farsight. There's no way the GC lets that stand. They'll send the Peacekeepers in"—he snaps his thin green fingers—"like that."

Maltor raises a hand, "Were you not following the news prior to our arrival at the summit? I think the Peacekeepers might be otherwise occupied."

Wil cocks his head, "No." He turns to Gabe, "Gabe?" The droid nods and moves toward the large wall display. He looks at the ceiling, mimicking Wil as he accesses the ship's computer over the wireless network. A moment later, the latest GNO Newsbreak the ship downloaded comes to life on the screen. They watch silently, except Bennie who manages to make a disturbing amount of noise while eating a calzone.

When the video stops and the display goes blank, Maxim turns to look at the crew and their guests, "Well, grolack. That has to be Farsight. Right?"

Wil puts his face in his hands for a minute, "Fuck. We thought it was Janus and *The Source*, but yeah it could be Farsight. We have no idea what Farsight found on Glacial—more than we thought. Or, hell it could be both. Is it possible *The Source* creature could control or somehow reach out to whatever Farsight scraped up off Glacial?" He runs a hand down his face, scratching at the stubble on his cheek. He takes a long pull of his grum, then sits the half empty glass on the table. "I don't know what's going on, but yeah, it doesn't look good. Two very horrible people have access to, well, monsters. We've seen what Farsight can do with the creatures. I don't want to see what Janus can get up to. With our comms down, we can't tell the GC what we know. Let's get to Duch and get him to transmit the data." He looks at Bennie, "Speaking of, after dinner can you get it bundled up into a nice package?" The Brailack nods. "After that, we head to Kal Nor. Maybe we can get the Peacekeepers to lend us a command carrier as an escort."

"You think we'll need an escort?" Zephyr asks.

Wil shrugs, "I don't think we'll get one, not from the Peacekeepers. We're still not that popular with certain Councilors, and the Peacekeepers seem to be a bit busy."

"Maybe Duch can help there?" Cynthia offers.

Gabe looks around the kitchen, "For what it is worth, I find it highly unlikely that *The Source* and Janus would be working with Farsight. We observed several living creatures from orbit, forty-two to be specific, not counting however many might have survived deeper inside the caverns. By the time Farsight arrived, we know that *The Source* creature was en route to Janus's fleet. It is likely we will be dealing with two unique enemies."

"Cheery," Cynthia says.

Gabe looks around the table, "Sorry."

FAVORS?_

"UH, WE'RE BEING TARGETED," Zephyr reports as the *Ghost* approaches Crildon Three, home of Rhys Duch's criminal empire. "How does he have so many surface-to-orbit emplacements on just that one island?"

"Rude," Bennie says.

Maxim looks up from his tactical station, "Were those here last time?"

Wil doesn't adjust their course, "Are we close enough for short-range comms?"

Cynthia checks her console, "Nothing yet."

Something on Zephyr's console beeps. It's an angry sounding beep.

Maxim opens his mouth, "Target lo—"

"Wait!" Cynthia says cutting him off, "I just picked up a signal off one of the satellites!" She starts working her console.

Zephyr's console is still beeping, and the beeping has somehow gotten more urgent. Just as suddenly as the angry beeping started, it stops.

"Got him," Cynthia says looking up. "We're cleared through."

Wil looks down at the plot Cynthia just sent to his console, "That was stressful."

Duch is waiting at the foot of the cargo ramp when the large cargo doors open. "Hi guys! You have to be more careful." He gestures to one of the ever-present combat drones that patrol his island as it zips past overhead, "Coming in hot without comms is dangerous."

Maxim grunts, "It wasn't our idea."

Duch waves the topic away, moving on quickly. "You didn't have to come all the way back here. I would have deposited the funds in your accounts."

Wil reaches the bottom of the ramp and extends his hand, grasping the Multonae man's forearm as he grasps Wil's. Wil smiles, "That's not why we're here." He looks around, not seeing any of the small beings that populate the world and work for the crime boss. He does see Duch's small Brailack assistant, Tah'tu who he waves at before turning back to Duch. "We have two favors to ask."

The rest of the crew walks down the ramp, Barbara and Maltor with them. Duch shifts his gaze to the others and settles on the two new Tygrans. "Barbara Mress! You're supposed to be dead!" He releases Wil's arm and moves to offer his arm to the Tygran woman. "How is this possible?"

She bows, "Rumors of my death are clearly exaggerated. Thank you for allowing us to land."

The crime boss winks, "For my friend Wil and the others, of course; though having the CEO of Tralgot owe me a favor is even more reason."

Barbara glances at Cynthia who smiles and shrugs.

Gabe leans down to Wil, "I will supervise Duch's people if that is acceptable to you, Captain. The repairs we made at the harvester were rushed and I would be more comfortable making sure the *Ghost* is in optimal condition before combat."

"Combat?" Maltor asks, overhearing. "Who said anything about combat?"

Gabe smiles, "There is always combat,"—he rests a hand on Maltor's shoulder—"always." Zephyr and Maxim nod.

Gabe grins, which is far less disturbing than his full smile, "Also, I do not trust Duch's people unattended on the ship."

Wil nods, whispering, "Good call." He pats Gabe's shoulder.

Duch smiles and extends a hand toward the waiting ground cars. "I assume one favor is fixing your busted comms?" He looks at Wil, then Gabe who nods. He grins, "I can take the cost out of what I got you for the last of the stuff I was moving." He hops in the first car with Wil, Barbara, and Maltor. Duch looks over to Wil as the car moves, "I got the last of it sold by the way, did pretty good if I do say so myself."

Wil nods, "That's good to hear, because our second favor is a bit bigger." Duch turns to look at him, saying nothing. "You happen to have a fleet lying around? Nearby, ideally."

"A fleet? Of starships?" the Multonae man asks, confused.

"No, dummy!" Bennie shouts from the second car. "Ocean cruise liners."

Wil spins in his seat, "Hey! Shut up back there!" He turns to Duch, "Yeah, Starships. Ones with guns, ideally."

"Are you planning to attack someone?" the Multonae man asks, sitting up stiffly.

"No, and we don't want to put your ships and crews at too much risk, but we need to get Miss Mress to Kal Nor station and there are good odds that Farsight Corporation will try to stop us." Wil snaps his fingers, "This might help." He lifts his wristcomm and finds the file he'd copied from the *Ghost* earlier. He played it for the Multonae man next to him.

When the video finishes and Duch looks up at Wil, then back to Barbara and Maltor, "Grolack." The two Tygrans nod.

Wil says, "Yeah. Farsight is waging war, but no one knows." He frowns, "It'd go a long way if we could broadcast this from here."

The other man holds up a hand, "No." He sighs, "Sorry, I like you guys but if I broadcast that data packet, it'll bring Farsight down on my head." He looks at Barbara, "The ships are a big ask, one I can't say for sure I can deliver, but I can't take the risk of attracting more attention." The car arrives. "I had the staff prepare a meal." He gets out of the car and walks toward the guest house the crew had stayed at the last time they visited Duch.

As Zash places the dessert course in front of everyone, Duch announces, "The repairs to the *Ghost* are complete. I'm told your droid friend is very overbearing."

Grell takes the pile of empty plates through a door Wil didn't notice last time they were here. He raises an eyebrow and is about to ask about it when Barbara says, "Mister Duch, I need your ships, what would it take to get them?" Duch is about to answer but Barbara continues, "Would a transport contract with Tralgot be of interest?"

Zephyr leans over to Maxim, "She doesn't mess around."

Maxim shakes his head, "Glad we're on her side."

Duch raises an eyebrow, "Not the strongest bargaining posture to throw out an offer like that right off the bat, Miss Mress."

Barbara inclines her head, "Just so, but time is of the essence. I can have Maltor draw up a two-cycle shipping agreement." She looks around, "I presume one of your"—she clears her throat—"businesses is shipping and transport?"

The Multonae criminal looks at Wil who smiles but says nothing, then looks at Barbara, "Miss Mress, I think we can probably work something out, for say, a three-cycle transport agreement, with exclusivity in two sectors, to be named later."

Maltor's eyes widen. Barbara takes a sip of her drink, something neon yellow with spherical ice chunks floating in it. Wil and Cynthia exchange a look. When Barbara puts her glass down, she smiles,

"Three cycles, one sector exclusivity, with an option to extend to three systems after a half cycle."

"Deal," Duch says, then snaps his fingers.

Grell rushes out, "Yah bahss?"

"PADD," Duch says not looking down at the purple-skinned henchman. When Grell pulls a PADD out of the satchel at his side, Duch takes it, taps a few commands into it, then offers it to Wil to pass to Barbara. "My standard boilerplate, I think you'll find it in order."

Cynthia leans to Bennie, "He's maybe less of an idiot than I thought."

Maxim leans toward Zephyr, "He had a multi-cycle shipping agreement with exclusive sector allotments, just sitting in draft on a PADD?" Zephyr shrugs.

"It's just because he looks like a human," the Brailack offers. Cynthia shrugs, nodding.

LONG DISTANCE_

"WIL, THERE'S A CALL FOR YOU," Cynthia says, from her station. The crew is on the *Ghost* getting ready to head out. Duch's fleet is in orbit waiting for them. It surprises everyone not just at how quickly the crime lord was able to assemble a fleet but at its relative well-armed-ness.

"Like from Duch or?"

"I think it's from Earth," she says looking at her console. "The encoding is weird, and the signal isn't very strong. It's downright weak, actually."

Wil taps his chin, then stands, "I'll take it in our quarters." He heads for the bridge hatch. "Let Duch and his folks know we'll leave as soon as the rest of his ships arrive." Cynthia nods, "On it."

Wil sits down in the seat next to the small workstation set in the bulkhead of the quarters he and Cynthia share. He adjusts the wall-mounted display screen then taps a control on the desk.

The screen comes to life, a grid of faces is looking back at him. Not the same faces he'd seen when he called home to check on their progress. Fewer than before. "Captain Calder," President Stiverson says from the center of the screen.

"How'd you figure out how to reach me?" Wil asks leaning forward.

"We've made progress on your goal," the President says. The screen flickers, artifacts glitching across it.

"It should be *your* goal: world peace, unity," Wil counters.

The President waves his hand, brushing the idea away. "We've made progress. The faces you see here are the founding members of the Earth Government Alliance. Those faces you don't see have licensed or sold their part of the data file. We have it all, obviously since we are now able to reach out to you." The President grins, his chin high.

Wil nods slowly, taking it all in, "Ok, that's good; I think. Not exactly the way I'd hoped, but better than nothing."

The Prime Minister of India raises her hand, "We"—she glances somewhere, likely to one of the faces on her own screen—"well, the US has also come clean. Not just to us, but to the world at large."

President Stiverson nods, "There's been a little light rioting in some cities, especially Colorado and Kansas."

"*Light rioting*?" Wil asks, incredulous.

The President narrows his eyes again waving his hand to dismiss the idea, "That happens when the truth comes out without proper planning. We're dealing with it, and polling shows that more voters are ok than not with the truth." The screen freezes, the President's scowl plastered on his face, then resumes.

Wil sighs, "Ok, then overall, I guess congratulations are in order." Most of the heads on his display bow slightly. "So, what's next for the *Earth Gov Alliance*, catchy by the way."

"We've begun construction of a central government facility, that's a year or two off, at least. For now, we're working on making life on Earth a little better for everyone," the Canadian Prime Minister answers.

Wil nods, "Ok, good. Hey, listen, things are a bit, well upheaved out here at the moment. So, it's good you're making progress, but..."

"Up heaved?" the British Prime minister asks haughtily.

"Yeah. Too much to explain now; we've actually got to get moving soon." He smiles, "For what it's worth, I'm proud, of you all."

The Chinese President smirks, "That makes it all worthwhile."

From the overhead speaker Cynthia says, "Wil, the fleet is ready."

He looks up at the ceiling, "Be right there." He turns back to the display, "I have to go, but now that you can reach me, feel free anytime." The screen freezes then resumes, artifacts slowly fading. "But maybe a first priority is an orbital subspace transmitter. Your signal is really weak."

The Japanese representative bows, "One is in the works. While your methods are at best questionable, Captain Calder, thank you."

"Wil?" the ceiling says.

"Gotta go." He taps the control on the desk and the display goes dark. He stands, "Coming."

"Good afternoon. I'm Klor'Tillen with a breaking news alert," the Brailack journalist says, his face betraying his concern.

"Word has just reached us here at GNO that Farsight Corporation has formed a trade alliance with the Weyland Combine, forming a corporate alliance larger than any other in the history of the Commonwealth." He taps the desk absently, "Weyland ships have been reported in orbit over Leku, which you may know as the home planet of the fourth most powerful corporation, Bonaventure Limited."

Klor'Tillen's co-host looks over, "This is a disturbing turn of events, especially after the incident at the corporate summit last week, where so many corporations, many of the most powerful in the GC lost their Chief Executives, including Weyland."

Klor'Tillen nods, "There is talk of the GC Council stepping in to enact sanctions on Farsight."

"It's also been reported that Farsight vessels have been seen near Kal Nor, home of Tralgot Corporation. Tralgot's CEO Barbara Mress is presumed dead, but the company has not confirmed as yet," the co-host says.

CHAPTER 17_

RUN_

"The fleet is formed up," Zephyr announces. The *Ghost* is in the middle of a dozen modified freighters and even two corvettes, older models to be sure, but actual military vessels. Each ship jumps to FTL, then the *Ghost* does the same.

"Impressive," Maxim says as the *Ghost* goes to FTL.

After ten minutes at FTL Cynthia says, "I have Duch on comms."

The main display changes from the view of the impromptu fleet hurtling through space faster than light to the smiling, floral-print-shirt wearing Multonae man. "Hey Wil"—he looks around—"hey guys." No one replies. "So, uh I've given the Captains their orders. Look I want to help you all—"

"You want the Tralgot contract," Bennie interrupts.

Duch grimaces, not a frequent sight, "Yeah sure, but still, I want to help you." He holds up a finger, "But I don't want to lose those ships or their crews."

"Big of you," Maxim mumbles. Wil glares at his friend.

The bridge hatch opens and Barbara walks in.

"All I'm saying is be careful. They're escorts, not your backup," the crime boss says, then adds, "Good luck." He looks at Barbara standing near the bridge hatch, "I look forward to our working relationship Miss Mress." The screen goes dark, then returns to the view of the stretched stars of FTL travel.

Barbara looks at Wil, "I have an update from Kal Nor. Jark may not know where we are, but he definitely seems sure he knows where we're going. Farsight cruisers are patrolling around the station. The fleet is outside our designated territory, so nothing we can do about it, or even legally object to. One of my vice presidents has called in some of our fleet." She looks around the bridge, "I'll be honest; our strength has never been military. Our fleet is not that big and not that powerful, a handful of cruisers and lighter vessels. Certainly no match for Farsight's, especially if Jark has more of those weird black frigates."

"Even one is dangerous," Bennie says.

"Great," Maxim growls.

She looks at the big Palorian, "I'm going back to my quarters. Now that comms are repaired and we're not on Crildon Three, Maltor and I are reaching out to allies and contacts in the GC Council." She presses the control to open the hatch and leaves.

Wil slouches in his command chair, resting his chin in on his fist. He looks at his console, "We'll be there tomorrow, midday." He turns his chair and stands, "Movie?"

Zephyr stands, "Gabe mentioned really wanting to watch"—she taps the thumbs of her right hand together at her side as she thinks—"Blown Fuse? Broken Robot?" She reaches up and scratches her forehead, "No that's not it, but that's what it's about, apparently. He found it in your archive."

Wil scratches his own forehead, "Broken robot?" He snaps his fingers, "*Short Circuit.*" He smiles, "Should be fun." He looks at Cynthia, "Want to see if our guests want to join?" She nods and leaves the bridge.

Maltor is standing near the sofa in the crew lounge, "This doesn't seem like the best use of our time."

Wil closes the refrigerator door, seven tall bottles of grum clasped precariously in his hands. He moves to the lounge area and distributes them to everyone, "There's not much else we can do. We're en route; you two have made your calls, right?" Barbara nods slowly. "So, we distract ourselves. We watch a movie, we sleep, and tomorrow when we reach Kal Nor, we're ready to go." He gestures to the large over-stuffed chair, "Sit."

He returns to the kitchen area and grabs two chairs. Gabe walks in from the engineering section in the aft-most part of the deck. "I am excited to watch this film with you all." He turns to Barbara and Maltor, "It is good to see you join us. Movie night has become a time-honored tradition among this crew and our various clients and guests."

Cynthia walks in from the stairwell from the crew berths. She sees Wil on one of the kitchen chairs, walks over taking the bottle from him, then walks over to the large chair where Bennie is sitting and picks him up. He makes an undignified noise as she deposits him next to Wil on the kitchen chair. She looks at Wil, "I am not sitting on that"—she points to the chair Wil is in—"for a whole movie." She winks. Bennie growls but says nothing.

As the screen dims and the studio logo comes up, Maltor asks, "What is this movie about?"

Wil smiles, "It's about—"

"Spoilers," Gabe says, his eyes briefly flashing his combat-mode red. Wil clamps his mouth shut.

FIGHT!_

"Everyone ready?" Wil asks from his command and pilot station.

"Tactical, good," Maxim replies.

"Comms, ready," Cynthia says, then adds, "Pirate fleet reports ready."

"Sensors and ops, ready," Zephyr adds.

Bennie looks around, "Uh, code slicing and hacking, ready, I guess." He looks back to Wil and shrugs.

From the ceiling Gabe says, "Engineering is ready."

Wil taps a control on the arm of his chair, "Babs and Maltor, good to go?"

"We are ready and strapped in. I am not certain I trust these jury-rigged restraints on your lounge chairs," Barbara replies.

"Best we could do to give you full situational access. This channel stays open, so call out anything you need us to know," Wil replies.

"Will do, Captain. Good luck, and please don't get me killed," the Tygran executive says, her voice light.

Wil looks over his shoulder at Cynthia, "You cool monitoring the smugglers and other undesirables on a separate channel?"

Cynthia nods, pointing to the earpiece in her cat-like ear.

Wil turns forward and nods, "Here we go." His voice is flat, hiding his nerves as best he can.

The stretched-out star lines of FTL travel vanish, replaced by dozens of starships and in the far distance, Kal Nor space station.

"Incoming comms from Kal Nor," Cynthia says, then adds, "Audio only."

The overhead speakers beep to announce the new open channel. "*Ghost*, this is Kal Nor space control. Transmitting approach coordinates. Please share with your escorts. The Tralgot fleet will attempt to open the corridor in five centocks."

"Acknowledged, Kal Nor space control," Wil says. The speakers beep.

On the screen, the fleet of modified frigates forms up around the *Ghost* and adjusts course per the instructions Cynthia just transmitted. The two corvettes take the lead. The Farsight fleet begins adjusting their course. Two cruisers move to intercept the approaching ships.

Wil looks over to Max, "Weapons free." He turns slightly, "Let our friends know." Cynthia nods, talking in a low voice to the small fleet around them.

As the first Farsight cruiser reaches engagement range, there are no comms or threats, they open fire. The smuggler fleet breaks, each ship veering off while returning fire.

"New contacts! Weyland Combine ships. Cruisers and some frigates," Zephyr announces. "They must have been loitering outside sensor range, waiting for a call."

The new arrivals immediately open fire on the nearest Tralgot ships just as the Tralgot ships closer to the *Ghost* open fire on the Farsight cruisers attempting to intercept. The Farsight cruisers return fire; missiles and beam weapons leap between ships, crisscrossing in front of the *Ghost* as she races towards Kal Nor.

Several blaster bolts strike the *Ghost's* shields rattling the small warship and everyone inside.

"Shields are down five percent but no damage; they're recharging," Maxim reports. The sound of the *Ghost's* blasters firing runs through the ship.

Wil looks at Bennie, "I think it's time to share what we know."

Cynthia interrupts, "Incoming comm, bounced off the Farsight ships."

Wil holds up a finger for Bennie to wait, the hacker nods, fingers poised over his controls.

A window on the main display appears, Jark Asgar filling the entire thing. "Captain Calder," he says.

"Little busy at the moment, Jark. What's up?" Wil pushes the controls forward diving the *Ghost* under the nearest Farsight cruiser, as Maxim rakes the shields with their blasters. Missiles leap from the bottom of the display towards a Weyland Combine frigate that is attempting to flank a Tralgot cruiser.

"This can all end amicably," Asgar says. He continues, "You've obviously put a few things together."

"Like for example, that you took the creatures you found on Glacial and somehow made your own custom monsters, not to mention coating your ships in their weird armored skin."

"Monsters?" Asgar shakes his head, "Hardly. Those creatures are marvels of evolutionary design. I don't know where they came from, but those creatures will keep my R&D departments busy for cycles. The armor for our ships is but the first discovery we've been able to bring to prototype."

"And your pet beastie? The one from the summit?" Wil asks.

Asgar grins, "Oh, that was a special project. Clearly it needs some work."

The *Ghost* shakes and something over Cynthia's console erupts in sparks. The Tygran woman ducks, then speaks into her comm piece. She looks up, pressing a control. "He's muted. Wil the smugglers are breaking. Two have already bailed on us, the others are too. Those corvettes are still here, for now."

"Fuck," Wil hisses, then nods. Cynthia presses the button again.

"What is it you want from us, Asgar? Tralgot isn't going to surrender to your pressure. Neither will the other mega corporations."

"You've been out of touch for a few days," the Hulgian man grins. "I've been busy since the summit. What I want is straightforward. Stand down. Hand over Miss Mress, and be on your merry way to wherever it is you go to get drunk between jobs."

"We'll never agree to an alliance, Jark," Barbara interjects, her voice coming through the overhead speakers. "Tralgot will not ally itself with Farsight, and we will resist you. I've already notified the GC Council of our intent to issue several lawsuits."

Asgar tuts, "Lawsuits? My dear Mress, we're so far past that it's embarrassing you haven't figured it out. Your fleet is nowhere near strong enough to repel us, and that ragtag group of smugglers and pirates you arrived with seems to have already abandoned you."

Something impacts the *Ghost's* shields causing everyone to lurch and grab the arms of their seats. More sparks erupt; this time from something over the main display.

From his station Maxim whispers, "Two Tralgot cruisers just bit it. Our shields are down forty percent, and two shield emitters have overloaded. Gabe is on it."

Wil glances at Bennie and nods.

The Brailack hacker nods, "This is familiar." He presses a few buttons. "Data pack transmitted to Kal Nor."

ELSEWHERE ON THE GHOST_

"BEST WE COULD DO to give you full situational access. This channel stays open so call out anything you need us to know," Wil says from the ceiling speakers in the kitchen and crew lounge.

Maltor looks at Barbara, pulling one of his hastily welded shoulder restraints. "This is worrisome," he says as something behind him groans, hopefully not a weld giving up.

She tugs her own restraints, "I assume this is better than being tossed around our quarters like the last time." Her assistant reluctantly nods.

On the kitchen table between them are several PADDs and two desktop model comm panels that Bennie kept in the storage area, having replaced the units in the berths with more compact wall-mounted units.

Maltor turns to his comm unit. On the screen are the almost two dozen captains and commanders of the Tralgot fleet near Kal Nor. An indicator in the corner of the display shows that the communications are encrypted. "Stand by. All ships are weapons free once the fighting starts." Nods from most of the small faces.

Barbara looks at her own comm panel, the Senior Vice President she left in charge while she was at the summit. "The Captain of the

Ghost has the data packet. When he transmits it, rebroadcast on all channels."

"Acknowledged, Miss Mress." The other man, a Trenbal she's known for years, closes the channel.

The ship shakes and something near the hatch that leads to the engineering spaces pops, smoke wafting through the vent above the hatch.

From the overhead speaker Zephyr says, "New contacts! Weyland Combine ships—cruisers and some frigates. They must have been loitering outside sensor range."

Maltor turns to his comm system, "Weyland ships are hostile. Squadron four, engage."

The ship shudders and the sound of the weapons system rumbles through forcing both Tygrans to increase the volume levels on their comm systems to hear those they're working with.

Gabe grabs a toolbox, leaves engineering, and takes the stairs down to the cargo hold. He crosses to the port side of the hold in seconds, able to sprint at an unbelievable speed. The heavy hatch that leads to the small engineering and repair space in the wing root groans as he effortlessly opens it. He enters, closing the hatch behind him, just in case of loss of pressure. Several indicators are blinking red. The ship shakes and Gabe thrusts his free hand out to the bulkhead to stabilize himself. A second later, his feet magnetize.

The port disruptor is overheating, despite the repairs he'd made on Crildon Three with those small beings Rhys Duch employed. He removes a panel and sees two of the flow regulators are already glowing white hot.

"Maxim, I will have to take the port disruptor offline briefly," he says, routing his words through the comm system to the bridge.

"Now?" the tactical officer growls, concentrating on something else while talking.

"Unfortunately, but I will be quick." He closes the channel and pushes the two levers next to the flow regulators disengaging the power bus connection to the weapons systems in the port nacelle. He grasps each flow regulator, removing and tossing them to the deck. From a small storage unit set in the opposite bulkhead he removes two new flow regulators, inspecting them.

He replaces the regulators and returns the levers to their open positions. "You have the port disruptor again," he tells Maxim.

"Thanks," the other man says, then closes the connection.

Gabe turns to another panel with a blinking red indicator and sets to repairing the damage.

Having listened to the insufferable Jark Asgar attempt to bully Captain Calder, Barbara says, "We'll never agree to an alliance, Jark. Tralgot will not ally itself with Farsight, and we will resist you. I've already notified the GC Council of our intent to issue several lawsuits." She turns to her comm system to the waiting Malkorite woman, "Now would be excellent." The other woman nods and the screen goes blank.

Opposite her, Maltor tells someone on his comm unit, "Squadron seven, reinforce one; that Weyland cruiser just got backed up by a Farsight frigate."

CORPORATE GROWTH_

"I COULD SET you up with a very lucrative transport contract," Jark offers.

Wil looks at Zephyr, "Are those the going currency or something?" She shrugs. He turns to Asgar, "No thanks. We're more interested in keeping a GC spanning monopoly from forming, hostilely it turns out."

"There's no way you can stop this," Asgar replies. "I've already formed alliances or otherwise tied up most of those who could oppose me."

Wil smiles, "Most, but not all." He adjusts their course as a salvo of missiles closes in. Most of the inbound projectiles miss, but enough of them strike the shields to cause something to explode over Maxim.

The big Palorian looks at his console, slamming a palm against it to remove the static, "Starboard shields are at fifteen percent."

As if on cue, though Wil is just as surprised as Asgar seems to be, almost two dozen ships of mixed size and design appear out of FTL. They spread out as they fly past Kal Nor, opening fire on Weyland and Farsight ships as they pass.

"Who the wurrin?" Asgar shouts as he looks to something or

someone off screen. He turns back to Wil, "I see you're not without surprises, but I have some of my own." He nods off-screen.

"Dren," Zephyr whispers. She turns to look at Wil, "Three of those black frigates just dropped out of FTL."

Wil sighs, and looks at Jark's grinning face, "You've been busy." The *Ghost* shakes again.

Zephyr whispers, "Gabe is working on the starboard shields. The new arrivals are broadcasting a mix of idents, but they're all small to medium-sized corporations from around the GC."

Wil looks at Asgar, "It's not just Tralgot who opposes this. Imagine when the GC Council finds out what you've been up to."

"Oh, did you think that transmission made it to Kal Nor?" This time the large Hulgian man laughs, "Oh, Captain Calder, you're so far out of your depth."

Down in the crew lounge Barbara swears. "We have to get that data to Kal Nor!"

Maltor nods and swipes away his fleet command screen to bring up another communication interface. "All channels are flooded with noise."

"See if you can help Zephyr identify the source of the jamming," Barbara instructs. She looks at the ceiling, "Zephyr tie in your sensors to Maltor's comm unit. We're looking for the source of the jamming; you worry about other things."

"Got it," Maltor says hunching to look more closely at his screen. The lights in the kitchen flicker and *Ghost* lurches hard enough that both Tygrans would have been tossed out of their seats if not for the homemade restraints.

Barbara and Maltor lock eyes, and the younger man says, "I stand corrected on the quality of these restraints."

The fans in the ceiling of the bridge are whirring loudly as they work to pull the acrid, burned electronics-smoke from the bridge.

Jark Asgar is still in the corner of the main display. "As entertaining as this is Captain Calder, I'm afraid I have other things to think about. Last chance; surrender Miss Mress now, and I'll leave Kal Nor alone. We can come to a mutually agreeable acquisition strategy."

A white bar appears across the top of the window that Jark Asgar is occupying on the main display indicating that the channel is muted, then from the overhead speaker Maltor says, "Captain, the jamming is about to cease, be ready to re-transmit." The white bar across Asgar's window disappears.

Before Wil can say anything, Barbara says over the bridge speakers, "Grolack you, Jark."

Wil looks at Bennie, tapping the mute control on the arm of his chair, "Change in plans, set your transmission to wide. Kal Nor can take care of sending it to Babs's contacts in the GC. Let's let the rest of nearby space know what happened. Oh, and compress it and send it to GNO directly." Bennie nods. Wil turns back to the main display, releasing the mute, "You know, Jark, you seemed like such a great guy, but it turns out you're just another greedy corporate profit-monger." On the main screen showing the ongoing battle, three Tralgot ships and five of the new mismatched arrivals turn on a single Weyland ship. It is smaller than a cruiser and Wil sees that it has been loitering just outside the main engagement area. Close enough to fire weapons, but far enough away to not likely be engaged.

The ship doesn't last long under the concentrated fire, despite the best efforts of other Farsight ships to intercede. The light cruiser suffers multiple explosions that rip it in half, secondary explosions further shredding the two halves. In seconds, the ship is nothing but an expanding debris cloud.

From the corner of his eye, Wil sees Bennie hit the transmit command, uploading the highly compressed data packet to any internex node he can find, as well as to Kal Nor. He turns to Wil and nods this time.

Jark clearly knows that the ship that was jamming is gone, he glares at Wil, "It was a, well, pleasure isn't the right term, to know you, Captain. Goodbye." The small window closes.

"What an asshole," Wil says.

CHAPTER 18_

SO MANY BAD GUYS_

Down in the kitchen, Barbara nods to her comm unit, "Thank you. This is our chance." She closes the channel and looks at Maltor. Her young assistant nods.

She looks at the ceiling, "Captain, we've uploaded the data everywhere we can think. I don't know if there are any Peacekeeper ships close enough to engage, but I've got what reinforcements I can muster on their way."

"Sounds good," Wil says to the ceiling, "We'll make the most of it." The *Ghost* shakes and something explodes somewhere else in the ship.

From the ceiling speaker Gabe says, "That was the cargo hold. It is open to space."

"Good thing we tied everything down," Bennie says.

Zephyr says, "After last time, yeah." The ship shakes again, and she focuses on her console. "We're outnumbered. There are only five Tralgot ships left and ten of the others."

Maxim fires a missile at one of the black-armored frigates. "Kal

Nor has weapons, what if we bring the remaining ships in close, let Kal Nor's shields reinforce us?"

Wil looks at the ceiling, "Babs? That work?"

There's a pause, "Yes, that should work! We're working with Kal Nor space command now. Issue the order, Captain."

Wil turns to Cynthia. She nods, "All forces allied with Tralgot, move towards the station. They'll reinforce us."

Wil brings the *Ghost* into a corkscrew over the top of a Farsight cruiser then pushes the sub-light throttles a bit more forward, pushing them closer to the relative safety of Kal Nor.

Maxim consults his screen, "I've got four missiles left."

Gabe is in the starboard wing root repair nook; the atmosphere vented when he opened the heavy hatch. He has crawled deeper into the repair crawlspace to access one of the overloaded shield emitters. When he opens the panel, the lack of oxygen keeps the burned wires from sparking. He reaches in and removes the back of the emitter where the power conduits connect. Thankfully, the design of the emitters allows them to be repaired more easily than many others that require the removal of the entire emitter. Moving the more delicate components to the removable section speeds repairs dramatically. He makes a note to send his thanks to the Ankarran shipwrights; he has thirteen such notes in a queue to send when he is ready.

He places a new module into the emitter assembly, quickly reconnecting the power bus. A light on the new module blinks green twice before remaining lit solid green.

"Starboard shields back online," Maxim says as the *Ghost* shakes. Despite the overhead fans, the bridge is clouded with lingering smoke.

"Sweet boneless zip zap," Zephyr says, then looks at Wil, "Kal Nor is powering up."

The main display shows several panels on the massive mushroom shaped station slide away to reveal blaster cannons that Wil has only ever seen on Peacekeeper Command carriers. From other panels, missile launchers slide out and lock into place. Immediately, the awesome firepower of Kal Nor opens up, wiping out two cruisers: Farsight and Weyland. One of the black-armored frigates is making an attack run on a damaged Tralgot cruiser when beam weapons from at least five heavy cannons rip into it. The ink black armor plates withstand the onslaught longer than any other ship could but then buckle allowing the beams to rip into the insides of the vessel. It explodes a moment later.

"Guess that armor has its limits," Maxim quips, eyes glued to the screen.

"Uh, why did we not do this in the beginning?" Bennie asks.

Wil shrugs but inclines his head, "Good question." He looks at the ceiling, "Babs, knowing about this might have saved a lot of lives."

There's an audible sigh from the ceiling speakers. One must be damaged because there's a crackle underlying the response, "Because now Farsight knows. Kal Nor went from possible target to a certain one. Asgar won't let this station stand now that he sees how powerful it is. We're trapped. I've ordered an evacuation."

To reinforce her statement, almost a dozen new cruisers arrive: some Farsight and Weyland but a few are Motrox and Bonaventure.

Wil groans. "Yeah, I see what you mean."

"Wait one!" Zephyr says biting her lip, "More contacts, lots of them."

Everyone on the bridge turns their attention to the main display. On it, the remains of the Tralgot fleet and its allies are gathered around the massive space station tucked between the two massive drums.

THIS WENT SOUTH FAST_

"PEACEKEEPERS!" Zephyr says, releasing a breath she didn't realize she'd been holding.

"Never thought I'd be happy to see these bozos," Wil says then looks at Maxim and Zephyr, "No offense."

"Ex-Peacekeeper," Maxim replies smiling.

On the main display, the Peacekeeper fleet, nearly twice as many ships as the fleet that was engaged in the Harrith incident years ago, spreads out.

"That... that is a lot of ships," Maxim says from his console.

Wil looks at his big friend, "I don't think I knew they had that many."

From the overhead speaker Barbara offers, "It turns out that all those attacks on Peacekeeper assets the last few weeks—at least a few witnesses seem to think Jark's new frigates are a dead ringer for the ships that have been causing so much trouble. They're looking for some retribution and to end this before it escalates further."

"I think Jark's ambitions may have exceeded his grasp," Wil says, watching the battle unfold. The Farsight ships and their allies hold together admirably for a few minutes, but the combined might of nearly two dozen Peacekeeper capital ships is a force to be reckoned with.

The hatch to the bridge opens and Barbara and Maltor walk in. As Wil spins in his chair to look at them, she says, "I wanted to watch this from up here." She rubs her lower back, "You really need better chairs for your dining area."

Maltor moves to lean against the bulkhead near Cynthia's station, "Agreed, my tail is killing me."

"Look!" Bennie shouts, pointing to the main display. One of the larger Farsight cruisers is breaking in half, secondary explosions rip through it. Before the metal of the dead Farsight cruiser even cools, a Peacekeeper command carrier explodes, a half dozen of Jark Asgar's sleek black armored frigates peel off in different directions.

"Damn!" Wil says leaning back in his seat.

"Do we know which one Jark is on?" Zephyr wonders aloud.

Bennie turns from watching the main display to his console, "Gimme a microtock."

Everyone turns to look at the Brailack as he works. After a few seconds he looks up, "Ok, maybe a bit more than a microtock; stop staring at me." He waves a hand dismissively.

Maxim says, "He can't be here, right? The combined Farsight and friends fleet is already half destroyed."

"I'm surprised he hasn't surrendered, or his Captains at least," Barbara says.

"Me too, actually," Wil says.

Bennie cuts in, "He's not here."

"What?" Barbara says walking towards Bennie's station.

Wil nods, "Yeah, what she said."

The Brailack hacker spreads his arms, "He's not here. I hacked into their battle net and tracked his data packets back to what I'm guessing is his command ship, about three light years from here."

Wil begins working his command console, "Let's go. Let's bring this fight to that big triceratops motherfucker."

Maxim looks back to Zephyr, "Tricera-whatnow?"

Wil brings the *Ghost* around and under a Tralgot cruiser, "Cyn, let the Tralgot folks know what we're doing." He looks to Bennie, "Send me the plot." The Brailack nods.

"On it," she says as Barbara leans down to grab a spare comm set.

The *Ghost* accelerates out of the protective bubble of Kal Nor, racing past a Weyland Combine corvette.

Cynthia glances at Barbara and Maltor then says, "Maybe we should drop off Miss Mress and Maltor?"

Wil shakes his head once, "No time. This"—he gestures to the battle on the main display—"will be over soon. I don't know what his plan is, but I'm guessing Asgar isn't planning to face justice."

Wil pushes the FTL throttles all the way forward. "Thirty minutes." He spins his command chair, "Babs, can you and Maltor work with your folks? This ends clean if Asgar is in cuffs."

The Tygran woman taps Maltor on the shoulder nodding, "We'll make calls." She pushes the release on the bridge hatch and as she crosses the threshold, she turns to look at Wil, "Let's make him pay."

Wil grins, "I knew I liked you." He turns back to face the main display and his command console.

Maxim clears his throat, "We still only have four missiles."

Wil grins, "We'll worry about that in twenty-nine minutes. We could arrive and Asgar might not be there."

CITIZEN'S ARREST_

"Dropping out of FTL in two," Wil announces to the bridge then looks at the ceiling, "Gabe, we good?"

"Good is a relative term, Captain. The reactor is fully functional, and I have repaired everything that I could."

"Ok, that sounds—"

"However, I would rate our combat effectiveness at sixty percent," Gabe finishes.

Wil looks at the rest of the crew who all shrug and exchange worried looks. He looks at the ceiling again, "Ok, so not great, but we'll make do."

"Indeed," the ceiling replies.

Wil watches the countdown then pulls the FTL throttles back, letting the *Ghost* fall back to normal space. The main display shows the stretched-out stars returning to normal.

"Two contacts," Zephyr announces, then adds, "A cruiser and something I've never seen before."

Maxim consults his console, "Yeah, that's not good." He looks across the small bridge to Bennie, "Let me guess, he's in the scary one."

The Brailack hacker looks at his big Palorian friend, nodding once. Over the overhead speaker Barbara says, "I got through to the Peacekeeper fleet commander back at Kal Nor, she's sending ships. They're a few centocks behind us."

Wil nods, "Ok, great. Thanks." He looks over his shoulder, "Cyn, hail them."

He turns to look at the main display, the two ships growing as the *Ghost* gets nearer. A few seconds later, the window appears with Jark Asgar in it. "Jark!" Wil says brightly.

"I'm impressed." He looks to the corner of the screen, towards where Bennie is sitting, "Your work, I assume." Bennie makes a rude gesture.

"This is over, Jark." Wil leans forward, elbows on his knees. "You have to see that. The Peacekeepers are mopping up the remains of your and your ally's ships. Everyone knows what you did at the Corporate Congress summit. It's over. I'm placing you under citizen's arrest."

Asgar raises a leathery eyebrow, "A citizen's what?"

Wil looks around, "Is that not a thing in the GC?"

Zephyr looks at him, "Well, since none of us know what that is, I'd say no."

Asgar slams a massive fist on the table he's seated at causing the camera pick up to wobble, "Shut up!" On the main display the two ships are adjusting course to intercept the *Ghost*. Asgar continues, "I've put in too much time, money, and effort for this to fail." He looks offscreen, then comes back, "This is just a minor setback. I've weakened the Peacekeepers—"

"Uh, they just kicked your ass," Wil interrupts.

"Destroy them!" Asgar shouts at someone before the small comm closes. The larger ship, the standard model Farsight cruiser opens fire with missiles. The smaller vessel, a corvette at best, but clad in the now familiar black chitin-like hull armor moves to flank the much smaller *Ghost*.

From behind Wil, Cynthia asks, "Uh, you had a plan of some sort, right?"

Wil doesn't answer other than to put the *Ghost* into a tight corkscrew that evades most of the inbound missiles—most but not all. Several of the anti-ship missiles impact against the *Ghost's* shields rattling the smaller craft.

Bennie is clutching his console, "I think his plan is that we die and Jark wins."

"That's a bad plan. A very bad plan!" Maxim shouts over the sound of the *Ghost's* weapons returning fire. "That's not the plan, right Wil?"

Wil pushes the sub-light throttles while pulling the flight controls back as hard as he can. The *Ghost* races past the large cruiser, taking hits from the point defense weaponry as they pass. "I'm trying to concentrate!" Wil snaps.

The *Ghost* bucks and shudders as she flies between the two hostile ships, taking weapons fire from all sides.

"Max, feel free to use those missiles however you see fit!" Wil shouts as he fights to keep control of the ship.

Sparks erupt from a panel under Zephyr, forcing her to lift her feet and turn away from the console. She looks at Wil as the lights on the bridge flicker, "You do have a plan, right?"

"Captain?" Barbara says from the overhead speakers, the concern in her voice is obvious despite the static crackling over the comms.

"Wil?" Cynthia presses.

The *Ghost* stops shaking as it clears the two hostile ships. "Hold on. Max, get ready." Wil pushes the controls, forcing the *Ghost* into a one hundred and eighty degree turn that causes the hull to groan. "Now, Max!"

The big Palorian nods and presses a control on his console. From the bottom of the main display two missiles leap away from the *Ghost*, followed by two more.

"That's it," Maxim says as the four missiles streak toward the cruiser. The *Ghost* is racing back toward the two ships. The first two missiles impact on the cruiser's shields lighting them up a bright blue as they absorb the explosions. The second two follow exploding against the shields.

"Contacts," Zephyr announces. She looks up from her console, "Peacekeepers and Tralgot."

Wil pulls the sub-light throttles back and brings the *Ghost* off its intercept course with the two Farsight vessels. He makes a slow turn looking at the others, grinning ear to ear, "And that was the plan."

Bennie looks at him eyebrow ridge quirked, "What? Get shot at until the Peacekeepers arrived?"

Cynthia chuckles as Wil makes a face. "Uh, no. We were distracting Jark and his goons to keep them here."

On the main display, the Peacekeeper task force has boxed in the two Farsight vessels. The ships are exchanging fire, but the Farsight cruiser is already venting atmosphere from several hull breaches. The sleek black vessel stops firing and powers down its engines.

"Incoming call," Cynthia says, tapping her console.

A comm window opens on the main display to show a Peacekeeper officer. She nods, "Greetings, Captain Calder. It seems you people can't stay out of trouble."

The bridge hatch opens and Barbara walks in.

Wil tilts his head, "We're just lucky I guess."

The fleet officer sees Barbara and nods, "Miss Mress, thank you for the heads up on this location. We'll have Asgar in custody shortly."

"Captain, make sure your troops are in full battle rattle," Maxim warns, "There's likely to be monsters on that black corvette."

"Monsters?"

Zephyr chimes in, "Long story."

Barbara holds her hand up, "My assistant is preparing a précis for you, Captain Storm."

The other woman nods. The comm window closes.

Barbara looks to Wil, "Any chance we can go home now?"

Wil looks over his shoulder and winks, "Let's take our clients home."

NEWSCAST_

"GOOD MORNING from GNO Studio eight. I'm Mon-El Furash."

"And I'm Megan," her co-host adds. "We have breaking news in the ongoing story of those mysterious attacks against Peacekeeper facilities across the Commonwealth in recent weeks."

Mon-El jumps in, "It turns out that Farsight Corporation, one of the largest mega-corporations in the GC, was behind it. CEO Jark Asgar has been taken into Peacekeeper custody after a battle between Farsight forces and the Peacekeepers."

"And let's not forget the role Tralgot and several other corporations played in this."

Mon-El nods, "Of course. We've learned that Tralgot CEO Barbara Mress was instrumental in all of this information coming to light."

Megan smiles, "Certainly interesting times we find ourselves in." She holds up two fingers an inch apart, "This close to a corporate war."

"Stay with us as we learn more about this unfolding story," Mon-El closes.

PUTTING THINGS BACK TOGETHER_

"Repairs are almost complete, Captain," Gabe says as he enters the conference room in the upper drum of Kal Nor station. The rest of the crew and Maltor are sitting around the table.

Wil nods to his engineer, "That's good. How're the other ships doing?"

Gabe moves to stand near Wil's seat, "From what I could gather, their repairs are progressing as well. One of Rhys Duch's corvettes departed an hour ago, Maltor ensured it was one of the first to be repaired."

Wil nods and looks at Maltor, "Thanks."

Maltor nods, "From the reports I've gotten, all ships that took part in the conflict will be fully repaired by the end of the day tomorrow."

Maxim whistles, "Your spaceport operates at a level of efficiency I've rarely seen outside the military."

The feline-featured younger man nods, "Thank you, I think."

A Peacekeeper cruiser glides past the large view port at the end of the room.

Barbara walks in; everyone turns to look at her. She takes a seat at the head of the table, "Farsight has been working on this for a while. I just heard from one of my contacts in the Peacekeepers; they've started interrogating Asgar and his staff. This goes deep, starting well before last cycle's Crucible incident. Their find on Glacial seems to have been a very happy coincidence for them."

"Lucky them," Zephyr deadpans.

"Poor Doppo," Wil says.

Maltor's feline-like nose wrinkles as he watches Wil, "I'm sure Asgar's assistant will be ok; he'll probably flip on his boss." Barbara raises an eyebrow but says nothing.

Maxim asks, "So, what now?"

Zephyr nods, "I get the impression this isn't simply *over*."

Barbara nods, "You're right. Now, the GC spends cycles pulling Farsight apart, spinning off what it can, selling off what it can't, all while trying to dig out all the secrets. I've been appointed the chairwoman of the special committee, actually." She smiles, her incisors showing. She holds up a hand, "Figuring out what to do with the Glacial creatures and the various nightmares Farsight created with their genetic material is an entirely different and probably more complicated problem to solve."

Cynthia grunts, "How many of those things were on Asgar's ship?"

"From what I could gather, the Peacekeepers lost an entire platoon when they boarded the ship. They had to eliminate all the creatures. None were able to be captured."

"Bastard," Wil growls sort of under his breath.

Barbara stands, "Well, the *Ghost* should be ready shortly. You're welcome to stay at Kal Nor as long as you like, on us." She smiles and looks at Cynthia, "Please don't be strangers."

Bennie seems to take an interest in the conversation suddenly, putting his PADD down, "Food? Maybe we can find a place with fried zergling."

Everyone sighs while nodding. Maltor and Barbara file out of the room ahead of the crew of the *Ghost*.

The End.

THANK YOU_

Thank you so much for reading Space Rogues 6: War and Peace

If you enjoyed it I'd love it if you left a review. Seriously, reviews are a big deal. They help readers find authors. They help authors show how awesome they are. :)

Reviews are social proof and go a long way to encouraging other readers to take a chance on an unknown.

OFFER_

As they say, there's no harm in asking, so here we go.

If you can help connect me with someone who can get Space Rogues
on a screen (Big or Little) I'll cut you in for 10% (Up to $10,000) of
whatever advance is paid.

Send me an email and we can discuss.
rights@johnwilker.com

STAY CONNECTED_

**Ever wonder what the inside of the Ghost looks like?
Where Wil's room is or what the lounge area looks like?**
Sign up for my newsletter at
johnwilker.com/newsletter
The 'Rogues Gallery' has subscriber only goodies like a complete set
of deck plans for the Ankarran Raptor Model 89

Visit me online at
johnwilker.com

If you like supporting things you love by sporting merch, well you're
in luck! I've launched a Space Rogues Shop, take a look.

Coming Spring 2020
Space Rogues 7: A Guy Walks Into a Bar
Pre-Order it now!

OTHER BOOKS BY JOHN WILKER_

Space Rogues Universe (in story chronological order)

- Space Rogues 1: The Epic Adventures of Wil Calder, Space Smuggler
- Space Rogues 2: Big Ship, Lots of Guns
- Space Rogues 3: The Behemoth Job
- Space Rogues 4: Stay Warm, Don't Die
- Space Rogues 5: So This is Earth?
- Space Rogues 6: War and Peace
- Space Rogues 7: A Guy Walks Into a Bar

Made in the USA
Las Vegas, NV
06 May 2022

48498418R00194